DOVER HORROR CLASSICS

THIRTY HOURS
WITH A
CORPSE

AND OTHER TALES OF THE GRAND GUIGNOL

MAURICE LEVEL

INTRODUCED AND EDITED BY
S. T. JOSHI

D1478848

DOVER PUBLICATIONS, INC.
MINEOLA, NEW YORK

DOVER HORROR CLASSICS

Bibliographical Note

Thirty Hours with a Corpse and Other Tales of the Grand Guignol, first published by Dover Publications, Inc., in 2016, is a new anthology of thirty-nine stories reprinted from standard sources. A new Introduction has been specially prepared for the present edition.

Library of Congress Cataloging-in-Publication Data

Level, Maurice, 1875–
   [Short stories. English]
   Thirty hours with a corpse, and other tales of the Grand Guignol / Maurice Level, introduced and edited by S. T. Joshi.
       p. cm. — (Dover horror classics)
   ISBN-13: 978-0-486-80232-9 (pbk.)
   ISBN-10: 0-486-80232-9 (pbk.)
   1. Horror tales, French. 2. Level, Maurice, 1875– — Translations into English I. Joshi, S. T., 1958– editor. II. Title.

PQ2623.E9A2 2016
843'.912—dc23

2015031477

Manufactured in the United States by RR Donnelley
80232901   2016
www.doverpublications.com

Contents

Contents

Introduction

MAURICE LEVEL (1875–1926) is the forgotten man of French literature. Although he published thirteen novels, dozens of plays, and hundreds of short stories, and was a star contributor to the celebrated Grand Guignol Theatre in Paris, Level today is virtually unknown. He does not appear in any English-language dictionaries or encyclopedias of French literature—and, incredibly, does not appear even in multi-volume and presumably authoritative French encyclopedias of French literature. Not a single article has been published about him in an academic journal, and the most basic features of his life are unknown. All we have is his work.

And yet, Level enjoyed remarkable popularity in the English-speaking world during the second and third decades of the twentieth century, when two novels, *The Grip of Fear* (1911) and *Those Who Return* (1923), were translated, along with a volume of short stories, first published in England as *Crises* (1920) and, later that same year, in the United States as *Tales of Mystery and Horror*. (To add to the oddity, Level's stories never appeared in a collection in French.) In 1921, H. P. Lovecraft, who admitted that he had not yet read any of Level's work, wrote a paean to him based solely upon his increasing reputation:

> Nay, I have never read a tale of M. Maurice's, but have yearned to do so ever since beholding the announcement of his book of tales in the reviews a year or so ago. . . . For M. Level I have only the respect most profound—I would that I could create plots as delicious as his! How relieving it is to fly from the pitiful commonplaces of futile, trivial, superficial, ethics-mad, mock-important, sentimental, romantic, false-idea'd, American namby-pamby Sunday-school tales, to something that actually digs under

the illusory surface of conventional values & feigned motives, & shakes the real fibres of the human animal![1]

Lovecraft goes on here at much greater length, but this should suffice to suggest what an impression Level's mere reputation made on an artist so sensitive to the weird, terrible, and unconventional as Lovecraft.

In "Supernatural Horror in Literature" (1927), Lovecraft's response is somewhat more subdued. In discussing the *conte cruel* ("cruel tale"), "in which the wrenching of the emotions is accomplished through dramatic tantalisations, frustrations, and gruesome physical horrors," he goes on to write: "Almost wholly devoted to this form is the living writer Maurice Level, whose very brief episodes have lent themselves so readily to theatrical adaptation in the 'thrillers' of the Grand Guignol."[2] The overriding fact that Level avoided the supernatural altogether in his work necessitated such a response, for Lovecraft had considerable doubts as to whether nonsupernatural horror, however "gruesome" or extreme, could ever be a legitimate branch of the "weird tale."

As mentioned, we know next to nothing of Level's life, except that he studied medicine for a time—a point that becomes evident in a number of his tales. It is unclear when he first became associated with the Grand Guignol Theatre, but his earliest published play appears to date to 1906. The history of the Grand Guignol Theatre has now been charted in a number of volumes,[3] and from them we learn much that is of indirect interest to the study of Level and his work. The theatre was founded in 1897 by Oscar Métérnier but was taken over two years later by Max Maurey. In spite of its reputation for focusing on death, madness, and eroticism, an average evening's program at the theatre

---

[1] H. P. Lovecraft to Myrta Alice Little (17 May 1921); *Lovecraft Studies* No. 26 (Spring 1992): 28–29.

[2] *The Annotated Supernatural Horror in Literature,* ed. S. T. Joshi (New York: Hippocampus Press, 2012), p. 53.

[3] See Mel Gordon, *The Grand Guignol: Theatre of Fear and Terror* (New York: Amok Press, 1988); Richard J. Hand and Michael Wilson, *Grand-Guignol: The French Theatre of Horror* (Exeter, UK: University of Exeter Press, 2002). The latter volume contains new translations of Level's *Sous la lumière rouge* (as *In the Darkroom*) and *Le Baiser dans la nuit* (as *The Final Kiss*).

usually included a comedy. (None of the Level stories that have been translated into English are comedies except, perhaps, a single example, "The Appalling Gift.") Otherwise, the program almost exclusively featured one-act plays, exactly of the sort suited to the intense, tightly constructed plots we find in Level's stories. The theatre's heyday chiefly occurred in the decade or two after World War I, but it declined in the 1930s, especially with the advent of talkies and of horror films; but it continued for decades, not shutting its doors until 1962.

Level was not the most prolific contributor to the Grand Guignol; that honor goes to André de Lorde, whose overall output includes more than 150 plays, novels, and other work. But Level's plays were among the theatre's biggest hits; one of them was *Sous la lumière rouge* (based on the story translated into English as "In the Light of the Red Lamp"), which premiered in 1911, while *Le Baiser dans la nuit* (based on the story "The Last Kiss") premiered the next year. It would appear that Level wrote his stories first, publishing them in magazines and newspapers (especially the Paris paper *Le Journal*), then adapted them into plays, sometimes with the help of a collaborator. So far as can be ascertained, only eight of his plays were actually published. One of them, *Lady Madeline* (1908), is of interest in being a stage adaptation of Poe's "The Fall of the House of Usher."

It is difficult to characterize Level's work, save to say that its relentless emphasis on crime, hate, vengeance, and their psychological effects constitutes his distinctive contribution to literature. This is the focus of the early novel *L'Épouvante* (1908), translated as *The Grip of Fear*, although its title simply means "terror" or "fright." In this work, a journalist, having stumbled upon an undetected murder, deliberately plants evidence implicating himself as the perpetrator of the crime, merely to experience the thrill of being hunted by the police. The journalist, Onesimus Coche, always imagines that he can reveal the truth to the police if matters go too far; but he finds that his emotions get the better of him as the noose tightens figuratively around his neck. He begins to crack under the strain, and it is said of him toward the end: "From the very start Coche had but one enemy: his own imagination."

But accomplished as this novel is, Level's reputation will probably rest on his tales, which if nothing else have all the compactness and "unity of effect" that Edgar Allan Poe believed was the signature feature of the short story. Level's immediate literary influences in this regard were probably Guy de Maupassant (who is cited in *Those Who Return*) and Villiers de l'Isle-Adam, a master of the *conte cruel*, whose work preceded Level's by a few decades; but these two writers themselves drew extensively upon the structural perfection of Poe's short stories as models for their own work, and Level manifestly did so as well. Without a wasted word, Level's tales progress from the first scene to the last in a manner that fully exhibits the conflict of emotions that is at their heart, but without the digressions and irrelevancies that often mar even the most accomplished of novels. Level's tales reveal such an economy of means that nothing could be added to or extracted from them without destroying their very fabric.

The emphasis on terror, even if it is of an unambiguously non-supernatural sort, makes the reading of Level's tales at times an excruciating experience. It is not that there is any excess of physical violence involved: "The Last Kiss" is probably the most extreme in this regard, with its unflinching display of the hideous effects of acid when thrown upon a man's (and, later, a woman's) face. "The Kennel" is hideous in its suggestion of a corpse being fed to hungry dogs. But beyond this, the terror in Level's tales is chiefly psychological: the terror of an impoverished prostitute being forced to service the executioner of her lover; the terror of a man coming upon definitive evidence that his lover was buried alive; the terror that a mother feels when she suspects that her newborn baby is the child of a madman. . . . Many of the scenarios Level constructs may seem somewhat contrived and artificial, but his purpose is to study the emotional extremes of those who find themselves confronted by madness, guilt, and paranoia.

There is a considerable social element in many of Level's tales—an element that similarly links them to the Grand Guignol's concern for naturalism, a literary movement that emphasized the plight of the outcast and impoverished and sought to display the harshness and injustice of a social fabric built upon radical inequities in wealth and social position. Many of Level's stories feature beggars or other characters on the margins of society who plunge into crime to exact vengeance upon a society that has left them no other means of combating economic inequality. "The Beggar" is prototypical in this regard: a beggar tries in vain to bring help to a man who is being crushed by an overturned cart, but he is driven away by the man's family because they believe he is only looking for a handout. In the end, the beggar can only express a certain wry satisfaction that the man's own family effectively caused his death.

In tales written during and after World War I, Level cleverly adapted his blood-and-thunder style to grim and poignant narratives involving the war. His surprise endings, featuring sudden twists and unexpected dénouements, work well when applied to war scenarios. The deep resentment by the humiliated French at German occupation and brutality is searingly displayed in several tales. It would be interesting to know if any of these were adapted for the Grand Guignol.

Maurice Level remained a figure of note even after his early death. His play *Le Baiser dans la nuit* was performed as late as 1938 at the Grand Guignol Theatre and was even adapted (loosely and without credit) as an EC comic. But beyond the three volumes already mentioned, none of his work appeared in English in book form subsequent to 1923, and only a few scattered tales appeared in English-language magazines in the later 1920s and 1930s. (Three of them appeared in the celebrated American pulp magazine *Weird Tales*.) But among devotees of psychological suspense and the macabre, Level's work has always retained a shadowy interest, and he has refused to fade away. The present volume, which contains virtually every short story by Level that has been translated into English, should confirm that that interest is well deserved. Few authors have displayed greater psychological acuity, greater craftsmanship in the manufacture of short stories, and a more unflinching gaze at the grotesque crimes that human passions are capable of engendering; and few have exhibited those crimes and those passions with loftier artistry.

—S. T. JOSHI

A Note on the Texts

This volume reprints, with a single exception, all the short stories by Level that have been translated into English. The first twenty-six stories are taken from *Crises* (1920). The next six stories are taken from *Tales of Wartime France*, translated by William L. McPherson (1918). The last seven stories are uncollected tales appearing in magazines. They are: "The Appalling Gift" (*Living Age*, 24 March 1923); "Night and Silence" (*Weird Tales*, February 1932); "The Cripple" (*Weird Tales*, February 1933); "The Look" (*Weird Tales*, March 1933); "The Horror on the Night Express" (*Mystery Magazine*, February 1934); "Thirty Hours with a Corpse" (*Mystery Magazine*, September 1934); and "She Thought of Everything" (*Mystery Magazine*, May 1935). No translators were given for any of these stories.

The one story by Level that has not been included here is "The Old Maids," published in *Jacqueline and Four Other Stories from the French* [no translator indicated] (1925). It is a fine tale (a translation of "Vieilles Filles"), but so obviously a mainstream story that its inclusion could not be justified here.

Where practicable, the translations have been revised by consultation with the original French texts.

—S. T. J.

The Debt Collector

Ravenot, debt collector to the same bank for ten years, was a model employee. Never had there been the least cause to find fault with him. Never had the slightest error been detected in his books.

Living alone, carefully avoiding new acquaintances, keeping out of cafés and without love-affairs, he seemed happy, quite content with his lot. If it were sometimes said in his hearing: "It must be a temptation to handle such large sums!" he would quietly reply: "Why? Money that doesn't belong to you is not money."

In the locality in which he lived he was looked upon as a paragon, his advice sought after and taken.

On the evening of one collecting day he did not return to his home. The idea of dishonesty never even suggested itself to those who knew him. Possibly a crime had been committed. The police traced his movements during the day. He had presented his bills punctually, and had collected his last sum near the Montrouge Gate about seven o'clock. At the time he had over two hundred thousand francs in his possession. Further than that all trace of him was lost. They scoured the neighborhood and waste ground that lies near the fortifications; the hovels that are found here and there in the military zone were ransacked: all with no result. As a matter of form they telegraphed in every direction, to every frontier station. But the directors of the bank, as well as the police, had little doubt that someone had lain in wait for him, robbed him, and thrown him into the river. Basing their deductions on certain clues, they were able to state almost positively that the coup had been planned for some time by professional thieves.

Only one man in Paris shrugged his shoulders when he read about it in the papers; that man was Ravenot.

Just at the time when the keenest sleuth-hounds of the police were losing his scent, he had reached the Seine by the Boulevards Exterieurs. He had dressed himself under the arch of a bridge in some everyday clothes he had left there the night before, had put the two hundred thousand francs in his pocket, and making a bundle of his uniform and satchel, he had dropped the whole, weighted with a large stone, into the river and, unperturbed, had returned to Paris. He slept at a hotel, and slept well. In a few hours he had become a consummate thief.

Profiting by his start, he might have taken a train across the frontier, but he was too wise to suppose that a few hundred kilometers would put him beyond the reach of the gendarmes, and he had no illusions as to the fate that awaited him. He would most assuredly be arrested. Besides, his plan was a very different one.

When daylight came, he enclosed the two hundred thousand francs in an envelope, sealed it with five seals, and went to a lawyer.

"Monsieur," said he, "this is why I have come to you. In this envelope I have some securities, papers that I want to leave in safety. I am going for a long journey, and I don't know when I shall return. I should like to leave this packet with you. I suppose you have no objection to my doing so?"

"None whatever. I'll give you a receipt . . ."

He assented, then began to think. A receipt? Where could he put it? To whom entrust it? If he kept it on his person, he would certainly lose his deposit. He hesitated, not having foreseen this complication. Then he said easily:

"I am alone in the world without relations and friends. The journey I intend making is not without danger. I should run the risk of losing the receipt, or it might be destroyed. Would it not be possible for you to take possession of the packet and place it in safety among your documents, and when I return I should merely have to tell you, or your successor, my name?"

"But if I do that . . ."

"State on the receipt that it can only be claimed in this way. At any rate, if there is any risk, it is mine."

"Agreed! What is your name?"

He replied without hesitation:

"Duverger, Henri Duverger."

When he got back to the street, he breathed a sigh of relief. The first part of his program was over. They could clap the handcuffs on him now: the substance of his theft was beyond reach.

He had worked things out with cold deliberation on these lines: On the expiration of his sentence he would claim the deposit. No one would be able to dispute his right to it. Four or five unpleasant years to be gone through, and he would be a rich man. It was preferable to spending his life trudging from door to door collecting debts! He would go to live in the country. To everyone he would be Monsieur Duverger. He would grow old in peace and contentment, known as an honest, charitable man . . . for he would spend some of the money on others.

He waited twenty-four hours longer to make sure the numbers of the notes were not known, and, reassured on this point, he gave himself up, a cigarette between his lips.

Another man in his place would have invented some story. He preferred to tell the truth, to admit the theft. Why waste time? But at his trial, as when he was first charged, it was impossible to drag from him a word about what he had done with the two hundred thousand francs. He confined himself to saying:

"I don't know. I fell asleep on a bench. . . . In my turn I was robbed."

Thanks to his irreproachable past, he was sentenced to only five years' penal servitude. He heard the sentence without moving a muscle. He was thirty-five. At forty he would be free and rich. He considered the confinement a small, necessary sacrifice.

In the prison where he served his sentence he was a model for all the others, just as he had been a model employee. He watched the slow days pass without impatience or anxiety, concerned only about his health.

. . . At last the day of his discharge came. They gave him back his little stock of personal effects, and he left with but one idea in his mind, that of getting to the lawyer. As he walked along he imagined the coming scene.

He would arrive. He would be ushered into the impressive office. Would the lawyer recognize him? He would look in the glass: decidedly he had grown considerably older, and no doubt his face bore traces of his experience. . . . No, certainly the lawyer would not recognize him. Ha! Ha! It would add to the humor of the situation!

"What can I do for you, Monsieur?"

"I have come for a deposit I made here five years ago."

"Which deposit? In what name?"

"In the name of Monsieur . . ."

Ravenot stopped suddenly murmuring:

"How extraordinary! . . . I can't remember the name I gave!"

He racked his brains . . . a blank! He sat down on a bench, and feeling that he was growing unnerved, reasoned with himself:

"Come, come! Be calm . . . Monsieur . . . Monsieur . . . It began with . . . which letter?"

For an hour he sat lost in thought, straining his memory, groping after something that might suggest a clue. . . . A waste of time. The name danced in front of him, round about him: he saw the letters jump, the syllables vanish. . . . Every second he felt that he had it, that it was before his eyes, on his lips. No! At first this only worried him; then it became a sharp irritation that cut into him with a pain that was almost physical. Hot waves ran up and down his back. His muscles contracted: he found it impossible to sit still. His hands began to twitch. He bit his dry lips. He was divided between an impulse to weep and to fight.

But the more he focused his attention, the further the name seemed to recede. He struck the ground with his foot, rose and said aloud:

"What's the good of worrying? It only makes things worse. If I leave off thinking about it, it will come of itself!"

But an obsession cannot be shaken off in this way. In vain he turned his attention to the faces of the passers-by, stopped at the shop windows, listened to the street noises; while he listened, unhearing, and looked, unseeing, the great question persisted:

"Monsieur? . . . Monsieur? . . ."

Night came. The streets were deserted. Worn out, he went to a hotel, asked for a room, and flung himself fully dressed on the bed. For hours he went on racking his brain. At dawn he fell asleep. It was broad daylight when he awoke. He stretched himself luxuriously, his mind at ease; but in a flash the obsession gripped him again:

"Monsieur? . . . Monsieur? . . ."

A new sensation began to dominate his anguish of mind: fear. Fear that he might never remember the name, never. He got up, went out, walked for hours at random, loitering about the office of the lawyer. For a second time the night fell. He clutched his head in his hands and groaned:

"I shall go mad."

A terrible idea had now taken possession of his mind: he had two hundred thousand francs in notes, two hundred thousand francs, acquired by dishonesty of course, but his, and they were out of his reach. To get them he had undergone five years in prison, and now he could not touch them. The notes were there waiting for him, and one word, a mere word he could not remember, stood, an insuperable barrier, between him and them. He beat with clenched fists on his head, feeling his reason trembling in the balance; he stumbled against lamp-posts with the sway of a drunken man, tripped over the curbstones. It was no longer an obsession or a torment, it had become a frenzy of his whole being, of his brain and of his flesh. He had now become convinced that he would never remember. His imagination conjured up a sardonic laugh that rang in his ears; people in the streets seemed to point at him as he passed. His steps quickened into a run that carried him straight ahead, knocking up against the passers-by, oblivious of the traffic. He wished that someone would strike him so that he might strike back; that he might be run over, crushed out of existence. . . .

"Monsieur? . . . Monsieur? . . ."

At his feet the Seine flowed by, a muddy green, spangled with the reflections of the bright stars. He sobbed out:

"Monsieur? . . . Oh, that name! . . . that name! . . ."

He went down the steps that lead to the water, and lying face downwards, worked himself toward the river to cool his face and hands. He was panting . . . the water drew him . . . drew his hot eyes . . . his ears. . . . He felt himself slipping, but unable to cling to the steep bank, he fell. . . . The shock of the cold water set every nerve a-tingle. He struggled . . . thrust out his arms . . . flung his head up . . . went under . . . rose to the surface again, and in a sudden mighty effort, his eyes starting from his head, yelled:

"I've got it! . . . Help! Duverger! Du . . ."

. . . The quay was deserted. The water rippled against the pillars of the bridge: the echo of the somber arch repeated the name in the silence. . . . The river rose and fell lazily: lights danced on it, white and red. . . . A wave a little stronger than the rest licked the bank near the moving rings. . . . All was still. . . .

The Kennel

As TEN o'clock struck, M. de Hartevel emptied a last tankard of beer, folded his newspaper, stretched himself, yawned, and slowly rose.

The hanging-lamp cast a bright light on the table-cloth, over which were scattered piles of shot and cartridge wads. Near the fireplace, in the shadow, a woman lay back in a deep armchair.

Outside the wind blew violently against the windows, the rain beat noisily on the glass, and from time to time deep bayings came from the kennel where the hounds had struggled and strained since morning.

There were forty of them: big mastiffs with ugly fangs, stiff-haired griffons of Vendée, which flung themselves with ferocity on the wild boar on hunting days. During the night their sullen bayings disturbed the countryside, evoking response from all the dogs in the neighborhood.

M. de Hartevel lifted a curtain and looked out into the darkness of the park. The wet branches shone like steel blades; the autumn leaves were blown about like whirligigs and flattened against the walls. He grumbled.

"Dirty weather!"

He walked a few steps, his hands in his pockets, stopped before the fireplace, and with a kick broke a half-consumed log. Red embers fell on the ashes; a flame rose, straight and pointed.

Madame de Hartevel did not move. The light of the fire played on her face, touching her hair with gold, throwing a rosy glow on her pale cheeks and, dancing about her, cast fugitive shadows on her forehead, her eyelids, her lips.

The hounds, quiet for a moment, began to growl again; and their bayings, the roaring of the wind and the hiss of the rain on the trees made the quiet room seem warmer, the presence of the silent woman more intimate.

Subconsciously this influenced M. de Hartevel. Desires stimulated by those of the beasts and by the warmth of the room crept through his veins. He touched his wife's shoulders.

"It is ten o'clock. Are you going to bed?"

She said "yes," and left her chair, as if regretfully.

"Would you like me to come with you?"

"No—thank you—"

Frowning, he bowed.

"As you like."

His shoulders against the mantelshelf, his legs apart, he watched her go. She walked with a graceful, undulating movement, the train of her dress moving on the carpet like a little flat wave. A surge of anger stiffened his muscles.

In this chateau where he had her all to himself he had in bygone days imagined a wife who would like living in seclusion with him, attentive to his wishes, smiling acquiescence to all his desires. She would welcome him with gay words when he came back from a day's hunting, his hands blue with cold, his strong body tired, bringing with him the freshness of the fields and moors, the smell of horses, of game and of hounds, would lift eager lips to meet his own. Then, after the long ride in the wind, the rain, the snow, after the intoxication of the crisp air, the heavy walking in the furrows, or the gallop under branches that almost caught his beard, there would have been long nights of love, orgies of caresses of which the thrill would be mutual.

The difference between the dream and the reality!

When the door had shut and the sound of steps died away in the corridor, he went to his room, lay down, took a book and tried to read.

The rain hissed louder than ever. The wind roared in the chimney; out in the park, branches were snapping from the trees; the hounds bayed without ceasing, their howlings sounded through the creaking of the trees, dominating the roar of the storm; the door of the kennel strained under their weight.

He opened the window and shouted:

"Down!"

:

For some seconds they were quiet. He waited. The wind that drove the rain on his face refreshed him. The barkings began again. He banged his fist against the shutter, threatening:

"Quiet, you devils!"

There was a singing in his ears, a whistling, a ringing; a desire to strike, to ransack, to feel flesh quiver under his fists took possession of him. He roared: "Wait a moment!" slammed the window, seized a whip, and went out.

He strode along the corridors with no thought of the sleeping house till he got near his wife's room, when he walked slowly and quietly, fearing to disturb her sleep. But a ray of light from under her door caught his lowered eyes, and there was a sound of hurried footsteps that the carpet did not deaden. He listened. The noise ceased, the light went out. . . . He stood motionless, and suddenly, impelled by a suspicion, he called softly:

"Marie Thérèse . . ."

No reply. He called louder. Curiosity, a doubt that he dared not formulate, held him breathless. He gave two sharp little taps on the door; a voice inside asked:

"Who is there?"

"I—open the door—"

A whiff of warm air laden with various perfumes and a suspicion of other odors passed over his face.

The voice asked:

"What is it?"

He walked in without replying. He felt his wife standing close in front of him; her breath was on him, the lace of her dress touched his chest. He felt in his pocket for matches. Not finding any, he ordered:

"Light the lamp!"

She obeyed, and as his eyes ran over the room he saw the curtains drawn closely, a shawl on the carpet, the open bed, white and very large; and in a corner, near the fireplace, a man lying across a long rest-chair, his collar unfastened, his head drooping, his arms hanging loosely, his eyes shut.

He gripped his wife's wrist:

"Ah, you . . . filth! . . . Then this is why you turn your back on me!" . . .

She did not shrink from him, did not move. No shadow of fear passed over her pallid face.

She only raised her head, murmuring:

"You are hurting me!—"

He let her go, and bending over the inert body, his fist raised, cried:

"A lover in my wife's bedroom! And . . . what a lover! A friend . . . Almost a son . . . Whore!—"

She interrupted him:

"He is not my lover . . ."

He burst into a laugh.

"Ha! Ha! You expect me to believe that!"

He seized the collar of the recumbent man, and lifted him up toward him. But when he saw the livid face, the half-opened mouth showing the teeth and gums, when he felt the strange chill of the flesh that touched his hands, he started and let go. The body fell back heavily on the cushions, the forehead beating twice against a chair. His fury turned upon his wife.

"What have you to say? . . . Explain! . . ."

"It is very simple," she said. "I was just going to bed when I heard the sound of footsteps in the corridor . . . uncertain steps . . . faltering . . . and a voice begging, 'Open the door . . . open the door' . . . I thought you might be ill. I opened the door. Then he came, or rather, fell into the room. . . . I knew he was subject to heart-attacks. . . . I laid him there . . . I was just going to bring you when you knocked. . . . That's all . . ."

Bending over the body, and apparently quite calm again, he asked, every word pronounced distinctly:

"And it does not surprise you that no one heard him come in? . . ."

"The hounds bayed . . ."

"And why should he come here at this hour of the night?"

She made a vague gesture:

"It does seem strange . . . But . . . I can only suppose that he felt ill and that . . . quite alone in his own house . . . he was afraid to stay there . . . came here to beg for help . . . In any case, when he is better . . . as soon as he is able to speak . . . he will be able to explain . . ."

M. de Hartevel drew himself up to his full height, and looked into his wife's eyes.

"It appears we shall have to accept your supposition, and that we shall never know exactly what underlies his being here tonight . . . for he is dead."

She held out her hands and stammered, her teeth chattering: "It's not possible . . . He is . . ."

"Yes—dead . . ."

He seemed to be lost in thought for a moment, then went on in an easier voice:

"After all, the more I think of it, the more natural it seems . . . Both his father and his uncle died like this, suddenly . . . Heart disease is hereditary in his family . . . A shock . . . a violent emotion . . . too keen a sensation . . . a great joy . . . We are weak creatures at best . . ."

He drew an armchair to the fire, sat down, and, his hands stretched out to the flames, continued:

"But however simple and natural the event in itself may be, nothing can alter the fact that a man has died in your bedroom during the night . . . Is that not so?"

She hid her face in her hands and made no reply.

"And if your explanation satisfies me, I am not able to make others accept it. The servants will have their own ideas, will talk . . . That will be dishonor for you, for me, for my family . . . That is not possible. . . . We must find a way out of it . . . and I have already found it . . . With the exception of you and me, no one knows, no one will ever know what has happened in this room . . . No one saw him come in . . . Take the lamp and come with me . . ."

He seized the body in his arms and ordered:

"Walk on first."

She hesitated as they went out at the door.

"What are you going to do?"

"Leave it to me . . . Go on."

Slowly and very quietly they went toward the staircase, she holding high the lamp, its light flickering on the walls, he carefully placing his feet on stair after stair. When they got to the door that led to the garden, he said:

"Open it without a sound."

A gust of wind made the light flare up. Beaten on by the rain, the glass burst and fell in pieces on the threshold. She placed the extinguished lamp on the soil. They went into the park. The gravel crunched under their steps and the rain beat upon them. He asked:

"Can you see the walk? . . . Yes? . . . Then come close to me . . . hold the legs . . . the body is heavy . . ."

They went forward in silence. M. de Hartevel stopped near a low door, saying:

"Feel in my right-hand pocket . . . There is a key there . . . That's it . . . Give it to me . . . Now let the legs go . . . It is as dark as a grave . . . Feel about till you find the keyhole . . . Have you got it?—Turn . . ."

Excited by the noise, the hounds began to bay. Madame de Hartevel started back.

"You are frightened? . . . Nonsense . . . Another turn . . . That's it!—Stand out of the way . . ."

With a thrust from his knee he pushed open the door. Believing themselves free, the hounds bounded against his legs. Pushing them back with a kick, suddenly, with one great effort, he raised the body above his head, balanced it there a moment, flung it into the kennel, and shut the door violently behind him.

Baying at full voice, the beasts fell on their prey. A frightful death-rattle: "Help!" pierced their clamor, a terrible cry, super-human. It was followed by violent growlings.

An unspeakable horror took possession of Madame de Hartevel; a quick flash of understanding dominated her fear, and, her eyes wild, she flung herself on her husband, digging her nails in his face as she shrieked:

"Fiend! . . . He wasn't dead! . . ."

M. de Hartevel pushed her off with the back of his hand, and standing straight up before her, jeered:

"Did you think he was?"

Who?

THAT DAY I had worked very late, so late that when at length I raised my eyes from my desk, I found twilight had invaded my study. For some minutes I sat perfectly still, my brain in the dull condition that follows a big mental effort, and looked round mechanically. Everything was gray and formless in the half-light, except where reflections from the last rays of the setting sun made little patches of brightness on table or mirror or picture. One must have fallen with particular strength on a skull placed on the top of a bookcase, for, looking up, I saw it clearly enough to distinguish every detail from the point of the cheekbones to the brutal angle of the jaw. As everything else became swallowed up in the fast-deepening shadow, it seemed to me that slowly but surely this head quickened into life and became covered with flesh; lips came down over the teeth, eyes filled the orbits, and soon, by some strange illusion, I had before me, as if suspended in the darkness, a face that was looking at me.

It was watching me fixedly, the mouth set in a mocking smile. It was not one of those vague floating images one sees in hallucinations: this face appeared so real that for a second I was tempted to stretch out my hand to touch it. Immediately the cheeks dissolved, the orbits emptied, a slight mist enveloped it . . . and I saw nothing but a skull like all other skulls.

I lit my lamp and went on with my writing. Twice or thrice I raised my eyes to the place where I had seen the apparition; then the momentary excitement it had caused died away, and my head bent over my desk, I forgot all about it.

Now, a few days later, as I was going out of my house, near my door I passed a young man who drew aside to allow me to cross the road. I bowed. He did the same and went on. But the face was familiar, and believing it was someone I knew, I turned to look after him, imagining he might have stopped. He had not, but I stood watching him till he disappeared among the passersby. "A mistake on my part," I thought, but to my surprise, I kept on asking myself: "Where the devil have I seen him? . . . In the drawing-room? . . . At the hospital? . . . In my consulting-room? . . . No . . . I concluded that he must resemble someone else and dismissed him from my thoughts. Or tried to—for in spite of myself I continued to endeavor to place him. I certainly knew the head well: its deep-set eyes, hard, steady gaze, clean-shaven lip, straight mouth, and square jaw made it too characteristic to be either forgotten or mistaken for that of another person. Where on earth had I seen it? During the whole evening it obsessed me, coming between me and what I looked at, giving me that feeling of irritation caused by not being able to remember a name or some melody that haunts you. And this persisted for a long time, for weeks.

One day I saw my Unknown again in the street. As I approached I almost stared at him. On his part he looked at me with the same frigid expression, with the cold look I knew so well; but he betrayed no sign of knowing me, did not hesitate a second, and avoided me by turning sharply to the right. My conclusion was the inevitable one. If I really knew him he must also know me, and meeting me face to face for the second time, would have shown it by a glance or movement as if to stop. There had been nothing of this: I was therefore the victim of an illusion.

And I forgot all about him.

Some time after this, late one afternoon, a man was shown into my consulting room. He was hardly over the threshold when, much surprised, I rose to greet him: it was my Unknown. And once again the likeness that had so obsessed me was so striking that, mechanically, I walked toward him with out-stretched hand as to an acquaintance. He showed surprise, and I almost stammered as I pointed to a chair, saying:

"Excuse me, but you are so extraordinarily like . . ."

Under his cold, intent gaze, I left my sentence unfinished, saying instead:

"What can I do for you?"

Sitting quietly with his two hands stretched on the arm of his chair, he did not reply immediately. I was beginning once more to cudgel my brains: "Where have I seen him?" when suddenly a thought, or rather an extraordinary vision flashed into my mind, a vision amazing enough almost to surprise me into crying aloud: "I know." At last I had succeeded in locating him—I had recognized on the shoulders of this living man the head that had appeared to me one evening in the darkness above my bookcase! It was not a resemblance: it was identically the same face. The coincidence was sufficiently curious to distract my attention from what he was saying, and he had been talking for some moments before I began to follow his case:

"I don't think I was ever normal. When I was quite young I began to feel different from other boys, to have sudden desires to rush away, to hide myself, to be alone; while at other times I longed passionately for society, for wild excitements that would make me forget myself. Sometimes, for little or no reason, I had sudden fits of temper that almost choked me . . . They sent me to the sea, to the mountains: nothing did me any good. At the present time I start at the slightest sound; a very bright light hurts me like a pain; and though all my organs are sound—I have been to several doctors—the whole of my body aches. Even if I sleep, I wake in the morning as tired as if I had been dissipating all night. Frequently a feeling of agony of mind for which there is no real cause makes my brain giddy; I can't sleep, or if I do, I have horrible nightmares . . ."

"Do you drink?"

"I have a horror of wine, of every kind of alcohol; I drink nothing but water. But I haven't yet told you the worst . . ." (he hesitated) . . . "what it is that is really grave in my condition . . . If anyone contradicts me even, about a trifle, for a look, a gesture, a nothing, a sort of fury takes possession of me. I am careful never to carry any weapon in case I might be unable to resist using it. It seems to me that at these times my own will leaves me, as if that of someone else takes its place; it drives me on, I cease to be my own master, and when I come back to myself I can't remember anything—except that I wanted to murder someone! If one of these crises takes me when I am at home, I can shut myself up safely in my own room, but if, as sometimes happens, I am out, I know nothing more till I find myself perhaps sitting on a bench alone at night in some strange place. Then, remembering the fury I felt and coupling it with the lassitude that has followed and the impossibility of recollecting what I have done, I begin to wonder if I have committed some crime. I rush home and shut myself up, my heart beats violently whenever the bell rings, and I have no peace of mind till some days have gone by and I feel sure that once again I have been saved from myself. You will understand, Doctor, that this state of things can't go on. I shall lose not only my health, but my reason . . . What am I to do?"

"There's nothing to be really alarmed about," I replied. "These are only the symptoms of a nervous condition that will yield to treatment. Let us try to find its cause. Do you work very hard?—No.—Is there anything in your life that is likely to cause great nerve-strain?—No.—Any excesses?—None.—You can tell a doctor anything . . ."

His tone was convincing as he replied:

"I have told you the truth."

"Let us look for other reasons. Have you any brothers or sisters?—No.—Your mother is alive?—Yes.—She is probably very high-strung?—Not at all.—And your father?—Is he strong, too?"

In a very low voice he replied:

"My father is dead."

"He died young?"

"Yes, I was just two years old."

"Do you know what he died of?"

This question seemed to affect him deeply, for he grew very pale. At this moment more than at any other I was struck by the extraordinary resemblance between him and the apparition. After a pause, he replied:

"Yes . . . and that is why my condition terrifies me. I know what my father died of: my father was guillotined."

Ah, how I regretted having pushed my investigations so far! I tried to glide off to something else; but we now understood each other. Endeavoring to speak naturally and hopefully, I gave him some general advice and some kind of prescription; then I told him that he must have confidence in himself, and be sure to come back to me soon. After I had gone to the door with him I said to my servant:

"I will not see anyone else today."

I was not in a state to listen to or examine a sick person. My mind was confused: the apparition . . . the resemblance . . . this confession . . . I sat down and tried to collect my thoughts, but in spite of myself my eyes kept fixing themselves on the skull. I looked in vain for the strange resemblance that had for so long puzzled me—I saw nothing but its mysterious mask. But I was unable to keep my gaze from it; the head drew me toward it . . . I ended by leaving my chair and going to lift it down.

Then it was that, raising it in my hands, I became aware of an extraordinary thing that had till now escaped my notice. The lower part of the back of the head was marked by a broad and sharp groove, an unmistakable gash such as would be made by the violent stroke of an axe, such as is made on the necks of those who are executed by the instinctive retreat of the body at the supreme moment from the knife of the guillotine.

It may have been nothing but coincidence. Perhaps it could be explained by saying that I had already seen, without noticing, my consultant in the street, and that, unknowingly, the face thus subconsciously registered in my memory had come before me when I was looking at the skull the night of the apparition . . . Perhaps . . . perhaps? . . . But there are mysteries, you know, that it is wiser not to try to solve.

Illusion

B LUE WITH cold, clutching at the bottom of his pockets the few pence he had earned that morning by opening and shutting the doors of cabs, his head bent toward his shoulder in an attempt to get some shelter from the biting wind, the beggar moved among the hurrying crowd, too weary to accost, too benumbed to risk holding out a bare hand.

Blown sideways in powdery flakes, the snow caught in his beard, or melted on his neck. He did not notice it, for he was lost in a dream.

"If I were rich, just for an hour . . . I'd have a carriage . . ."

He stopped, thought for a moment, shook his head, and asked himself:

"And what else? . . ."

Visions of various kinds of luxury passed through his mind. But every time he formulated a wish, he shrugged his shoulders.

"No, that's not it . . . Is it then so difficult to get just one minute of real happiness? . . ."

As he trudged along in this way he saw another beggar who was shivering under the protecting doorway of a house, his features drawn, his hand outstretched, his voice so weak it was lost in the noises of the street as he droned:

"Help, if you please . . . Please help me . . ."

Close by him sat a dog, a poor bedraggled cur that trembled as it barked, feebly trying to wag its tail. He stopped. At the sight of this other brother in affliction, the dog yelped a little louder, rubbing its nose against him.

He looked with attention at the beggar, at his rags, his gaping shoes, his poor hands blue with cold, at the set, livid face with closed eyes, at the gray placard on his breast which bore the one word: "Blind."

Feeling that a man had stopped before him, the blind man took up his plaintive cry:

"Help, Monsieur . . . Pity the poor blind . . ."

The beggar stood motionless. The passersby quickened their steps, turning their heads away. A woman loaded with furs and followed by a servant in livery who held an umbrella over her came out of the door of the house and walking quickly on the tips of her toes as she protected her mouth with her muff, was swallowed up in her carriage.

The blind man kept on murmuring his monotonous appeal:

"Help . . . Please spare me a copper . . ."

But no one paid any attention to him. After a time the beggar took some coppers from his pocket and held them out. Seeing the action the dog barked with pleasure. The blind man closed his trembling fingers on the halfpence and said:

"Thank you, Monsieur . . . may God reward you . . ."

Hearing himself addressed as "Monsieur," the beggar was on the point of replying:

"I'm not 'Monsieur,' mate. I'm just another poor devil as miserable as yourself . . ."

But he restrained himself, and knowing only too well how the poor are spoken to, answered:

"It is very little, my poor fellow . . ."

"You are very kind, Monsieur . . . it is so cold, and you must have taken your hands out of your pockets for me. It is bad weather for the infirm . . . If people only knew . . ."

A great pity welled up in the heart of the beggar as he muttered:

"I know . . . I know . . ."

Then, forgetting his own poverty in the face of this greater affliction, he asked:

"Were you born blind?"

"No . . . it came as I grew old . . . At the hospital they told me that it was caused by age . . . cataract, they called it, I think . . . But I know better . . . I know that it wasn't only age that brought it . . . I have had too many misfortunes . . . I have shed too many tears . . ."

"You have had a great deal of trouble?"

"Oh, Monsieur! . . . In one year I lost my wife, my daughter, my two sons . . . all that I loved . . . all I had to love me. I almost died myself, but gradually I began to get better . . . But I wasn't able to work any more . . . Then it was poverty . . . destitution . . . Some days I don't have anything to eat at all. I've had nothing since yesterday but a crust of bread, and I gave half to my dog . . . With the money you gave me, I shall get some more for tonight and tomorrow."

As he listened the beggar turned over the coppers in his pocket. He was trying to count them, distinguishing by touch the difference between the pence and halfpence. He had elevenpence-halfpenny. He said:

"Come with me. It's too cold here. I will see that you have something to eat."

The blind man reddened with pleasure, stammering:

"Oh, Monsieur . . . you are too kind . . ."

"Come . . ."

Careful that the other should not feel how wet his own clothes were, how thin, he took him by the arm, and they set off. The dog, its head up, its ears cocked, led the way through the people, pulling sharply at its chain when they crossed a road where there was traffic. They walked on like this for a long time, finally stopping before a little restaurant in a back street.

The beggar opened the door and said to the blind man:

"Come in . . ."

Choosing a table near the stove, he made him sit down and took a chair near him.

Some workmen, all of them silent, were hungrily emptying the small thick plates before them. The blind man took the lead off his dog and held his hands out to the fire, sighing:

"It's very comfortable here . . ."

The beggar called the girl who was waiting and ordered some soup and boiled beef. She asked:

"And what will you have?"

"Nothing."

When the soup, which smelled very appetizing, and the meat were before him, the blind man began to eat slowly and in silence. The beggar watched him, cutting little bits of bread that he held under the table to the dog. The soup and meat finished, he said:

"Have something to drink. It will put some strength into your legs."

Later, he called the servant:

"How much?"

"Tenpence-halfpenny."

He paid, leaving the remaining penny for the girl, and helped his companion to rise. When they were back in the street, he asked:

"Do you live far from here?"

"Where are we?"

"Near St. Lazare station."

"Far enough. I sleep in a shed on the other side of the river."

"I'll go part of the way with you."

The blind man kept on thanking him. He replied:

"No . . . no . . . it's not worth mentioning . . ."

Without knowing why, he felt happy, supremely happy, happier than he ever remembered feeling. As he walked along, lost in dreamy thoughts, he forgot that he himself had been without food since yesterday, that he had no place to sleep in that night; he forgot his miseries, his rags, that he was a beggar.

From time to time he said gently to the blind man:

"Am I going too quickly? Are you very tired?"

The blind man, humble and grateful, answered:

"No . . . oh, no, Monsieur . . ."

He smiled, happy to hear himself addressed in that way, soothed alike by the illusion he was giving the other and his own odd sensation of being a rich, charitable person . . .

On the quay, feeling the dampness of the air from the river, the blind man said:

"Now I can find my way alone. I have my dog."

"Yes, I will say goodbye," replied the beggar in a solemn voice.

For a strange thought had taken possession of him: the illusion that he had so often and so ardently desired, had it not become a reality? Had he not at last enjoyed the sensation of perfect happiness? Had not this last hour given him more joy than any of his wildest dreams of wealth and rich food and love? This blind man had no suspicion that he had been leaning on the arm of a beggar as poor as himself . . . had he not been able to believe himself rich, and could he hope ever again to feel the deep, unmixed joy of tonight?

But the elation did not last long. Suddenly realities came back. He said a second time:

"Yes . . . I will leave you now."

They had reached the middle of the bridge. He stopped, felt once more in his pockets to see if by any chance a halfpenny remained there. Not one . . .

He grasped the blind man's hand, pressed it warmly, while the other said:

"Thank you once again, Monsieur. Will you tell me your name so that I can pray for you?"

"It's not worthwhile. Hurry out of the cold. It is I who am very happy. Goodbye . . ."

He went a little way back, stopped, looked fixedly at the dark expanse of water below him, and once again in a louder voice said:

"Goodbye . . ."

Then suddenly he leaped up on the parapet . . .

There was a great splash . . . then cries of "Help!" . . . "Run to the bank of the river!"

Pushed roughly about by the people who rushed up, the blind man cried:

"What is it? What has happened?"

A street urchin who had almost knocked him over shouted without stopping:

"A beggar has made a hole in the water."

With a weary gesture he shrugged his shoulders, murmuring:

"He at least had the courage, he had! . . ."

Then, touching his dog with the toe of his boot, he drudged on, tapping the ground with his stick, his face turned up to the sky, his back bent . . . without knowing . . .

In the Light of the Red Lamp

SEATED IN a large armchair near the fire, his elbows on his knees, his hands held out to the warmth, he was talking slowly, interrupting himself abruptly now and again with a murmured: "Yes . . . yes . . ." as if he were trying to gather up, to make sure of his memories: then he would continue his sentence.

The table beside him was littered with papers, books, odds and ends of various kinds. The lamp was turned low: I could see nothing of him except his pallid face and his hands, long and thin in the firelight.

The purring of a cat that lay on the hearth-rug and the crackling of the logs that sent up strangely shaped flames were the only sounds that broke the silence. He was speaking in a faraway voice as a man might in his dream.

"Yes . . . yes . . . It was the great, the greatest misfortune of my life. I could have borne the loss of every penny I possess, of my health . . . anything . . . everything . . . but not that! To have lived for ten years with the woman you adore, and then to watch her die and be left to face life alone . . . quite alone . . . it was almost more than I could bear! . . . It is six months since I lost her . . . How long ago it seems! And how short the days used to be . . . If only she had been ill for some time, if only there had been some warning . . . It seems a horrible thing to say, but when you know beforehand the mind gets prepared, doesn't it? . . . Little by little the heart readjusts its outlook . . . you grow used to the idea . . . but as it was . . ."

"But I thought she had been ill for some time?" I said.

He shook his head. "Not at all, not at all . . . It was quite sudden . . . The doctors were never even able to find out what was the matter with her . . . It all happened and was over in two days. Since then I don't know how or why I have gone on living. All day long I wander round the house looking for some reminder of her that I never find, imagining that she will appear to me from behind the hangings, that a breath of her scent will come to me in the empty rooms . . ."

He stretched out his hand toward the table. "Look, yesterday I found that . . . this veil, in one of my pockets. She gave it to me to carry one evening when we were at the theatre, and I try to believe it still smells of her perfume, is still warm from its contact with her face . . . But no! Nothing remains . . . except sorrow . . . *though there is something*, only it . . . it . . . In the first shock of grief you sometimes have extraordinary ideas . . . Can you believe that I photographed her lying on her deathbed? I took my camera into the white, silent room, and lit the magnesium wire: yes, overwhelmed as I was with grief, I did with the most scrupulous precaution and care things from which I should shrink today, revolting things . . . Yet it is a great consolation to know she is there, that I shall be able to see her again as she looked that last day."

"Where is this photograph?" I asked.

Leaning forward, he replied in a low voice: "I haven't got it, or rather, I have it . . . I have the plate, but I have never had the courage to touch it . . . Yet how I have longed to see it!"

He laid his hand on my arm: "Listen . . . tonight . . . your visit . . . the way I have been able to talk about her . . . it makes me feel better, almost strong again . . . would you, will you come with me to the dark room? Will you help me develop the plate?"

He looked into my face with the anxious, questioning expression of a child who fears he may be refused something he longs to have. "Of course I will," I answered.

He rose quickly. "Yes . . . with you it will be different. With you I shall keep calm . . . and it will do me good . . . I shall be much happier . . . you'll see . . ."

We went to the dark room, a closet with bottles ranged round on shelves. A trestle-table littered with dishes, glasses, and books ran along one side of the wall.

By the light of a candle that threw flickering shadows round him, he silently examined the labels on the bottles and rubbed some dishes.

Presently he lit a lamp with red glass, blew out the candle, and said to me:

"Shut the door."

There was something dramatic about the darkness relieved only by the blood-red light. Unexpected reflections touched the sides of the bottles, played on his wrinkled cheeks, on his hollow temples.

He said: "Is the door closely shut? Then I will begin."

He opened a dark slide and took out the plate. Holding it carefully at the corners between his thumb and first fingers, he looked at it intently for a long time as if trying to see the invisible picture which was so soon to appear.

With great care he let it glide into the bath and began to rock the dish.

I cannot say why, but it seemed to me that the tapping of the porcelain on the boards at regular intervals made a curiously mournful sound: the monotonous lapping of the liquid suggested a vague sobbing, and I could not lift my eyes from the milk-colored piece of glass which was slowly taking on a darker line round its edges.

I looked at my friend. His lips were trembling as he murmured words and sentences which I failed to catch.

He drew out the plate, held it up to the level of his eyes, and said as I leaned over his shoulder:

"It's coming up . . . slowly . . . My developer is rather weak . . . But that's nothing . . . Look, the high lights are coming . . . Wait! . . . you'll see . . ."

He put the plate back, and it sank into the developer with a soft, sucking sound.

The gray color had spread uniformly over the whole plate. His head bent over it, he explained:

"That dark rectangle is the bed . . . up above, that square"— he pointed it out with a motion of his chin—"is the pillow: and in the middle, that lighter part with the pale streak outlined on the background . . . that is . . . Look, there is the crucifix I put between her fingers. My poor little one . . . my darling!"

His voice was hoarse with emotion: the tears were running down his cheeks as his chest rose and fell.

"The details are coming up," he said presently, trying to control himself. "I can see the lighted candles and the flowers . . . her hair, which was so beautiful . . . the hands she was so proud of . . . and the little white rosary that I found in her Book of Hours . . . My God, how it hurts to see it all again, yet somehow it makes me happy . . . very happy . . . I am looking at her again, my poor darling . . ."

Feeling that emotion was overcoming him and wishing to soothe, I said:

"Don't you think the plate is ready now?"

He held it up near the lamp, examined it closely, and put it back in the bath. After a short interval he drew it out afresh, re-examined it, and again put it back, murmuring:

"No . . . no . . ."

Something in the tone of his voice and the abruptness of his gesture struck me, but I had no time to think, for he at once began to speak again.

"There are still some details to come up . . . It's rather long, but as I told you my developer is weak . . . so they only come up one by one."

He counted: "One . . . two . . . three . . . four . . . five . . . This time it will do. If I force it, I shall spoil it . . ."

He took out the plate, waved it vertically up and down, dipped it in clean water, and held it toward me:

"Look!"

But as I was stretching out my hand he started and bent forward, holding the plate up to the lamp, and his face, lit up by the light, had suddenly become so ghastly that I cried:

"What is it? What's the matter?"

His eyes were fixed in a wide terrified stare, his lips were drawn back and showed teeth that were chattering: I could hear his heart beating in a way that made his whole body rock backwards and forwards.

I put my hand on his shoulder, and unable to imagine what could possibly cause such terrible anguish, I cried for the second time:

"But what is it! Tell me. What's the matter?"

He turned his face to me, so drawn it no longer seemed human, and as his bloodshot eyes looked into mine he seized me by the wrist with a grip that sent his nails into my flesh.

Thrice he opened his mouth trying to speak; then brandishing the plate above his head, he shrieked into the crimson-lit darkness:

"The matter? . . . the matter? . . . I have murdered her! . . . She wasn't dead! . . . the eyes have moved! . . ."

A Mistake

"Doctor," said the man, "I want you to examine me and tell me whether I am suffering from tuberculosis. I want to know the truth. I have enough courage to hear the worst without flinching. I consider, too, that it is your duty to speak with perfect frankness, and that it is my right to know my exact condition. Will you promise to do as I ask?"

The doctor hesitated, pushed back his armchair, leaned against the chimney-piece beneath which burned a large fire of logs, and replied:

"I give you my word. Will you undress yourself?"

While the patient took off his clothes, the doctor questioned him:

"You feel weak! You have night-sweats! . . . You have had them, but don't know. Do you cough much? Little fits of coughing early in the morning? . . . Are your parents still alive? Do you know what they died of? . . ."

The man, his chest bare, said:

"I am ready."

The doctor began to sound him. The sick man followed the examination carefully, listening attentively as he stood with his heels together, his arms drooping, his chin raised. In the silent room the taps of the finger sounded like a hollow scale. Afterwards came the auscultation, long and careful. When he had finished; the doctor gave him a little slap on the shoulder and smiled:

"Dress yourself. You are very highly strung, essentially nervous, but I can assure you there is nothing wrong, absolutely nothing . . . You don't seem particularly glad to hear it?"

The man, who was dressing himself, stopped, his arms in the air, his head half out of the front of his shirt: there was a piercing expression in his eyes, and it was with a mocking laugh that he replied:

"Oh, yes, I am . . . Very glad . . ."

He put on the rest of his clothes in complete silence. The doctor was at his desk, writing a prescription. He stopped him with a gesture: "Useless . . ."

He took a louis from his pocket, put it on the corner of the table, sat down, and in a voice that trembled slightly began to talk:

"Now for a little conversation. Eighteen months ago, a patient came here asking you, just as I did a few minutes ago, to tell him the truth. You examined him, quickly, it is true, then told him that he was tubercular, that his state was very grave—Oh! don't protest, don't defend yourself, I am certain of all I say—and that he must never marry, much less have children."

"I don't remember," murmured the doctor, "but it is possible . . . I have so many consultants . . . But I can't quite see what you are leading up to . . ."

"To this: that I was that consultant. I lied to you when I said I was unmarried. I was married and the father of children. When the door shut behind me, you never gave me another thought. I was only a negligible unit among the thousands of unhappy creatures who die every year of consumption. But for me your diagnosis had awful consequences."

He passed his hand over his eyes and went on:

"When I got home my wife and little girls were waiting for me. It was winter, but indoors it was the essence of comfort. A big fire blazed on the hearth. Warmth, sweetness, happiness . . . all were there. Till that day I had loved the hour of return, the rest with my dear ones grouped round me: I loved my wife's embraces, the kisses of my children, and all day long I looked forward to the moment when I should be free to forget with them the worries of business and all my troubles. When my wife held her lips up to me that evening I drew back, and I pushed away my little girls when they ran to me.

"The seed you had sown in my mind was beginning to grow.

"We sat down to dinner. During the meal I tried to hide my preoccupation. But I was sad; heartbroken, thinking of the beloved beings I should soon have to leave, of my home deprived of its support, of the children who would grow up fatherless.

"To others who know themselves condemned there remains the consolation of being able to press to their hearts those they must leave behind: they face the Hereafter filled with the happiness such compensation means. But I! . . . A permanent danger to everyone I went near, I carried Death in me. Still alive, I was cut off from the number of the living: I had no longer any right to the joys of other men.

"When bedtime came my children clustered round me as they did every evening.

"I pushed them away. My mouth, my horrible mouth, must never go near theirs again. Presently I went to bed. Slowly all became quiet in the house and the streets. I put out my lamp and lay awake near my wife, whose quiet breathing I could hear.

"The interminable hours of a sleepless night dragged by. I pressed my hands on my chest, trying to discover with my fingers the weak spots in my lungs. I had no pain, hardly enough discomfort to make me believe in the truth of your verdict. Such unreasonable revolts are natural. The wish father to the thought, I ended by believing that you had made an error of judgment. I said to myself: 'It's impossible: I will consult another doctor . . .'

"Suddenly I heard coughing in the next room. I started. The cough, which came from my children's room, sounded again, dry, sharp and ending in a sort of rattle. Terrified, I stretched out my hand to my wife, but I was afraid to wake her, and I waited. The coughing began again. I got up quietly and went into the room where the children slept. In the glimmer of the night-light, I could see them lying in their beds. It seemed to me that the older one was flushed. I touched her hand. It seemed hot. I bent over her. She coughed several times and turned restlessly on her pillow. I stayed beside her a long time: she kept coughing. I went back to bed, but hardly had I lain down when a terrible thought took possession of me: 'Like me, she is tubercular!'

"I had no doubt about it. I accepted it as a fact."

He leaned forward, and his hands grasping his knees, asked:

"At that moment you had no idea of what you had done, had you?

"The next day was unbearable. I dared not tell my wife that our child was ill. I had not the courage to call in a doctor. I was afraid of what he would say, of what I knew he was going to say: I was ashamed of myself, and cowardice kept me silent.

"But my mind did not stand still. It was no longer only a question of contagion. A still more terrifying specter confronted me: that of Heredity. My children had inherited my physical condition, just as they had my eyes, my hair. Even if they had escaped that awful law, the mere fact of my being near them had contaminated them.

"Imagination, you say! Nonsense. You and the whole fraternity, haven't you taken pains to educate the ignorant public through the newspapers and magazines, by conferences! . . .

"All that I had read and heard surged up in my memory.

"One after another my wife and little daughters would gradually fade, dragging out martyred lives till the fatal end came . . . And I, I should watch it all: in their faces, in their wasting bodies, I should follow the progress of the disease. No science could alter the inevitable."

He lifted his finger and spoke in a deep, low voice.

"Then—follow me carefully—living haunted by this thought, I grew to believe that there are cases when it is a man's duty to stop suffering which he knows to be inevitable: that he has the right to undo what he has done, to suppress, make an end of beings condemned to physical torture, the right to be the Destiny that saves them from such a fate.

"You shudder, you are afraid of understanding, . . . Yes, with my own hands I killed my children and my wife, killed, you hear me, killed them. I poisoned them, and did it so quickly and cleverly no one ever suspected me.

"At first I meant to put an end to myself as well, but I deserved punishment, not for having killed them, for I believed my action a legitimate one, but for having brought them into the world. And what greater expiation could I have imposed on myself, than that of bearing alone, full of misery, the burden of the existence from which I had saved them, the sufferings from which I had set them free?

"And now, see what happened. Some weeks after they were gone strength began to come back to me. The pain in the side went, the blood-spitting ceased. I ate with appetite. I began to put on flesh. Yes, I began to grow fat!

"At first I believed that in some mysterious way the progress of the disease had momentarily stopped so that it might reassert itself later with greater violence. But after some months I was obliged to recognize facts: I was growing better, I was cured. I say 'cured.' Had I ever been tubercular?

"This thought, vague at first, took shape. Do you understand what it meant? If I were tubercular, what I had done was necessary. If I were not, I had murdered without excuse, for no reason.

"I gave myself a year to make sure, hoping that the arrested disease would reappear, trying by every kind of imprudence to set it working again. Useless. Then came the conviction, the certainty, that you had been wrong, had been guilty of a shameful error of judgment. An overwhelming sadness took possession of me. I had deliberately ruined my life, killed innocent creatures, plunged myself in the years of mourning through which I was dragging my way—and why? Because of your mistake. And I have come here today to hear you yourself confess it, that mistake!"

He rose and crossed his arms on his chest.

"Could you have admitted it more stupidly? You didn't see my eyes just now when you assured me that there was nothing wrong with me, 'absolutely nothing.' No, for if you had seen them you would have trembled with fear, you would have read in them what I am going to tell you . . ."

The doctor was very pale as he stammered:

"My God, I am not infallible . . . Nowadays this idea of tuberculosis has become an obsession, creeps into everything . . . It influences one unconsciously . . . one is apt to give importance to a sound that may be accidental, something temporary . . . I may have been wrong . . . the greatest physicians have made mistakes in their diagnoses . . . I will examine you again . . ."

The man burst into a terrible laugh:

"You will, will you! . . . For what kind of a fool do you take me? You run yourself on to the point of a sword, and you think you can get free by a graceful twist? There is nothing wrong with me! You have told me so. Nothing, nothing, nothing! This time—and for the best of reasons—I will accept your word without question.

"But you have made me into an assassin, and you are my accomplice. Unconscious accomplice? I agree with you. You were the brain, and I, I was the arm. And as Justice is everlastingly the same, I—'the highly strung, the essentially nervous!'—I judge, I condemn and I execute. You first. Myself afterwards."

Two shots rang out. The servants rushed in to find the two bodies lying on their backs.

Some brain and blood had splashed on the table and made a crimson mark on an unfinished prescription that ran:

> Bromide 15 grams
> Distilled water. . . .

Extenuating Circumstances

IT WAS from the newspapers that Françoise learned that her son had been arrested.

At first she was unable to believe it; it was too monstrous.

Her lad, her little lad, so well-behaved, so shy, who just a month ago had spent his Easter leave with her; her son a thief and a murderer? . . . She seemed to see him standing before her again in his soldier's uniform, his round young face smiling and kind; she felt again on her wrinkled cheeks his hearty goodbye kisses, and, filled with happy and peaceful memories of him, she shrugged her shoulders, repeating:

"Of course it's a mistake. It's someone else."

Still, there it was, written with a big headline: "Crime of a Soldier." It had happened in his barracks, and his name was there in full.

Bewildered, she crouched in her chair, her spectacles pushed up on her forehead, her hands clasped, her mouth trembling as she talked to herself in the warm silence of the kitchen, her eyes looking vaguely at the old dog lying by the open door, at the tall clock whose slow tick-tock gravely marked the time.

Someone came in. She started violently, crying: "Who's there?" Recognizing a neighbor and wishing to hide her agitation, she added:

"I was asleep . . . It's hot . . ."

Habitually reserved and silent, today she went on talking, talking, asking questions and making replies, fearing that she herself might be questioned. As she uttered her disjointed sentences, her one thought was: "Does she know?"

Unable at last to think of anything else to say, she relapsed into silence. With an odd expression, the neighbor said:

"Is it long since you had news of your son?"

"No . . . This morning."

She did not say how! But as she spoke there came to her an overwhelming desire to be reassured, to be comforted, to hear a voice echo her indignant: "It's a mistake! It's not my lad—how could it be? . . ."

She held out the paper, and trying to speak easily:

"Have you seen this? . . . Queer, isn't it?" Her throat dry, the tears welling up in her eyes, she added:

"I was so stupid . . . When I saw it first, it gave me quite a turn! . . . What a fool! . . ."

The neighbor still remained silent. She repeated:

"But it's strange, isn't it? . . . It's strange! . . ."

"Yes, it's odd there should be two of the same name in the same regiment."

With a great sigh of relief, the old woman cried:

"That's just what I say! . . . That's it! . . . there are two of them . . . It's not mine! . . ."

"I don't know anything about that," answered the woman. "I'm only asking you . . . It's to be hoped there are . . . because if it's your lad . . . They are saying it was him that robbed the cooper . . . yes, the three hundred francs that were stolen when he was home at Easter."

The mother drew herself up stiffly, white as death, her fists clenched:

"How dare they! . . . He never did it . . . never, never! . . . Aren't you ashamed of yourself? . . . What have we done to you that you put everything on us? . . . My poor little lad . . . Oh, but you shall all see! . . ."

And without shutting the door behind her, without even putting on her sabots, she hurried, almost running, to the railway station.

She arrived at the town just as it was striking seven. In the train, instead of diminishing, her fears had grown. She was no longer saying: "It is impossible!" but "Suppose it is true! . . ." The journey had seemed endless, with the villages and fields rushing past her, the telegraph poles rising and falling giddily like a swing. When the train stopped she began to tremble, almost feeling that the moment to know the truth had come too quickly. She was murmuring Paters and Aves, adding her own supplications to the prayers that came mechanically to her lips:

"O, Kind Virgin, you could never have let such a thing happen, could you? . . . The beautiful prayers I shall say to you presently! . . ."

Behind the iron gate the courtyard of the barracks stretched white in front of the square buildings. Soldiers were sitting on the steps, chatting in the evening calm. Her boy had taught her the different ranks. She stopped, saying timidly:

"Excuse me, Sergeant, I want to ask you something. I want to know . . ."

She hesitated, not daring to show her fear.

"It's this. It's about my son . . . Jules Michon of the 3rd Company . . . I want to know if . . . if I can see him . . ."

She tried to smile:

"I am his mother . . . his mother . . . No? But why? . . . Where is he? . . . Is he ill? . . . Then why can't I? . . . Yes, I know . . . No, I don't know . . . He has been arrested . . . At the police station? . . . No? . . . In . . . in prison . . . you say? . . . He is to be tried by court-martial? . . ."

She hid her face in her hands.

Holy Virgin, it was true then! Holy Virgin . . .

Staggering, she turned away. At the military prison she learned that her son was in solitary confinement, and the word "solitary" increased her terror. She imagined him alone, forever shut away from everyone, fastened in. They told her to go and see a lawyer. From him she learned the exact state of affairs. There was no possible doubt about it. Her boy had killed someone to rob him; they had found the money—nearly six three hundred francs—in his mattress. He had confessed.

After much weeping and useless begging to be allowed to see him, she went back to the village. Everyone knew. Shrinking from what they might say to her, dreading their looks, she did not go home till midnight. Like a poor animal who fears blows and hides itself, she no longer dared to go out, keeping her shutters closed, trembling as she lifted the paper that was pushed under her door every morning. From it she learned not only all the details of the crime, but that her son was accused of something else. All the evidence seemed to prove that it really was he who had robbed the cooper. But that—never! She would swear it was not true . . . But eventually she began to have doubts about even that.

At the end of a month she went back to the lawyer. She no longer asked to see her son. Not, great God, that she had ceased to love him . . . She was ashamed . . .

"What will they do with him, Monsieur? You won't let them take him from me . . ."

"My poor woman, I am very much afraid they will . . . If only I could find some extenuating circumstance . . ."

"What's that? A circumstance . . . what does it mean?"

"It means something that will lessen the crime in the eyes of the judge. Here is an example: A man steals; if it can be proved that he did it because he was in great poverty, because his children were starving, that would be an extenuating circumstance. In his case there's nothing of the kind. It's not even his first offense. That other robbery—he denies it—but— Well, well, I will do everything that can possibly be done."

Françoise went home wearier and more heartbroken than ever, her mind tortured by those new words: "Extenuating circumstances." How, where, could she find some excuse that would move the judges to clemency? . . . There was none. She could see nothing but the crime; nothing could lessen its horror.

The day of the trial came. She set out again, the last step in the ascent of her Calvary. In the train she prayed, invoking all the saints, while through her empty brain there resounded the words, so often repeated: "Extenuating circumstances . . . Extenuating circumstances . . ."

She waited in the dark, gloomy room with the witnesses who lowered their voices because of her presence. When her turn came she walked into the box with faltering steps, her eyelids blinking in the clear light, and in a moment her eyes were on her boy, who bowed his head over a handkerchief with big blue squares and burst into short, sharp sobs . . . She drew herself up stiffly and faced the judge.

She herself had asked to go into the witness box. Standing there, she wondered vaguely why she had insisted. She knew nothing at all about it; she had nothing to say. Why was she

there? . . . For no reason at all except that she was his mother.
Was it not she who had borne him . . . nursed him . . . caressed
him . . . brought him up? . . . Was he not hers, her very own? . . .
But no, not now; today he did not belong to her.

To all the questions she replied by signs or unintelligible words.
There was dense silence in the court. An infinite pity went out
toward the old, black-robed peasant woman, bowed by sorrow.

"He is your only child?" said the judge.

"Yes, Monsieur."

"Did you have anything to complain of when he lived with you?"

"Oh no, Monsieur!"

"Had he any bad companions?"

"Never. His father, who was liked and respected by everyone,
would not have allowed it . . . Neither would I . . . We were very
highly thought of . . ."

"We know . . . we know . . ."

Then, turning to the prisoner:

"You knew it, too, and that is why, screening yourself behind
the good reputation of your parents, you took advantage of your
stay with your mother to commit robbery . . . How could anyone
suspect the son of such honest people? . . . Others may be able
to say: I am not wholly responsible. I lived with people who set
me a bad example. You . . . you have no such excuse."

At this the old woman seemed to make a violent effort. A
strange light shone under the tear-swollen lids of her small eyes,
and, her head bowed, without a gesture, in a voice that was
almost steady, she spoke.

"Forgive me, Monsieur. I see I must tell you the truth. My
poor lad is guilty of much, very guilty . . . But he is not the only
one . . . I told you just now I had nothing to reproach myself
with . . . I lied. That three hundred francs of the cooper's, it was
I who stole them, me . . . When my Jules came home at Easter,
I told him I had done it . . . It frightened him, poor lad . . . he is
very young . . . he saw his mother might lose her honor and her
reputation . . . and it was to get the money back and stop my
being arrested that he stole that other money . . . He was interrupted . . . he lost his head . . . and he struck the blow without
knowing what he did."

She was silent for a moment, out of breath: then went on in a lower tone:

"I lied . . . I am a wicked woman. It was I who set him the bad example . . . It is me you must arrest . . . Is that an extenuating circumstance for him? . . . Forgive me, Monsieur . . ."

More bowed than ever, the shoulders drooping, the head lower, she seemed to shrink to nothing . . .

The son escaped with hard labor for life. She—soon afterwards she died, scorned by all the village. They said a hasty mass for her and laid her in a remote part of the graveyard, a corner where even on the sunniest days the shadow of the church or belfry does not reach.

This story was told me by her grave, which had nothing to ornament it but a cross of weatherbeaten wood and a single wreath of rusty beads, twisted and broken, on which, however, I could distinguish the words:

"To Françoise Michon. From the judge who tried her son."

The Confession

I STOOD STILL for a moment before the open door, hesitating, and it was only when the old woman who had been sent to bring me said for the second time, "It is here," that I went in.

At first I could see nothing but the lamp screened by a low-drawn shade; then I distinguished on the wall the motionless shadow of a recumbent body, long and thin, with sharp features. A vague odor of gasoline and ether floated round me. But for the sound of the rain beating on the slates of the roof and the dull howling of the wind in the empty chimney, the silence was death-like.

"Monsieur," said the old woman gently as she bent over what I now saw was a bed, "Monsieur! . . . the gentleman you asked for is here."

The shadow raised itself, and a faint voice said:

"Very well . . . leave us, Madame . . . leave us . . ."

When she had shut the door after her, the voice went on:

"Come nearer, Monsieur. I am almost blind, I have a buzzing in my ears, and I hear very badly . . . Here, quite close to me, there ought to be a chair . . . Pardon me for having sent for you, but I have something very grave to tell you."

The eyes in the face that craned toward me were wide open in a sort of stare, and he trembled as he faltered:

"But first, are you Monsieur Gernou? Am I speaking to Monsieur Gernou, leader of the bar?"

"Yes."

He sighed as if with relief.

"Then at last I can make my confession. I signed my letter Perier, but that is not my real name. It is possible that if Death, so near me now, had not already changed my face, you might vaguely recognize me . . . But no matter . . .

"Some years ago, many long years, I was Public Prosecutor for the Republic . . . I was one of the men of whom people say: 'He has a brilliant future before him,' and I had resolved to have one. I only needed a chance to prove my ability: a case at the assizes gave me that chance. It was in a small town. The crime was one that would not have attracted much attention in Paris, but there it aroused passionate interest, and as I listened to the reading of the accusation I saw there would be a big struggle. The evidence against the prisoner was of the gravest nature, but it lacked the determining factor that will frequently draw a confession from the criminal—or the equivalent of a confession. The man made a desperate defense. A feeling of doubt, almost of sympathy ran through the court, and you know how great the power of that feeling is.

"But such influences do not affect a magistrate. I answered all the denials by bringing forward facts that made a strong chain of circumstantial evidence. I turned the life of the man inside out and revealed all his weak points and wrong-doings. I gave the jury a vivid description of the crime, and as a hound leads the hunters to the quarry, I ended by pointing to the accused as the criminal. Counsel for the defense answered my arguments, did his best to fight me . . . but it was useless. I had asked for the head of the man: I got it.

"Any sympathy I might have felt for the prisoner was quickly stifled by pride in my own eloquence. The condemnation was both the victory of the law and a great personal triumph for me.

"I saw the man again on the morning of the execution. I went to watch them wake him and prepare him for the scaffold, and as I looked at his inscrutable face I was suddenly seized with an anguish of mind. Every detail of that sinister hour is still fresh in my memory. He showed no sign of revolt while they bound his arms and shackled his legs. I dared not look at him, for I felt his eyes were fixed on me with an expression of superhuman calm. As he came out of the prison door and faced the guillotine, he cried twice: 'I am innocent!' and the crowds that had been prepared to hiss him suddenly became silent. Then he turned to me and said: 'Watch me die, it will be well worth while' . . . He embraced the priest and his lawyer . . . It appears that he then placed himself unaided on the plank, that he never flinched during the eternal moment of waiting for the knife, and that I stood there with my head uncovered. It appears . . . for I, I did not see, having for the moment lost all consciousness of external things.

"During the days that followed my thoughts were too confused for me to understand clearly why I was full of some trouble that seemed to paralyze me. My mind had become obsessed by the death of this man. My colleagues said to me:

"'It is always like that the first time.'

"I believed them, but gradually I became aware that there was a definite reason for my preoccupation: doubt. From the moment I realized this I had no peace of mind. Think of what a magistrate must feel when, after having caused a man to be beheaded, he begins asking himself:

"'Suppose after all he were not guilty! . . .'

"I fought with all my strength against this idea, trying to convince myself that it was impossible, absurd. I appealed to all that is balanced and logical in my brain and mind, but my reasonings were always cut short by the question: 'What real proof was there?' Then I would think of the last moments of the criminal, would see his calm eyes, would hear his voice. This vision of the scaffold was in my mind one day when someone said to me:

"'How well he defended himself; it is a wonder he did not get off . . . Upon my word, if I had not heard your address to the Court I should be inclined to think he was innocent.'

"And so the magic of words, the force of my will to succeed were what had quieted the hesitations of this man as they had probably triumphed over those of the jury. I alone had been the cause of his death, and if he were innocent I alone was responsible for the monstrous crime of his execution.

"A man does not accuse himself in this way without trying to put up some sort of a defense, without doing something to absolve his conscience, and in order to deliver myself from these paralyzing doubts I went over the case again. While I reread my notes and examined my documents, my conviction became the same as before; but they were *my* notes, *my* documents, the work of my probably prejudiced mind, of my will enslaved by my desire, my need to find him guilty. I studied the other point of view, the questions put to the accused and his answers, the evidence of the witnesses. To be quite sure about some points that had never been very clear, I examined carefully the place where the crime had been committed, the plan of the streets near the house. I took in my hands the weapon the murderer had used, I found new witnesses who had been left out or neglected, and by the time I had gone over all these details twenty times I had come to the definite conclusion, now not to be shaken, that the man was innocent . . . And as if to crown my remorse, a brilliant rise in position was offered me! It was the price of my infamy.

"I was very cowardly, Monsieur, for I believed I did enough in tendering my resignation without assigning any reason for it. I traveled. Alas! forgetfulness does not lie at the end of long roads . . . To do something to expiate the irreparable wrong I had caused became my only desire in life. But the man was a vagabond, without family, without friends . . . There was one thing I could have done, the only worthy thing: I could have confessed my mistake. I had not the courage to do it. I was afraid of the anger, the scorn of my colleagues. Finally I decided that I would try to atone by using my fortune to relieve those who were in great trouble, above all, to help those who were guilty. Who had a better right than I to try to prevent men being condemned?— I turned my back on all the joys of life, renounced all comfort and ease, took no rest. Forgotten by everyone, I have lived in solitude, and aged prematurely. I have reduced the needs of life to a minimum . . . For months I have lodged in this attic, and it is here I contracted the illness of which I am dying. I shall die here, I wish to die here . . . And now, Monsieur, I have come to what I want to ask you . . ."

His voice became so low I had to watch his trembling lips to help myself to understand his words.

"I do not wish this story to die with me. I want you to make it known as a lesson for those whose duty it is to punish with justice and not because they are there *to punish in any case*. I want it to help to bring the Specter of the Irreparable before the Public Prosecutor when it is his duty to ask for a condemnation."

"I will do as you ask," I assured him.

His face was livid, and his hand shook as he gasped:

"But that is not all . . . I still have some money . . . that I have not yet had time to distribute among those who have been unfortunate . . . It is there . . . in that chest of drawers . . . I want you to give it to them when I am gone . . . not in my name, but in that of the man who was executed because of my mistake thirty years ago . . . give it to them in the name of Ranaille."

I started.

"Ranaille? But it was I who defended him . . . I was . . ."

He bowed his head.

"I know . . . that is why I asked you to come . . . it was to you I owed this confession. I am Deroux, the Public Prosecutor." He tried to lift his arms toward the ceiling, murmuring:

"Ranaille . . . Ranaille . . ."

Did I betray a professional secret? Was I guilty of a breach of rules that ought to be binding? . . . the pitiful spectacle of this dying man drew the truth from me in spite of myself, and I cried:

"Monsieur Deroux! Monsieur Deroux! Ranaille was guilty . . . He confessed it as he went to the scaffold . . . He told me when he bid me goodbye there . . ."

But he had already fallen back on the pillow . . . I have always tried to believe that he heard me.

The Test

NOT A muscle quivered as the man stood with his gaze fixed on the dead woman.

Through half-closed eyes he looked at the white form on the marble slab; milky-white it was, with a red gash between the breasts where the cruel knife had entered. In spite of its rigidity, the body had kept its rounded beauty and seemed alive. Only the hands, with their too transparent skin and violet fingernails, and the face with its glazed, wide-open eyes and blackened mouth, a mouth that was set in a horrible grin, told of the eternal sleep.

An oppressive silence weighed on the dreary, stone-paved hall. Lying on the ground beside the dead woman was the sheet that had covered her: there were bloodstains on it. The magistrates were closely watching the accused man as he stood unmoved between the two warders, his head well up, a supercilious expression on his face, his hands crossed behind his back.

The examining magistrate opened the proceedings:

"Well, Gautet, do you recognize your victim?"

The man moved his head, looking first at the magistrate, then with reflective attention at the dead woman as if he were searching in the depths of his memory.

"I do not know this woman," he said at length in a low voice. "I have never seen her before."

"Yet there are witnesses who will state on oath that you were her lover . . ."

"The witnesses are mistaken. I never knew this woman."

"Think well before you answer," said the magistrate after a moment's silence. "What is the use of trying to mislead us? This confrontation is the merest formality, not at all necessary in your case. You are intelligent, and if you wish for any clemency from the jury, I advise you in your own interest to confess."

43

"Being innocent, I have nothing to confess."

"Once again, remember that these denials have no weight at all. I myself am prepared to believe that you gave way to a fit of passion, one of these sudden madnesses when a man sees red . . . Look again at your victim . . . Can you see her lying there like that and feel no emotion, no repentance? . . ."

"Repentance, you say? How can I repent of what I have not done? . . . As for emotion, if mine was not entirely deadened, it was at least considerably lessened by the simple fact that I knew what I was going to see when I came here. I feel no more emotion than you do yourself. Why should I? I might just as well accuse you of the crime because you stand there unmoved."

He spoke in an even voice, without gestures, as a man would who had complete control of himself. The overwhelming charge left him apparently undisturbed, and he confined his defense to calm, obstinate denials.

One of the minor officials said in an undertone:

"They will get nothing out of him . . . He will deny it even on the scaffold."

Without a trace of anger, Gautet replied:

"That is so, even on the scaffold."

The sultry atmosphere of an impending thunderstorm added to the feeling of exasperation caused by this struggle between accusers and accused, this obstinate "no" to every question in the face of all evidence.

Through the dirty window-pane the setting sun threw a vivid golden glare on the corpse.

"So be it," said the magistrate: "You do not know the victim. But what about this?"

He held out an ivory-handled knife, a large knife with clotted blood on its strong blade.

The man took the weapon into his hands, looked at it for a few seconds, then handed it to one of the warders and wiped his fingers.

"That? . . . I have never seen it before either."

"Systematic denial . . . that is your plan, is it?" sneered the magistrate. "This knife is yours. It used to hang in your study. Twenty people have seen it there."

The prisoner bowed.

"That proves nothing but that twenty people have made a mistake."

"Enough of this," said the magistrate. "Though there is not a shadow of doubt about your guilt, we will make one last decisive test. There are marks of strangulation on the neck of the victim. You can clearly see the traces of five fingers, particularly long fingers, the medical expert tells us. Show these gentlemen your hands. You see?"

The magistrate raised the chin of the dead woman.

There were violet marks on the white skin of the neck: at the end of every bruise the flesh was deeply pitted, as if nails had been dug in. It looked like the skeleton of a giant leaf.

"There is your handiwork. Whilst with your left hand you were trying to strangle this poor woman, with your free right hand you drove this knife into her heart. Come here and repeat the action of the night of the murder. Place your fingers on the bruises of the neck . . . Come along . . ."

Gautet hesitated for a second, then shrugged his shoulders and said in a sullen voice:

"You wish to see if my fingers correspond? . . . and suppose they do? . . . What will that prove? . . ."

He moved toward the slab: he was noticeably paler, his teeth were clenched, his eyes dilated. For a moment he stood very still, his gaze fixed on the rigid body, then with an automatonlike gesture, he stretched out his hand and laid it on the flesh.

The involuntary shudder that ran through him at the cold, clammy contact caused a sudden, sharp movement of his fingers which contracted as if to strangle.

Under this pressure the set muscles of the dead woman seemed to come to life. You could see them stretch obliquely from the collarbone to the angle of the jaw: the mouth lost its horrible grin and opened as if in an atrocious yawn, the dry lips drew back to disclose teeth encrusted with thick, brown slime.

Everyone started with horror.

There was something enigmatic and terrifying about this gaping mouth in this impassive face, this mouth open as if for a death-rattle from beyond the portals of the grave, the sound only held back by the swollen tongue that was doubled back in the throat.

Then, all at once, there came from that black hole a low, undefined noise, a sort of humming that suggested a hive, and an enormous blue-bottle with shining wings, one of these charnelhouse flies that live on death, an unspeakable filthy beast, flew out, hissing as it circled round the cavern as if to guard the approach. Suddenly it paused . . . then made a straight course for the blue lips of Gautet.

With a motion of horror, he tried to drive it away; but the monstrous thing came back, clinging to his lips with all the strength of its poisonous claws.

With one bound the man leaped backwards, his eyes wild, his hair on end, his hands stretched out, his whole body quivering as he shrieked like a madman:

"I confess! . . . I did it! . . . Take me away! . . . Take me away! . . ."

Poussette

E VERY MORNING as the clocks of the town struck six, the old maid left her house, shutting the door carefully behind her, and grasping tightly in her hand an old prayer book with broken corners and greasy pages, she crossed the road quickly and hurried to the neighboring church to hear the first mass.

There, in the almost empty nave, kneeling on her prie-dieu, her hands clasped, her head trembling, the murmur of her prayers mingled with the voice of the priest. When the service finished she went quickly home.

Her face was thin, and her narrow, obstinate forehead was covered with lines, but her deeply set eyes flamed with a strange fever.

As she walked she mumbled prayers and counted the beads of her rosary. Her heels made no sound on the pavement, and round her there floated a vague smell of incense and damp stones as if the long years of churchgoing had impregnated her yellow fingers and pointed knees with the odor of the old vestry and the vaults.

She lived alone in a suburb in a little house full of old-fashioned furniture, ancient portraits, and religious emblems; her only companion was a gray cat she called Poussette, a thin old cat that lay half asleep all day, glancing with an indifferent eye at the movements of the flies, sometimes rising lazily to look through the windowpanes at a leaf carried on the wind.

The old maid and the old cat understood each other. Both of them loved their hermitlike existence, the silence of the long summer afternoons with the shutters closed, the curtains drawn. They were afraid of the streets which seemed to them full of dangers.

Hidden behind the *persiennes*, the old maid watched the passers-by, listening to their footsteps dying away in the distance, and the cat stretched out its neck, drew itself up on three

47

legs and turned away from the other cats that crouched by the doors, licking themselves with their heads bent back, or disappearing like dark flashes as they ran away.

In bygone days when the warm, fragrant silence of night seemed to bathe the motionless trees in love, the cat would sometimes stretch out its neck toward the gardens, replying to the calls of the males whose shadows moved on the roofs; and excited by their entreaties, she would rub her flanks against the legs of the chairs.

Then the old maid used to snatch her up, shut her in the bedroom, open the window and cry in a voice of hate:

"Go away! . . . Get away! . . ."

The miaulings would cease for a moment, and when they broke out afresh and the shadows began to leap again, she would shut the shutters, draw the curtains closely, and shrinking in her bed, draw the cat under the clothes so that it should not hear the noise, stroking it between the ears to soothe it to sleep.

A fury took possession of her at the mere thought of the caresses of love. Proud of her virginity, she hated all that was not chaste, and the function of the flesh seemed to her a diabolical thing by which the Tempter soiled, made vile both beast and man. She reddened with anger when she saw lovers arm-in-arm in the moonlight, birds flying after each other at night, doves joining their beaks at the edge of their nest.

At one time the cat had been beautiful, with shining fur and firm, round limbs, and neighbors had more than once asked its mistress:

"Will you lend her to us? She and our cat would make such beautiful kittens."

"No! I wish to keep her. for myself . . ." she had answered, frowning as she drew the creature against her flat chest.

By degrees the animal had become ugly. Its sterile flanks had fallen in. In the cloisterlike atmosphere Poussette seemed to have forgotten her instinct. Her ardent flesh had slowly but surely lost its virility, and she no longer seemed to hear the insistent calls of the males.

One summer night, however, she became restless, left the armchair where she slept, and began to prowl about in the shadow. Outside on the roof-gutters the cats were miauling.

She stretched out her paws, dug her claws into the carpet, beat her sides with her tail, and responding suddenly to a surge of nature, slipped out through the half-open door into the garden.

When she found herself with the others, the long-repressed instinct woke into vibrating life. Her jaws distended, her claws clinging to the slates, she flung herself among the males, her cries mingling with their calls, yelling joyfully as they bit her.

The noise awakened the old maid and she sat up in bed to listen. Never had the cries of the Flesh sounded so loudly, rung so triumphantly in her ears. She got up quickly to protect her animal from them, and not finding her on the armchair, called:

"Poussette! . . . Little Poussette! . . . Come here! . . . Come! . . ."

Usually one word brought the cat to her side. This time there was no response. Looking about, she found that the door was half open, and she was seized with fear, not that someone might have broken in, but the fear that Poussette had escaped. She struck a match, and while the little blue flame flickered without giving any light, she murmured:

"It's not possible! . . . My God! . . . Poussette! . . ."

But when the candle was lit, she gave a cry of rage.

Poussette was not there.

Out into the garden, full of flower-scent and moonlight, she rushed, calling, calling . . .

Upon the roof, the cat, now appeased, was gently rubbing itself against the side of its companion; it looked fixedly, disdainfully, at her for a moment, then fell back to its caressings, its head bent forwards, its body stretched out.

At six o'clock, when the old maid set out for church, Poussette was still missing.

The service finished, she hastened back, forgetting to tell her beads. She had paid but scant attention to the mass, kneeling and rising mechanically, her mind tortured by memories of the night.

She found the cat lying on a chair, sleeping so soundly that it scarcely moved an ear when it was called.

Livid with rage, she seized it by the neck and flung it on the floor. The surprised animal stood still for a second, yawned, arched its back, sat down, blinked its eyelids, then, its whole body slack, rolled itself up and went to sleep again.

From that moment the old maid kept it at a distance,

shrinking from it as from something impure. If it approached, she pushed it away with her foot:

"Get away! Get away!"

Sometimes, livid with rage, she lifted it up between her thin fingers, glared into its eyes and flung it on the ground; or if the cat got in her way, she seized and beat it on the head, on the shoulders, the flanks, above all on the flanks, finding in this chastisement a ferocious and holy joy. The beast submitted to all this without a sign of revolt.

This went on for six weeks. The old maid avoided her neighbors as might a mother who dreads hearing the name of an unworthy child.

One morning when she had beaten the cat harder than usual and was belaboring its belly, the beast leaped up, its paws raised, its fur bristling.

"Ah!" cried the old maid. "You are going to begin scratching me now, are you? We'll see about that . . ."

But hardly had she raised her hand when the cat made a bound toward her face, digging its claws in her cheeks.

Terrified, she gave a loud shriek and fled to her bedroom, her face covered with blood.

For her Poussette was now a diabolical animal, and she dared not open her door, fearing she would see again its flaming eyes and threatening teeth.

Kneeling on her prie-dieu, she shuddered:

"The Demon is after me! . . . The Demon is here in this house! . . ."

At night she crouched in her bed with her eyes open, her chin on her knees, listening to every sound, feeling no fatigue as she muttered:

"The Demon! . . . The Demon! . . ."

Soon she had no longer the strength to speak, and her lips trembled over words she could no longer hear.

When nearly a week had gone by, surprised not to see her at mass, the priest called at her house. Some of the neighbors joined him as he stood knocking at the door.

"Something must be wrong. We would have gone in to see if we could do anything for her, but we dared not, she is so rude . . . with you it will be different . . . She will be glad to see you . . ."

They knocked at the shutters; no reply. They knocked again; silence.

"Yes, something must be wrong," murmured the priest.

He turned the handle of the door. It opened, and the neighbors followed him in.

Everything was in order. In the dining-room the remains of breakfast were still on the table. Some coffee, covered with a gray skim, was in the bottom of a cup. Flies buzzed round a piece of sugar, and little curls of butter, very yellow, were melting on a plate.

"Perhaps she is in her bedroom?" hazarded a woman.

They opened the door. At first they could not see anything, for the shutters were closed and the curtains closely drawn. The woman bent her head to listen and whispered:

"There is someone here! . . . Listen . . . someone is breathing."

A man went forward, drew the curtains, opened the window and pulled back the shutters; a flood of sunshine poured in.

The old woman was crouching in a corner near the foot of the unmade bed; she had nothing on but a chemise that showed her thin chest, and her disordered hair hung about her. Seeing the figures bending over her, she hid her face, which was covered with caked blood, in her hands, shuddering as she moaned:

"Satan! Satan! The Demon! . . ."

The priest tried to take her hand, to speak to her:

"Don't you know me? . . . It is I . . . your priest . . ."

But she only cried the louder, her nails digging into her forehead:

"Satan! The Demon! The Demon!"

He shook his head and said sadly:

"Alas, our poor friend has lost her reason! She, so pious! Who would have thought it possible? What can have happened to her? Look! She has been tearing her face with her own hands. Go and bring a doctor: I will stay here with her."

While they hurried out on their errand and the old maid continued to mutter in a hoarse voice: "The Demon! The Demon! . . ." the priest went back to the dining-room where he stooped with a smile to caress the cat. It was lying stretched out on its side, its chin up, its eyes half closed, purring as it offered its rose-colored teats to three kittens . . .

The Father

WHEN THE last spadeful of earth had been shoveled in and the last handshake given, the father and the son went home, walking slowly, as if every step were an effort. They were silent, for there had suddenly fallen on them the great weariness that follows an effort that has been too long sustained.

The house, still impregnated with the scent of flowers, calm again after the agonies, the comings and goings of the last few days, seemed strangely empty and new. The old servant who had come home before them had put all in order. They had the feeling of having returned after a long journey, but there was no joy in the homecoming, nothing of that deep sigh that means: "Ah! How good to be in one's own place again . . ." Yet outwardly all was as before. Curled up in a ball, a cat purred softly before the fire, and the winter sun shone with mild brightness on the windowpanes.

The father sat down by the fire, shook his head and sighed: "Your poor mother . . ."

Two tears rolled down the kind, round face that was a little congested by sorrow, the cold of the street, and the warmth of the room.

Presently, moved by the desire to hear something more than the purring of the cat, the tick-tock of the clock and the crackling of the wood in the grate, conscious, perhaps, of a kind of satisfaction in still being alive while others had gone forever, he began to talk:

"Did you see the Duponts? They were all there; the presence of the grandfather touched me very much . . . Your mother was very fond of them all . . . How was it your friend Bremard wasn't there! . . . But perhaps he was; in such a crowd one can't see everyone . . ."

He sighed again: "My poor lad" . . . his thoughts turning with redoubled tenderness to this big son of twenty-five who sat silently near him, his mournful eyes fixed on the fire.

The old servant came quietly in, so quietly they did not hear her open the door.

"Come, come, sir, you musn't sit here like this! You must have something to eat."

They raised their heads.

It was true. They must eat. Life must go on as before. They were hungry, not with the delightful hunger of the days when it is a pleasure to sit down to a well-spread table, but with the hunger of the animal whose stomach is empty. Till now a kind of self-consciousness had held them back. As she spoke they looked at each other silently, both desiring, yet fearing, the first tête-à-tête at a table made too large by the empty place.

And the father, the tears again rising in his eyes, murmured:

"Yes, you are quite right . . . Get dinner ready . . . You must eat something, my boy . . ."

The son nodded and rose.

"I will change my coat, then I will come."

He went out, shutting the door behind him. His steps went automatically toward his mother's room, and his hand was on the door-handle when the old servant approached, saying in a low voice:

"Monsieur Jean, I have something for you . . . a letter your mother gave me eight days ago just after she knew she couldn't get well . . . She told me to give it to you . . . when it was all over . . . Here it is."

Surprised, he stopped and stared at her. She was looking at him in a curious, hesitating way; the fingers in which she held the envelope were trembling, and instantly he had the conviction that some great secret, some great sorrow, was about to be revealed to him.

His throat contracting, he said:

"Give it to me . . ." and went into the room.

Without noticing what he was doing, he turned the key in the door.

The room, the bed too flat, the curtains too far drawn, the grate fireless, and the furniture arranged in too orderly a way, had already a look of being disused, deserted.

For some time he stood turning the letter about in his fingers, transfixed by the sight of the living handwriting of the dead woman, the dear, familiar writing that here on the slightly crumpled envelope showed itself less firm than usual.

Through a partition of curtained glass he could hear the comings and goings of the servant who was laying the table in the next room.

He tore open the envelope and read:

My beloved child,

I feel that the moment for the eternal farewell is very near. I go without fear, almost without regret, knowing you are a man now and for a long time have been able to get on without my help. My conscience tells me I have been the best of mothers. Yet a very grave secret lies between us, one I have never had the courage to tell you, but which it is essential you should know.

The woman you have so much loved and, above all, respected, she to whom you ran with every childish trouble, to whom you have brought all the perplexities of your manhood, your mother, my darling, has been guilty of a great sin. You are not the son of the man you have always called 'father.'

There has been in my life a great, an immense love, and my chief fault has been that I have never confessed it. Your father, your real father, is alive. He has watched you grow up, and he loves you. You are now old enough to decide the big things of life for yourself. You can completely change your life if you wish to do so. You can be rich tomorrow if you have the courage that has always failed me. I know I am doing a cowardly thing . . . but having acted so badly during my life, it seems inevitable I should end in the same way. A hundred times I have been on the point of leaving the house, taking you away with me. But I have not had the energy to do it. The slightest thing would have given me that energy: a suspicion . . . a harsh word . . . But there has never been anything . . . Not a cloud . . .

He ceased reading, overcome by the revelation.

His mother had consistently deceived her husband! . . . She had been able to live a lie all these years. She had been able to go on talking and smiling without in any way betraying either her wrongdoing or any kind of repentance. And he, till now pitiless toward the weakness of women, he for whom all pride, all joy, all veneration had been summed up in the word: "Mother! . . ." he had grown up there an intruder, a living insult to the good man whose attitude toward him had invariably been one of kindness, of tenderness! . . .

All his childhood rose before him. He saw himself again a tiny child walking about the street clinging to his father's hand . . . He grew older . . . For months a very severe illness had held him between life and death, and he saw again his father sitting by his bedside, tears in his eyes as he tried to smile . . . Time went on . . . Business troubles had come, and memories were of a still more touching kind . . . the conversations he had overheard at night after he had been tucked into bed. The mother very quiet; the father saying: "I will retrench in every possible way . . . I will give up smoking . . . I will give up cafés and my club . . . My clothes are still quite good . . . Whatever happens the child must not suffer . . . The bad moment will soon pass . . . If I economize in every way we shall be able to prevent his feeling it . . . These little ones have all their lives to suffer in . . . it is cruel to sadden them while they are young! . . ."

And this was the man she had deceived.

He sat down and buried his head in his hands. A phrase in the letter came back to him: "You are old enough now to decide the big things of life for yourself."

It was true. He had not the right even to hesitate. The idea of money never crossed his mind. It was just a question of having the courage she had lacked. He would leave the house without saying anything about it . . . He would go away somewhere, far away, and never come back. In that way the shame, the shame that he now knew of, would go with him. How could he ever sit down again at that table without flushing as he heard the kind voice calling him: "My dear boy," and talking fondly of the "poor mother"? . . .

He had decided, but he was sobbing:

"Oh, mother mother . . . What have you done! . . ."

It was goodbye to the quiet home life, the daily return to a house made sacred by memories; he could not, must not, had not the right to carry on the lie.

As he sat down, lost in his sad thoughts, a sound came from the dining-room.

"Poor boy . . . He feels it so keenly . . . He is in his mother's room . . . Let him stay there if he wants to . . . How it has changed our lives . . . I feel as if I have grown old, old. Thank God I still have him. He is a good boy; he won't leave me."

He raised his head, biting his lips. The father went on talking, and as he listened his thoughts went off in another direction. The course on which he had decided seemed less easy, his duty not so clear.

"He won't leave me . . ."

Had he the right to abandon this poor soul, to leave him to grow old alone in a deserted home? . . . To go away—was that all he could do to repay his unfailing kindness, his efforts for him, his self-denial?

But he was not his son . . . His presence under his roof had in it something intolerable, odious . . . Yet he must decide at once; if he hesitated it would be too late.

He was still holding his mother's letter. He went on reading it:

"The slightest thing would have given me that energy: a suspicion . . . a harsh word . . . But there has never been anything . . . not a cloud . . ."

Behind the partition, the voice of the father was saying: "Yes, I have lived twenty-seven years with her, and during the whole of that time there was never a cloud . . ."

The same words . . . the same phrase . . . He went back to the letter:

"And now I am going to tell you the name of your real father. It is . . ."

The paper trembled in his fingers. If he turned the page the name would be forever engraved in his eyes, in the depth of his being . . . and then . . . he could no longer . . .

The voice called gently:

"Come along, dear lad, dinner is waiting on the table . . ."

He drew back his head and shut his eyes for a second. Then he took a match, raised his arm, and set fire to the paper. He watched it burn slowly, and when the flame got down to his nails, he opened his fingers. A square of black ash fell on the floor. A little white corner burnt itself out . . . Nothing was left . . .

He opened the dining-room door, looked for a moment at the good man who stood waiting for him, the mild face full of affection, the eyelids swollen, the hands tremulous—and with a gesture like that of a child, he flung his arms round the stooping shoulders as one might embrace a beloved being they had imagined they would never see again. And there was a catch in his voice that sounded like a sob as he said:

"Father! My dear old father!"

"For Nothing"

CERTAINLY THIS Jean Gautet did not look like a dangerous criminal.

He was a sickly little being of uncertain age with an air of premature suffering. The eyes that wandered about behind the spectacles which from time to time he adjusted on his nose with a quick movement were quiet and mild; he had the look of a child who fears being scolded rather than that of an assassin.

But arrested a few hours after he had committed the crime, he had not even attempted to defend himself, had confessed the moment the policeman laid a hand on his arm. Since then he had taken refuge in almost complete silence.

"Why don't you explain your action?" said the judge at length. "Seeing you declare you did not know your victim, seeing you did not steal anything from his house, why did you kill him?"

"For nothing . . ."

"You must have had a reason . . . No one goes to a man's house and drives a knife into him without a motive . . . Why did you do it?"

"For nothing . . ."

"Had he harmed you in any way? . . ."

This time he flinched, lowered his eyes, made a vague gesture and murmured:

"No . . ."

But suddenly changing his tone, he added:

"Well, yes! . . . It wasn't for nothing . . . There was a reason . . . If I have kept silent all this time it is because I didn't explain at first, and it was hard to do it afterwards . . . Some confessions are very difficult to make . . .

"I am an illegitimate child. My mother had to work very hard to keep me. I had a joyless childhood . . . Too many tears were

58

shed in my home. At school they called me the 'Bastard.' I didn't understand, but I soon found it meant something very sad, for when I asked my mother about it she hid her face in her hands and cried. Instinctively I avoided using the word again. She never complained and never told me her story till she lay on her deathbed . . . I was then fourteen years old.

"At fourteen I found myself alone in the world, without relatives, without friends, tired of life before I had begun to live.

"Just at first it was not so hard. I found a place where they fed me and gave me a bed. From time to time they gave me old clothes. The years passed . . . When I was twenty I became dependent on myself, and then I learned what poverty meant . . . For two years I had to keep myself entirely on a pound a week, and as I wasn't a laborer—I was a clerk in a wholesale house—it was necessary for me to be properly dressed . . . To get clothes I had to economize in what I spent on food. I could only afford one meal a day—and there was very little of that . . . Sometimes I became faint and giddy in the streets, had to lean against a wall to keep myself from falling . . . hunger, of course . . .

"One morning when I got to the office, my employer said to me:

"'I am not pleased with the way you are doing your work. For some time you have been making mistakes. You don't seem to concentrate on what you are doing . . . Then you are careless about your appearance, and I don't like that. My clerks must look neat and respectable.' He touched the frayed revers of my coat. 'That's not the way to come to this office.'

"I tried to make excuses, but he wouldn't listen.

"'Nonsense! A man need never be ragged.'

"The other clerks were coming and going as he spoke, and I felt the blood rush to my head at the thought that they might hear . . .

"That day I had nothing at all to eat.

"When the stomach is empty, the brain works. The tears kept coming into my eyes as I bent over my desk. I wept from hunger and shame, and as I sat there in despair there came to me for the first time the idea that I could not be alone in the world seeing that my father was still alive. After all, I had a father. The thought comforted me and strengthened me. I resolved to go and find him. I would explain my position to him. He was rich, and he would be sure to help me when he knew my circumstances. Was I not his son?

"Next day I rang his bell. I felt almost tenderly disposed toward him. He was a little bowed old man with a pallid face and shuffling walk; everything about him showed he was ill, worn out. He said:

"'Who are you? What do you want?'

"The tone of his voice froze me. I stammered as I tried to explain the object of my visit. But hardly had I begun when, trembling, he interrupted me.

"'Not so loud . . . Lower your voice . . . Someone may hear . . .'

"He got rid of me as quickly as possible, pushing me toward the door with vague words.

"'Leave me your address . . . I will see what I can do for you . . . Yes . . . I will see . . . I am ill . . . I will write to you . . .'

"I went home trying to collect my ideas.

"I waited a whole week; he made no sign. I dared not go back to him, fearing I might upset him again. I told myself he could never let me die of hunger. I took to walking near his house. As far as I could without letting them guess my secret, I got the neighbors to talk.

"'Oh!' said one of them, 'if you are hoping to move him in any way, you'd better give it up at once . . . He has no more heart than a paving-stone. In any case, his money won't be of any use to him much longer. He is so ill he can hardly drag himself about . . .'

"I risked asking whether he had any relatives or friends.

"'Friends!' The man shrugged his shoulders. 'As to relatives, he may have a great-nephew in some corner in France, but he won't get anything. Everything he has will go to the woman who has been his housekeeper for fifteen years. She boasts about it. She declares he has often told her that not a halfpenny of his money is to go to his family, that he was not such a fool as to let his death make them rich, that she shall have everything. You will guess whether she counts the coppers.'

"Suddenly I began to hate my father. Was he not the cause of all my misfortunes?

"I went away and wandered about the streets, paying no attention to where I was going. A sense of injury blotted out every other feeling. I must have been walking a very long while when, almost fainting with hunger, I went into a low eating-house, near the fortifications I think it was . . . When I had paid the bill I had not one farthing left, and there were still six days before the end of the month. What was to become of me? As I wondered, my fingers touched the knife I had used to cut my bread. It was a long knife, thin, pointed—I don't know why I took it, but I did.

"I am not trying to excuse myself or lessen my crime, but the feeling of having that knife in my pocket, close against my side, turned my brain . . . I grasped the handle . . . I tried the blade with my fingers . . . And without knowing how or why it happened, I found myself standing in front of my father's house.

"I didn't argue with myself about it; there was no fighting against any horrible ideas. I wasn't thinking at all. Deliberately, without any kind of hesitation, I rang the courtyard bell . . . The door opened. I muttered the first name that came into my head . . . and I went up the stairs.

"When I got to the door of my father's flat, I stopped, vaguely aware of the madness of what I was doing. If I rang, no one would open the door at that hour of night . . . If I made any noise, the neighbors would come out to see what was the matter . . . I should be flung downstairs.

"I felt in my pocket for the key of my own door and slipped it quietly in the keyhole. It went in without a sound . . . I turned it as easily as a burglar would . . . Something gave way . . . The door opened. Stupefied by the coincidence of the key of my door exactly fitting his, I stood perfectly still in the dark for some seconds, asking myelf for the first time what I was doing there.

"At the same moment I saw a line of light on the carpet. Very quietly I opened a second door.

"A man—my father—was sitting with his back to me. He did not raise his head.

"A lamp with a lowered green shade lit the table over which he was bending. All the rest of the room was in deep shadow. He was writing. I could only see his bald head and thin shoulders. Holding my breath, I stole behind him and drew myself up on tiptoe. A large sheet of paper lay on his blotter. I read:

'THIS IS MY WILL.'

Underneath there were three lines of smaller writing. The words the neighbors had spoken flashed into my mind, and I seemed to see the greedy old servant who had taken the place that ought to have been my mother's.

"A frenzy ran through me. So I, his son, I who was going to die of hunger, I was beside him, starving at the very moment when with a few strokes of his pen he was going to do this abominable thing, make it irrevocable. Not a farthing would come to me, his own flesh and blood, who would die for need of it . . . All was for the old harridan who was counting the minutes till he died . . . It was impossible. He should not do it . . . I bent forward and read:

" 'I leave all I possess, money, houses . . .'

"I ground my teeth. He started violently, turned his head, and seeing my face, which at that moment must have been terrifying, cried out, with an instinctive movement covering the paper with his arm as if to prevent my seeing it.

". . . The knife was in my hand . . . I drove it forward, and with a force that seemed to make my own bones creak, sent the blade through his neck above his collar . . .

"Then I realized what I had done . . . I rushed away . . . You know the rest . . ."

He took off his eyeglasses and dried his eyes. Drops of sweat were running down his face; he was trembling violently.

The judge, who had been watching him closely, unfolded a large sheet of paper stained with a brown mark, and said:

"And you read nothing else on this page?"

He shook his head.

"Well, listen. I will read the rest to you:

" 'THIS IS MY WILL.

" 'I leave all I possess, money, houses, and furniture to Jean Gautet, my son, asking him to forgive me for having been the bad father I—'

"You didn't leave him time to finish."

The murderer drew himself up with a jerk, his eyes wild, his mouth gaping as he stammered:

"To my son? . . . Me? . . . I? . . ."

There was a pause; then he burst into a shriek of wild laughter, beating his head, and swaying about as he yelled:

"I am rich! I am rich!"

He had gone mad.

In the Wheat

WITH LONG strokes, slow and rhythmic, Jean Madek thrust his scythe into the wheat, and at the touch of the blade the sheaths that quivered at the end of the stalks fell down softly with a long *froufrou* like silk.

He advanced, measuring his steps by the supple balance of his arm, and behind him the ground showed itself brown, spotted here and there by groups of stones, bristling with thick-set sprigs of reddish straw.

His old mother followed close behind him, her back bent as she gathered up the scattered stalks, and seeing only her feet dragging their heavy sabots, her two wrinkled, knotted hands and her body covered with rags, one might have imagined she was some animal crouching on its four feet.

The sun mounted in the horizon. A heavy heat weighed on everything, wrapping the country in torpor, and the field looked like a large piece of ripe fruit, its sap rising in a penetrating perfume.

Gleaning steadily, the old woman grumbled:

"What's your wife doing as late as this? When's she coming?"

"She'll bring dinner at twelve o'clock."

The old woman shrugged her shoulders:

"At least she's not overtiring herself! . . ."

"She's like everyone else. Whether she's here or at the farm, she's at work."

"Oh! Work of that sort! . . ."

Then, as if talking to herself as she continued to scrape the ground:

"Our master isn't here either this morning. Perhaps he stayed behind to give her a hand? . . ."

The man held back his scythe:

"What do you mean by that?"

"Me? . . . Nothing . . . Words . . . Something to say . . ."

Jean went on with his work. The old woman began again as if speaking to herself:

"My dead husband wouldn't have had it . . . When he went to the fields, I didn't stay behind to keep the master company."

A second time the reaper raised his head.

"Why are you telling me that?"

"I was thinking, inside me, that your father was more suspicious than you are . . ."

The son straightened himself with a jerk.

"What is it? What do you mean? You must have some reason for talking like this . . ."

"If you must have it, then," blurted the old woman from her stooping position, "people are gossiping about you and about Céline . . . Nasty gossip, too!"

"Who gossips?"

"No one . . . and everyone . . . What's more, you can't blame them: they can't help seeing what's under their noses."

"Lies!"

Without seeming to hear him, the old woman pushed aside a clod of earth with her foot and continued:

"I'm telling you for your good. I'm your mother, and I oughtn't to hide anything from you . . . You can be angry if you like. But you've had your warning."

"I tell you it's all lies. Céline is a good housewife, never tired of work; she has everything she wants . . . Why should she be unfaithful? Why? . . ."

The old woman made a vague gesture: "Who can tell?"

Changing her tone, she went on:

"Besides, I'm not saying she is . . . I'm only speaking for the good of both of you. She is young, she likes to amuse herself, to dress smartly, to go to market on Saturdays. Temptation often takes people quickly. At the beginning they see no harm in it. They let someone give them a ribbon, a fichu, a comb for the hair, a watch-chain . . . And to be able to wear them, they say they were bargains, got for next to nothing . . . that they picked them up on the road. Perhaps it's true . . ."

Every one of the slow words struck into the husband's brain. He thought of his wife's return one evening after she had accompanied the master to the town. He pictured her as he saw her the following Sunday with her lace fichu and moiré ribbons. Above all, he saw the gold chain she said she had picked up on the road . . .

The monotonous voice of the old woman continued:

"It's not her that I'm meaning, of course! But a husband isn't always there: he's in the fields: he goes off to do his month's military service . . ."

The man was no longer listening. His two hands crossed on his scythe, his eyes vague, he was absorbed in the recollections that crowded into his mind. All kinds of little incidents gave weight to the insinuations of the old woman: the master, a known libertine, very hard on all his workers, but always particularly amiable to him: the wife coquettish. And suddenly he remembered that in a week he would have to leave for a long month with his regiment.

At the bottom of the field, under the big trees, a call rang out, and raising himself, Jean Madek saw the head and shoulders of his wife emerging from the gold of the plain, and a few steps behind her, swinging his short, thick stick among the corn, the master with his red face and big, shady-brimmed hat.

And a laughing voice cried:

"Here's the pittance!"

One by one the workers rose out of the corn, sat down under a tree and began to eat their dinner.

Jean sat silent, slowly cutting his black bread into pieces.

"Why are you so quiet, Madek?" said the farmer.

"Are you ill?" added the wife.

"No, but the sun strikes hard. It must have been better in the house?"

The master broke into a laugh:

"You're about right there!"

The meal finished, everyone lay down for a nap. They would start work again when the sun had lost a little of its ardor. Madek did not sleep. Lying on his stomach, his chin in his hands, he was lost in thought . . .

As two o'clock struck, the men got up, went back to the field, and once more over the gold of the corn, unruffled by any breeze, there sang the rhythmic sound of the scythes.

When they were all at work the master stretched himself slowly, and in a sleepy voice shouted to the wife of Madek:

"Come and give an eye here, Céline; have you by any chance a needle with you?"

"Yes, master."

"Then come and put a stitch in my blouse. The cows are in the meadow. There's plenty of time before you need fetch them. The sun has turned. It's too hot here just now. I'm going over there under the apple tree. Come to me when you've finished your sheaf. Come by the path so as not to beat down the corn."

They smiled stealthily at each other. But Madek, who was watching, had seen. He made a movement as if to speak, then he lowered his head and went on with the reaping.

The old woman had gone. It was now his wife who was following him. When she had tied up her sheaf he said, without turning:

"Didn't you hear what the master said to you?"

"Yes, I did . . ."

"Then what are you waiting for?"

"I'm just going . . ."

She fastened up her hair, which had come undone while she stooped; and, her two hands flat on her hips, her waist swaying under her bright petticoat, she strolled along the path, a corn-flower between her teeth.

He watched her being swallowed up in the verdure as one is swallowed up in the sea, and when she had quite disappeared in the shadow of the apple tree that stood out on the horizon, he set to work again.

His movements had lost their quiet ease of the morning. He went forward in jerks, stopping sharply, then on again, his head lowered, his jaw clenched, an ugly frown on his forehead.

All the old woman had said was fermenting in him like new wine, fizzing in his temples, filling him with a sort of drunken rage. At first there had been doubt; then had followed certainty, which had taken deeper root because of the incidents that had just happened.

He was advancing, and before him he seemed to see his wife and the master laughing and kissing each other in the shadow of the apple tree.

He was advancing, throwing the weight of his whole body into his arms. Behind him the sheaves fell, and the field that his scythe devoured seemed to grow larger. Never in the earliest vigor of his manhood had he been able to work like that.

From a distance, a fellow-worker called: "Are you going to cut it all today?"

Without looking up, he replied:

"Perhaps."

When he was only a few yards from the apple tree he stopped, listening intently; murmurs reached him. A voice, the voice of his wife, said:

"No . . . He might be able to see us . . ."

And another rougher one replied:

"Keep still! He's at the other end of the field. It'll be half an hour before he gets here . . . Come closer! . . ."

For some seconds he stood as if transfixed, livid under his sunburn; then, with a sharp gesture of decision, he went on reaping. But he had slowed down. The sweep of the scythe was almost noiseless. The wheat fell to the earth without a sound. When he was almost under the tree he heard the sound of kisses. Pulling himself up to his fullest height, with a furious movement he lifted the scythe. The blade leapt up, gleaming white in the sun, came down and plunged . . . Two horrible shrieks rang out, and two frightful things, two heads, bounded up and fell again, bespattering the stalks that broke with a grating sound . . .

The scythe flew up out of the corn-waves, all red . . .

Madek threw it away, and waving his bloody hands in the air, roared:

"Help! . . . An accident . . . They were there! . . ."

The Beggar

IT WAS growing dark, and the beggar stopped at a ditch by the side of the road and looked for a corner where he could spend the night. He rolled himself up in a sack that was his nearest approach to an overcoat, placed the little packet he carried on the end of his stick under his head for a pillow, and exhausted by fatigue and hunger, sank down and watched the stars prick through the dark sky.

The road, which was bordered by woods, was deserted. The birds were asleep in the trees. Away in the distance the village made a big black patch, and a lump came into the old man's throat as he lay there in the calm and silence.

He had never known his parents. Picked up out of charity, he had been brought up on a farm, but at an early age he had taken to the road looking for work that would provide him with food. Life had been very hard on him. He had never known anything of it but miseries: long winter nights spent under the shadow of mills; the shame of begging, the desire to die, to go to sleep and never wake again. All the men he had come in contact with had been suspicious and unkind. His great trouble was that everyone seemed to fear him; children ran away when they saw him; the dogs barked at his dusty rags.

But in spite of it all he bore no one any ill-will; he had a simple, kindly nature dulled by misfortune.

He was falling asleep when horse-bells sounded in the distance. He raised his head and saw a bright light moving above the ground. He watched it without interest. He could distinguish a heavy wagon and a big horse. The load was so high and so broad it seemed to fill the road. A man walked near the horse humming a song.

Soon the song ceased. The road was uphill. The hoofs of the horse struck and grated violently on the stones. With voice and whip the man urged the animal on:

"Gee up! . . . Up."

It was pulling with all its strength, its neck stretched out. Twice or thrice it stopped, almost fell on its knees, got up again and made an effort that strained its hide from shoulder to hind-quarters.

But it was winded, and the wagon stopped. The wagoner, his shoulder against the wheel, his hands on the spokes, cried still louder: "Up! Gee up . . . up there! . . ."

In vain the horse strained all its muscles: the cart did not move.

"Up there! Up . . ."

Its feet apart, its nostrils throbbing, the animal stood still, trembling with the strain of keeping the front of its hoofs in the soil so that it should not be dragged back by the enormous load. As he bent over the wheel the wagoner caught sight of the beggar sitting on the edge of the ditch, and hailed him:

"A hand, comrade! The brute won't go any further. Come and help to give a push."

The beggar got up and pushing with all his feeble strength cried with the other:

"Up, up! . . ."

It was useless.

Quickly exhausted and full of pity, the beggar said:

"Let him get his breath. It's too heavy for him."

"Not a bit of it. He's a cowardly brute. If I give in to him now, he'll never pull another load up a hill. Up there! Gee up! . . . Get a stone to wedge up the wheel. We'll make him go across the road to get a move on."

The beggar brought a big stone.

"Like this," said the wagoner. "I'll stay at the wheel. Here's the whip. Take the bit, head to the left, and lash his legs as hard as you can. That'll bring him to."

Stung by pain, the horse made a big effort. The stones ground and flashed under his feet.

"That's it! That's it!"

But as the horse strained to one side, the wagoner, bending to push the stone under the wheel, slipped. The horse was drawn back. The man gave a cry and fell.

He was on his back, his face convulsed, his eyes wild, his two elbows digging into the soil, his strong hands clutching the rim of the wheel as he tried to stop it from passing over his chest.

In a voice of agony he shouted:

"Pull him forward! Pull him forward! He's crushing me . . ."

Guessing, without seeing, what had happened, the beggar belabored the horse with both lash and handle. But the unwilling animal sank on its knees, rolled on its side, and the cart tilted forward, the shafts on the ground; the lantern upset and went out, and nothing could be heard in the darkness but the sharp breathing of the horse and the stifled moan of the man:

"Go forward . . . go forward . . ."

Unable to get the animal up, the beggar rushed to the wagoner trying to free him. But he was firmly held by the wheel. By a prodigious effort he was managing to keep it an inch or two from his body; a slip, a loss of strength, and it would mean being crushed to death . . . He himself understood this so clearly that when he saw the beggar bending over him, he yelled:

"Don't touch! Don't touch! . . . run to the village . . . quick . . . to my father's house . . . the Luchats . . . the first farm to the right . . . tell them to bring . . . help . . . I can keep like this for ten minutes . . . quick . . ."

The beggar ran up the hill at full speed. He rushed into the village, which lay straight in front of him. All the shutters were closed. There were no lights; not a soul to be seen anywhere. Dogs barked furiously as he passed, but he heard nothing, saw nothing, his mind concentrated on the awful vision of the man who was lying at the bottom of the hill holding off the great weight that was sinking down on him.

At last he stopped. Before him the road stretched out on the level. At his right a building stood behind a courtyard. A shaft of light came from the window. This must be the house. He hammered on the shutters with his fists.

A voice asked:

"Is that you, Jules?"

Completely out of breath because of the pace he had come at, he had no voice to reply; he could only keep on knocking. He heard the creaking of a bed, steps on the boards. The window opened, and the head of a sleepy man appeared in the square of light:

"Is that you, Jules?"

He had recovered enough voice to pant: "No, but I have come to . . ."

The farmer did not let him finish.

"What the devil are you doing here? Waking people at this hour of the night!"

He shut the window with a bang, muttering:

"A dirty tramp . . . A good-for-nothing . . ."

Stupefied by the brutality of the voice and action, the beggar stood transfixed . . . He thought:

"What did they think I wanted? What harm was I doing . . . I suppose I did disturb their sleep . . . If they only knew, poor things . . ."

He knocked timidly on the shutter again.

From inside the voice cried:

"Still there! . . . Wait a bit! You'll be sorry if I get up to you."

He had got his breath again, and with it came courage.

"Open the window . . ."

"Go about your business . . ."

"Open the window! . . ."

This time the window opened, and so quickly he had to jump on one side to get out of the way of the shutter. The farmer stood there, furious, a gun in his hand.

"Do you hear what I say, you starveling? If you don't clear out and quickly, it's an ounce of lead you get."

The hard voice of a woman called from the bed:

"Fire at him . . . a good riddance for everybody if you do! They're no good for anything but thieving, those tramps . . . and worse than thieving . . ."

Frightened by the gun that was pointed at him, the beggar retreated into the darkness. He trembled and for a moment forgot the poor wretch who was perhaps at that very moment dying on the road. For the first time a bitter anger rose in him. Never before had he felt so despised and rejected.

Suppose he had been starving, suppose he had knocked to beg for shelter? Had he not a right to a litter of straw near the cattle? to a crust of bread with the dogs? . . . Apparently his rags did not cover even a human being, seeing that the rich could threaten to kill him . . .

His first impulse was to raise his stick and beat upon the shutter, then he reflected:

"If I knock again he will fire . . . If I call, it will rouse the village and they will have knocked me senseless before I can explain what I want. If I go somewhere else for help, it will be just the same . . ."

After a moment of hesitation he set off at a gallop to go back and try to save unaided the comrade of a few minutes. He ran wildly, urged forward by the fear of what might have happened while he was away . . . What would he see when he got there . . .

This terror lent him the strength of the legs of a young man, and he was soon back near the place where the wagon had stopped. He cried:

"Comrade!"

No reply. He called again:

"Comrade!"

The darkness was so dense he could not find the horse . . . But he heard a neighing and went forward. The animal, still on its side, was lying a few steps from him, the wagon tilted forwards.

"Comrade! Comrade!"

He bent down, and as the moon came out from behind a cloud he saw the man with his arms spread out like a cross, his eyes shut, blood coming from his mouth. The wheel, which seemed enormous, was buried in his chest as in a rut.

Unable to do anything more for the poor mutilated creature, his anger against the parents blazed up more fiercely than before. A desire for revenge gripped him; he ran back to the farm, and this time he had no fear of the gun, no feeling but one of savage joy as he beat on the shutters.

"Is that you, Jules?"

He made no reply. When the window opened and he saw the farmer's face and again heard the question, he replied:

"No! It's the starveling who came here before to tell you your son lay dying on the road."

The terrified voice of the mother mingled with that of the father:

"What does he say? . . . What does he say? . . . Come in . . . quick, quick . . ."

But he pulled his hat down over his eyes and walked slowly away as he murmured:

"I've something else to do now . . . There's no need to be in such a hurry. You are too late . . . It was when I came before that you ought to have made haste. He's got the whole load of hay on his ribs now."

"Quick, quick, father!" sobbed the woman. "Run! Run!"

As he drew on some clothes, the father shouted:

"Where is he! . . . Listen . . . Come back . . . For the love of God tell . . ."

But the beggar, his stick on his shoulder, was lost in the darkness.

And the only reply was the call of a cock that had been awakened by the voices and crowed from a dunghill, and the howling of the dog that raised its head and bayed at the moon.

Under Chloroform

"As for me," declared pretty young Madame Chaligny, "if ever I were obliged to have an operation and it was absolutely necessary to give me an anaesthetic, I would not place myself in the hands of any doctor I didn't know personally . . . When I come to think of it, it seems to me that it would be ideal to be chloroformed by a man who was in love with you."

At this the old doctor, who had been sitting listening in silence, probably because they were speaking of his profession, shook his head.

"No, Madame, no. You are quite wrong there. That is the very last man you ought to choose."

"Why? With a man who loved her a woman would feel completely at ease; her thoughts would be concentrated on him, and she would not run the risk of having her mind distracted in a way that might prove dangerous at such a moment. There must be even a sort of rare voluptuousness in sinking into unconsciousness with beloved eyes gazing into yours . . . Then, think of the enchantment of coming to . . . of the return to consciousness . . ."

"Don't make any mistake about that return," smiled the doctor. "There's very little poetry about it. The sick person emerges painfully from the heaviest of all intoxications, and at such a moment the prettiest woman in the world lacks charm and runs the risk of disenchanting the most ardent lover."

After a little silence, he added gravely:

"She runs a still more terrible risk—that of never returning at all."

As everyone protested he went on:

"I will tell you a story to illustrate what I mean, an old and very sad story. I am the tragic hero of it, and if I am able to speak

75

of it today, it is because the telling can no longer compromise anyone. I am the only one left of those who played a part in it, and you will lose your time if you try to discover the names of people who are now in their graves. I am seventy years old; I was twenty-four then, so you see . . .

"I was house-surgeon at a hospital when I first met the woman who was the great and only love of my life. I would have done the maddest things to be able to see her; to keep her happy, out of the reach of any trouble, I was capable of making any and every sacrifice; I would have killed myself without regret rather than have a breath of suspicion touch her.

"We were very young. They had married her to a man twenty years older than herself, and I can say with truth, though the words sound strange from the mouth of an old man, that she loved me as much as I loved her.

"We had found complete happiness in each other for some months, discreetly, and without causing the slightest remark, when one morning I received a hasty line from the husband begging me to come and see his wife who was ill. I rushed to the house. I found her in bed, very pale, with the anxious face, blue-circled eyes, pinched nose and lifeless hair I had so often seen at the hospital. The night before she had been seized with violent pains in the side; they had put her to bed, and since then she had lain there moaning, hiccoughing between her sobs, warding off with terrified gestures any hand that approached her, her appealing eyes begging no one to touch her.

"There was not an hour, not a minute to lose. We sent for my chief, and it was decided to operate there and then.

"You must have been through it to understand the difference between calmly preparing to operate on people you don't know, and the horror of doing it for someone very dear to you.

"While they were getting the next room ready for the operation, my poor little darling beckoned to me, and trying to keep the pain out of her voice whispered:

"'I'm not afraid . . . Don't worry about me . . . you will put me to sleep, won't you? . . .'

"I protested with a gesture, but she persisted:

"'I beg you to do it. You must . . . No one but you . . .'

"I had neither the time nor the strength to say no. They came and carried her away.

"Then began my Calvary.

"While my chief and the other doctors and nurses moved about the room, I took the bottle of chloroform and the compress.

"She started back as she inhaled the first few drops, then smiled at me and gave herself up without further resistance. But she did not go off properly. Perhaps it was that, too moved to measure it carefully, I gave too little chloroform, letting too much air pass between the handkerchief and her lips. Also I could not help thinking of all the accidents that might happen, of the cases of syncope I had seen or heard of, and it was not astonishing that my eyes were not as sharp as usual, my fingers uncertain . . .

"My chief, his sleeves turned up, his streaming hands stretched out, came up:

" 'Has she gone off?'

"The sound of his voice braced me. It took my mind to the hospital, and I pulled myself together as I replied:

" 'No, sir, not yet.'

" 'Hurry . . .'

"I bent over her asking:

" 'Can you hear me? . . .'

"She opened her eyes and lowered the lids twice to say 'yes.'

" 'Is there a buzzing in your ears? . . . What can you hear?'

"She murmured:

" 'Bells . . .'

"As she spoke she seemed to shrink a little. One of her arms fell inert on the table; her breathing grew even, her face paler, and little blue veins appeared at the side of the nose. I bent over her: her breath was sibilant, and heavy with the smell of chloroform: she was asleep.

" 'You can begin now, sir,' I said to my chief.

"But when I saw the knife move along the white body, leaving behind it a red line, my agitation returned. As I watched them cut and pinch her flesh, it seemed to me that they were cutting and pinching my own. My hand stole up mechanically and stroked her face. Suddenly her legs moved with an instinctive gesture of defense, and she moaned.

"My chief straightened himself:

"'But you haven't got her under.'

"I poured some drops of chloroform on the compress; they made a large gray stain on the fine batiste.

"The operator bent over her again.

"But again she moaned and began to mutter incoherent syllables.

"How I longed for it all to be over; longed to see her come to herself, to have done with the awful nightmare! She was now motionless, but she continued to moan and mutter, and suddenly among the murmurings she pronounced distinctly a name, mine: Jean.

"A shudder ran through me. Speaking as if in a dream she went on:

"'Don't worry . . . I'm not afraid . . .'

"Great God, it was I who was afraid!

"Not so much afraid that she would never come to, that she would die in my arms, but afraid that in her delirium she would betray our secret.

"She began to stammer words that increased my fear. Hardly knowing what I was doing, I said:

"'Sir, she is not completely under . . .'

"'Because she chatters? . . . What does that matter so long as she doesn't move? . . .'

"At that moment her voice rose clearly, every word distinct:

"'I'm not afraid . . . You are with me . . . You put me to sleep . . .'

"There was no knowing what she might say next, and terrified, I administered more chloroform . . . Four, five times, tilt on tilt, I poured it on the compress and held it to her face. Her voice, now uneven, came to me muffled by the handkerchief I held against her mouth.

"'I am asleep . . . I can hear the bells . . . When I am well again we will go for walks together as we used to . . .'

"I lost my head. I thought that her husband, who was in the next room and probably near the door, would hear, that the others would understand. She, so proud, she whom no suspicion had ever touched, who till then had been above all suspicion, would be dishonored.

"To get her quite under, to try to keep her silent, I tilted the bottle, I tilted it again. The compress became heavy in my hand.

" 'We shall be together . . . at night,' chanted the voice. 'And you will take me in your arms again . . . you will . . .'

"I lost my reason. What would the next words be? I poured . . . I poured . . . I no longer knew what I was doing.

"Then came the moment when I found that the bottle was empty. I realized that I had given too much. Terrified, I flung the compress away; with a hasty finger I lifted one of her eyelids and saw that the pupil of the eye was fixed, dilated so that there was nothing left of the iris but a transparent ring. I wanted to shout: 'Stop! . . .'

"The word was strangled by the contraction in my throat.

"At the same moment I heard the voice of my chief, short and anxious:

" 'What's this . . . What . . . the blood-pressure is low.'

"With a violent movement he pushed me away:

" 'But she's not breathing . . . Some oxygen . . . some ether . . . quick . . .'

"Alas! Too late.

"Her poor head rolled lifeless; her blue eye, the eyelid still up, was glazed and looked at me with an empty stare . . .

"We tried everything, but nothing was any good. Syncope, the horrible white syncope, as we call it, had taken her from me."

For a few moments he sat lost in thought, then went on:

"I know perfectly well that such accidents happen frequently; that no one is safe from the treachery of chloroform. But I also know that if I had not loved her and had done my work with cold indifference; if I had not been overwhelmed by the double anguish of holding her life in my hands and hearing her unconsciously betraying the secret that would ruin her, I should not have to reproach myself with causing her death . . ."

He was silent. A wave of sadness passed through the room as if it had been carried in on the chilly autumn wind that blew against the damp window.

Madame Chaligny, her head on the back of her armchair, sat gazing into space like a person lost in a dream.

The party broke up early that night.

The Man Who Lay Asleep

WORN OUT with fatigue, half dead with hunger, Ferrou got to the gates of Paris as night was falling. For eight days he had dragged himself from village to village, getting strength from the desire to see once again, now that he was out of prison, the great city with its broad streets and the narrow roads which night suddenly peoples with moving and silent forms. For five years he had thought of nothing but his return, storing up hate and a desire for murder strong enough to make his first action the purchase of a knife he had sharpened in the dark on the stone edge of a well. As he walked along, his fingers were constantly on the handle.

Lights were appearing in the windows of some houses that stood in their own gardens. One of these remained dark, and but for the smoke that rose from a chimney, it might have been empty. The rare passers-by hurried along; here and there in the distance streetlamps flickered. It was quite dark now, a cold, dreary winter's night. Ferrou stood still: push on to Paris? He had not the strength; sleep where he was, in the cutting wind, with no covering but his rags? Impossible. He had left behind him the country stables where the straw makes a warm bed for vagabonds; there were no more village inns . . . and even if there were? . . . he had not a halfpenny in his pocket. For a second time the little house without lights attracted his attention. He was alone, he was cold, he was hungry, this shelter was as good as any other . . . He walked through the garden, listened, drew back a window shutter and found that the window was unfastened. He opened it, and at a bound was in the house. The window shut, he felt about in the dark, touching a bed, a small table; the drapery of a hanging wardrobe gave way to his hand; he raised it, felt the clothes beneath it, let it fall again. Then he found a door, opened it, and a savory smell of cooking tempted his nostrils.

"No good," he thought, "there's someone in the house. I must clear out . . ."

He turned to go, then stopped. Go where? To die of hunger on the road? If anyone came in, he could hide. Then, his thoughts running off into another channel, he said to himself:

"You are cold, and it is warm here; you are hungry, and hot food will soon be ready; you have no money, and there is sure to be a full stocking hidden somewhere. You will probably have time to do all you want before anyone disturbs you, and if you are disturbed . . ."

He opened his knife, tried the point on the palm of his hand, the edge on his nail, and murmuring: "The first who tries to stop me! . . ." went into the kitchen, lifted the lid of the pan, pricked the meat, and sneered:

"Not cooked enough; I will come back . . ."

But as he turned away there was a sound of steps outside. He heard the latch of the garden-gate lifted, the crunching of the gravel, and quickly, just as a key turned in the door, he slipped into the other room, raised the wardrobe-hanging and crouched down among the clothes. Not too soon: a man was coming into the house. This man lit a lamp, threw his coat over a chair, and began to pace the room. From his hiding place Ferrou saw him coming and going. He was a big man with large hands and square shoulders; his heavy, measured steps gave an impression of strength.

"The devil!" thought Ferrou. "It's not when the stomach has been empty for a week that a man is in a state to attack a lump like that!"

The man sat down and, his head resting on his hands, seemed to be thinking deeply. The bell sounded; he rose, saying:

"Is it you, Marie?"

"Yes. I went to bring the boy home from school. He hadn't taken his raincoat, and it's snowing."

The man took the child on his knee, stroking his hair. From the kitchen the woman said:

"I didn't hurry. You are earlier than usual; it's only half-past six. You didn't find your friends at the café?"

"Yes. But we had special work this afternoon, and tonight I must go out."

"Well, everything's ready. We can begin at once."

"Go on without me; I'm not hungry. I will lie down on my bed; you must wake me at eleven o'clock."

"All right. Come, little one, supper's ready. Let your father rest, he is tired."

The child went out of the room, and the man stretched himself on the bed.

"It is half-past six," thought Ferrou, "and he doesn't clear out till eleven. Five hours of this!"

Through the half-open door came the clatter of plates and the sound of the two voices. Now and again Ferrou was tempted to leave his hiding-place, to spring on the sleeping man, to stab him; then, imagining the unequal struggle, the noise, the too long and dangerous massacre of three beings, the woman and child clinging to his arm like cats, paralyzing his movements, he decided to wait. Once the man was gone, it would be easy to settle the woman and child. He had abandoned all idea of a quiet robbery. His stomach was too empty and his heart too full of hate to be satisfied with so little. His weakness made him ferocious; he had a knife, and it was there to be used.

When the meal was finished, the woman put the child to bed and washed up the crockery. In the silence that followed nothing could be heard but the tick-tock of the clock and the irregular breathing of the sleeper, who turned and tossed on his bed. It struck ten; he arranged his plan of attack. In an hour the man would go . . . Afterwards, he would be master of the place.

The thought of the coming massacre gave him more joy than the hope of the plunder. All was still. The man and the woman, the one sleeping, the other reading, had no suspicion that in the shadow a man lay in wait. Gradually a drowsiness stole over him, and he started when a voice said:

"It's eleven o'clock."

He rubbed his eyes and slowly stretched himself. The man got up, put on his shoes, and thrust his arms through the sleeves of his coat.

"Above all, don't catch cold," said the woman. "I have heated some coffee; will you have it?"

"Yes."

While he was sipping it, the woman went on:

"Won't you put on your other overcoat?"

Ferrou felt that she was stretching her hand toward the hanging and started. But when the man replied: "No, this one will do very well," he breathed again, and still shaking with fright, said to himself:

"You, you hellcat, you shall pay for that presently! . . ."

She went on:

"You haven't forgotten anything? What time will you be back?"

"About seven or eight o'clock as usual."

He was ready. Standing up, the collar of his overcoat buttoned up, he seemed bigger and stronger than before. Behind his curtain Ferrou was growing unnerved: "You are never going then! . . ." The man, his hand on the handle of the door, turned back.

"Don't forget to fasten the bars of the shutters and bolt the door."

The sound of wheels grated on the road and stopped.

"Here they are," said the man.

He went out and began to talk to the newcomers in the garden.

"You haven't forgotten anything? Yes.—The coach-house properly shut?—Yes, yes.—Let's be off then. Go in, Marie; it's snowing, it's a very bad night."

"Worse than you think!" snarled Ferrou.

His knife was burning his fingers; he longed to have done with it all. But the man still lingered. His voice rang clear through the cold air:

"Pass me the lantern. Let me see if everything is in its place."

Suddenly his voice, till then very kind, rose angrily:

"Just look how you have fastened that! The sheath is not even buckled. And it's badly balanced. In less than a quarter of an hour half the blade would be on the ground. You'd have mud in the slides and on the posts. Come, give a hand!"

Ferrou listened, mocking:

"The finest porcelain, at least, to need so much care."

The man went on:

"What have you been thinking about? At the first jolt, the tub would have tipped off."

Ferrou ceased sneering. A cold shiver ran down his back. The Blade . . . the Posts . . . the Tub . . . Separately, these words meant nothing . . . Put together . . . they suggested, might mean a terrible thing . . . Where was he? . . . Who was this man who had lain sleeping there and was now saying these words to the other man?

The voice softened:

"There, that will do. It would have been a fine thing if you had blunted the knife of the guillotine."

Trembling, Ferrou repeated: "The knife of the guillotine! . . ." and his teeth began to chatter. In a flash, these last words had brought the whole of the awful thing before him. He seemed to hear the mysterious noises that come in the night to wake those who are condemned to death, the hammer-knocks of the sinister carpenter; he seemed to see the pale faces of the assistants who enter the cell; the big red posts set up outside in the gray dawn of the morning . . .

"Ready," said a voice—the voice of the man.

Then Ferrou, gasping with fear, biting his fingers to stop himself from shrieking, stammered, forgetting that he might be heard:

"The executioner! I have been watching the executioner sleep!"

The cart had set off at a good pace and the woman was just going to shut the door, but forgetting that he had crouched there for hours waiting to kill, he flung away his knife, knocked her out of his way with a thrust of his shoulder, rushed into the garden, leaped over the fence and began to run blindly down the road, fleeing from Paris whose distant noises and familiar odors would soon be augmented by the sound of cracking bone and crushed flesh and the fusty smell of blood.

Fascination

ONE HOUR ago I was a prisoner. And what a prisoner! It was not a question of my honor or my liberty: it was my head that was at stake.

I have known terrible nights haunted by the nightmare of the guillotine. I have trembled as some ghastly fascination made me lift my clammy hands to my neck to trace the narrow line the knife would make there. I have shuddered at the hostile murmurs of the crowd. The hoarse roar: "To the scaffold with him!" has rung and echoed in my ears.

But that is all over now. I am free. Once again I have seen the noisy streets and the bright lights of the shops. Presently, quite at ease, I shall dine. Sitting by the fire I shall smoke my pipe, and tonight I shall fall asleep quietly in the warm bed that is waiting for me.

And yet never have I felt myself so much of a criminal as at this moment just after my judges have acquitted me. I am wondering what aberration prevented them from knowing the kind of being I really am. The power of systematic denial stupefies me, and I feel that if I am to regain my clearness of mind, I must write down the truth I have hidden for the last three months with a cleverness and cynicism that have ended by almost making me believe my own lies.

For I really am a murderer; I killed a woman.

Why? . . . I do not know. I have never been able to understand why I did it.

Certainly not because of jealousy; I did not love her. Not to rob her; I am rich, and the few francs they found on her could never have tempted me. Nor was it done in anger . . .

We were in this room. She was standing near that mirror; I was sitting just where I am at this moment. I was reading. She said to me:

"Let's go out . . . Let's go for a stroll in the Bois."

Without raising my eyes, I replied:

"No, I'm tired. Let's stay here."

She insisted. I persisted in my refusal. She kept on insisting, and her voice aggravated me. She spoke very angrily, sneering at my inertia, laughing scornfully, shrugging her shoulders. Several times I tried to stop her:

"Will you be quiet? . . . I beg you to be quiet . . ."

She continued. I got up and began to pace the room, and as I walked up and down I saw on the mantelshelf a little revolver that I used to carry in my pocket at night. I took it up mechanically. The moment I touched it an extraordinary frame of mind took possession of me. The voice of my mistress which had till then merely aggravated me, unnerved me to an extent I cannot describe. It was not what she was saying that irritated me; it was her voice, just her voice. If she had been jibbering meaningless words or reciting beautiful poetry, I should have felt just the same exasperation. An irresistible longing for quiet, for complete repose, seized me. How, why did my mind connect this imperious desire for the silence I could not command with the revolver I held in my hand? . . . I only know that I imagined myself brandishing the weapon, pressing the trigger, and I also saw the woman fall, without a cry . . .

As a rule such ideas are only giddy hallucinations that flash through the brain and are gone as quickly as they came. But this time it seemed as if this particular vision had caught into my mind in the way a jagged fingernail will catch in floss silk, getting more securely entangled as one tries to free it. I placed the revolver on the table. I could not help looking at it. I tried to turn my head away; my eyes drew me toward it.

It lay there before me a little lifeless thing, with its ivory butt and shining barrel. Twice, thrice, I stretched out, then drew back my hand. The desire was stronger than my will. I was obliged to touch it, to seize it.

It is impossible to understand the temptation that assails one in the face of certain kinds of danger. I remember that one day when I was in the park of the Buttes Chaumont I was obliged to hold on to the parapet of the place they call "The Suicide's Bridge" to prevent myself from leaping off into space. Several times when I have been alone in a railway carriage I have felt a sick longing to pull the alarm-signal. The nickel knob drew me toward it, seemed to beg to be pulled. It was in vain I told myself that such an action would be absurd, that I should be heavily fined or punished for doing it; had not the chance stoppage of the train or the flashing by of another suddenly diverted my thoughts, I am certain I should have succumbed to the temptation.

Well, at that moment I was overwhelmed by the same irresistible impulse. My eyes and my hands ceased to obey my will. I seemed to be watching myself as if I were someone else, to be following the movements of that other person without knowing what they were leading up to.

Was she still talking? . . . Was she silent? . . . I do not know. The only thing I am certain of is that I walked toward her with the revolver in my hand, that my wrist rose, and when it was on a level with her forehead, I pressed the trigger. There was a sharp noise like the crack of a whip. I saw a red mark, very small, under the right lid, and the woman fell, inert, like a petticoat that has been unfastened and slips down on the carpet.

Then, instantly, my reason came back to me. A wild terror dominated me. I rushed about the room like a madman without even thinking of looking at my victim, and some base instinct of cowardice forced me to open the door and run down the staircase shouting:

"Help! . . . She has killed herself! . . ."

At first everyone believed it was suicide. Later the experts found that very improbable. I was arrested. The trial was a long one. I could have explained everything in a few words. I need only have said:

"This is how it happened."

I persisted in obstinate denial. And as, sooner or later, they always find some motive to account for a criminal action, I was eventually acquitted.

Reviewing it all calmly now, I am wondering if I was wrong to go on lying. If I had told the jury what I am writing now, would they have believed me? Would they have absolved me from blame? I believe I was right to deny it. Imperfectly understood, certain truths can very easily seem like lies . . .

My God, how good it is to be free, to be able to come and go as I like.

From my window I see the street, the houses and the trees . . . It was here on this very spot the thing happened. They did not want to give me this room. I insisted on having it. I am not afraid of ghosts. Besides, I can write this better here than I should have elsewhere. One can visualize a past incident so much more realistically in the place where it happened.

. . . Somehow this confession has completely relieved my mind. My soul seems clean once again as if it had been washed.

I shall try to forget the nightmare it has all been. I will go and live in the country somewhere far away from Paris. Soon everyone will have forgotten even my name. I shall be another man, living another existence, with the ways and habits of a peasant . . . I shall cease to recognize myself.

There is one thing above all that I want to get rid of: the revolver they gave back to me in court this morning. It reminds me too forcibly of things I must forget. If I need a weapon I will buy another.

It is close beside me as I write, and the sight of it hurts me. Yet what a little thing it is . . . It is pretty . . . it looks like a toy, a charming ornament . . . incapable of doing any harm.

. . . I have just taken it in my hand. It is very light, very smooth to the touch. It is also very cold . . . It frightens me a little . . . It is so mysterious, this sleeping weapon . . . The danger of a knife is apparent; you see the sharp blade, can feel the pointed end . . . Here, nothing: you must have used it to—I will not keep it . . . I will not keep it . . . I will sell it at once, tomorrow . . . Sell it? . . . I will give it away . . . No, I will not. I will throw it away . . .

Yet, after all, why should I, so long as I don't see it for some time? I am looking at it too much . . . It is natural enough, too . . . It lies there like a silent witness . . . Decidedly I do not like it. I will get rid of it instantly.

. . . I keep on writing and the revolver is still before me.

People who commit suicide must sit just like this writing their last wishes. I wonder what their sensations are . . . I believe I know exactly. At first they dare not look at the revolver . . . then once their resolution has been made, they probably cannot take their eyes from it, sit looking at it, fascinated . . .

Does it really need so much courage for a man to kill himself?

The worst part must be the simple act of stretching out the hand, grasping the weapon, and feeling its chill . . .

. . . But no, I am holding it in my left hand . . . I place the barrel against my temple . . . The sensation is not at all disagreeable . . . A little shiver . . . then the steel grows warm against your flesh . . .

No, that cannot be the most horrible moment . . . it must be the second when one presses the trigger . . . the last order the soul gives the body . . .

Who knows? . . . Perhaps even that is nothing . . . Once the glamor has got hold of you, you feel irresistibly drawn on.

I understand that perfectly . . .

. . . You almost feel as if you no longer exist . . .

. . . You are no longer conscious of any sensation . . .

. . . The Unknown calls you . . .

. . . And you press the trigg . . .

The Bastard

SEATED ON his stool, an elbow on the table, the man ate his supper slowly, a long interval between every spoonful of soup. The woman was standing by the big open hearth, now and again pushing the blazing twigs into place with her sabot. She talked incessantly, paying no attention to the obstinate silence with which her remarks were received.

"Is it true that the Chaputs have got rid of their old hens? that the Rizoys' butter has turned?"

Without raising his head he murmured: "I don't know."

"And you—what sort of prices did you get?"

"Bah!"

"Why are you so short tonight? What's the matter with you?"

He put his spoon down. His arms stretched out before him, his two fists on the table, he drew a deep breath as if he were on the point of lifting a heavy sack.

"The matter . . . the matter . . ."

He stopped, drew back the plate he had pushed away, cut himself a piece of bread, shut his knife, and drying his mouth with the back of his hand, said:

"Nothing."

She insisted:

"You're put out about something . . ."

For a time there was silence, broken only by the sound of the rain and the wind outside. The fire blazed cheerfully, throwing big lights and shadows on the walls.

Presently the woman said:

"Have you finished your soup? Would you like anything else?"

He shook his head, and his "no" was short and sharp. Ignoring his tone, she began to talk again, telling him the gossip of the village, dwelling on details in the way one would if a man had

90

been absent for a long time and wanted to hear about everyone and everything.

"Do you know about the Heutrots' dog? The big brown dog? They say it's gone mad. While they were getting a gun to shoot it, it ran away and no one knows where it is."

The man whistled between his teeth. She burst out:

"Is that all you've got to say? I don't know what's the matter with you tonight . . . Been to the inn, I suppose . . . though usually when you've been there you come home in a good temper, ready to talk! Tonight not a word: you've eaten your food as if it was poison, and you haven't even asked where the boy is."

He turned slowly toward her, and looking straight in her eyes, asked:

"Is it long since you saw Big Jacquet?"

She was raising her leg to push back a log that had rolled too far forward; the abrupt question seemed to transfix her, and she stood with her foot in the air as she stammered:

"Big Jacquet? . . . Not for a long time . . . Why?"

"I thought he came here today . . ."

"He didn't."

"What are you lying for? The postman told me he saw him come out of here this morning."

She tried to retract:

"That's right . . . he looked in for a moment as he passed . . . I'd forgotten . . . Why should I remember such a small thing? . . ."

She shrugged her shoulders and turned away. But the man wanted to talk now.

"Stay where you are," he said roughly. "I have something to say to you!"

She tried to turn it off, but she had grown very pale and her voice was uncertain.

"What are you looking at me like that for?"

He placed his hand heavily on her shoulder.

"Sit down. This has lasted long enough. It's got to be settled sooner or later . . . I'm tired of being the laughing-stock of the village . . . with them all talking about it even when I'm there.

God knows I've tried not to believe it . . . but I've had too much of it. I want to know the truth. Big Jacquet is your lover."

She started violently.

"How have you the face to say such a thing! . . ."

"It's no words I want. I want proof. I know now, you see, I know."

He repeated the "I know! I know!" several times, emphasizing the words by striking his chest heavily at each repetition. Now that he had made the accusation, his anger blazed out. He banged his big hands on the table, shouting imprecations and threats. The woman was trembling, too terrified by this unchained fury to attempt to defend herself with any conviction.

"You thought it would go on like this always, that I was too stupid ever to find out. You'll see whether I am stupid or not . . . And that's not all. Whose child is he, the boy? Which of us is his father?"

She snatched up her apron and hid her face in it, sobbing:

"How can you talk like that . . . how can you . . ."

He seized her wrists; his eyes were bloodshot and it was through clenched teeth that he hissed:

"Which of us is his father? Which of us is his father?"

"How could it be any one but you?" she gasped between her sobs. "You know it as well as I do."

In spite of himself he was moved by her words, by her tears, and his voice softened a little.

"I know nothing about it . . . Nothing at all . . . Answer . . ."

Though she was nearly frightened out of her wits, she saw that her husband was weakening, and feeling she was getting the upper hand she raised her voice:

"For your sake as well as mine, I refuse to take any notice of such a question."

But anger had mastered him again. The accumulated wrath of months had only subsided for a moment to burst forth with renewed violence. His voice was little more than a hoarse whisper as he said, his arm raised threateningly:

"Listen . . . You will tell me the truth or—take care! There'll be murder in this house. I want to know who the father of that child is . . . We'll settle about you and me afterwards . . . But I'll know about the child now. Do you hear—at once. Do you think

I am going on bringing up another man's bastard, breaking my
back in the sun and rain to leave him a few acres of land? Do
you hear? Do you understand? There'll be murder in this house,
I tell you. You and him and the village between you all, you'll
end by driving me mad. I'm done with it! . . . It's got to stop . . .
You had nothing but the chemise you stood in when I married
you, and long before that they used to see you lying about
behind the mills with Jacquet . . . When the child was born eight
months to the day after the wedding, you told me it was the
fright you got when the cow went astray. I believed you . . . but
I know better now. They've taken care to open my eyes. He isn't
mine, that child! If he is, swear it. Then I shall know what to do.
Swear—swear before God!"

Her face was hidden in her hands; her teeth were chattering.
She made no reply.

"You whor—"

At this moment the door opened and the child came in, his
sabots covered with mud, the hood of his cape over his head.
The threatening attitude and loud voice alarmed him. The man
did not finish the word. His arm fell, and his voice faltered as he
pushed his wife from him, ordering:

"Go to bed."

Then he turned to the boy, trying to soften his voice as he
said:

"You stay here."

The frightened child took off his cloak, placed his sabots in a
corner near the door, and stood motionless.

The man went to a stool near the fire where he sat for some
time lost in thought, his elbows on his knees. Presently he raised
his head and beckoned to the boy.

"Come here . . ."

He drew him between his knees, and taking the small head in
his hands looked intently at his face in the light of the lamp. He
stared with desperate intensity, every nerve strained in the
effort to see whom the child resembled. A wave of tenderness
rushed through him at the contact with the frightened little
creature. He felt he would rather never see the child again than
find in him any resemblance to the Other. But some influence
he could not control riveted his eyes to the face, fastened his

fingers in the hair, pressed his knees tightly against the slim
form . . . Neither could he master a feeling of hate that burned
deep down in his heart. At first he hesitated, but desire for the
truth proved irresistible. The eyes, the small eyes deep-set in
their sockets, they were the eyes of the Other . . . The mouth
that seemed to be always smiling . . . his mouth; the front teeth
with the spaces between them, above all, the hair, the dry, stiff
hair that stood up in ruddy disorder . . . all, everything, down to
the smallest detail . . . Nothing was lacking. God in Heaven! . . .
It was true then. She had deceived him, the whore! She had
foisted her lover's child on him.

The evidence was there, shrieking at him . . . No need for
further proof . . . the living one stood before him . . . But he still
struggled against certainty, fighting with himself, not wanting to
believe, trying to reason away conviction . . .

He loved this child he had believed his own; he had watched
it grow up out of babyhood; it called him "father," and he was
never so happy as when it was running beside him in the fields
. . . Could any one feel like that toward the child of another man?
. . . Surely there was something unique in the feeling a man has
for his own flesh and blood, a tenderness he could never have for
the child of another man? . . . The eyes, the hair, the teeth, the
mouth might seem the same—but was he not imagining it?

. . . A noise like a moan broke the silence. He listened . . . It
sounded again . . . then there came a sort of scratching outside
the door, a growl. He pushed the child away, and the boy sat
down by the fire and began to play with the twigs. He went to
the window, opened it, peered out, and shut it again quickly.

He had seen a large dark mass crouching across the threshold. He knew all the dogs in the village, and by the pointed nose
and eyes that glittered in the shadow he had recognized the
Heutrots' dog.

He took his gun from the corner, put two cartridges in it, and
was on the point of opening the window to fire when it occurred
to him that the noise would frighten the child. He placed the
gun on the table, saying:

"Go and find your mother and tell her not to be frightened. I
am going to fire at the Heutrots' dog."

The child turned toward him. Kneeling before the fire, he was in the full light, and as he made a quick movement his likeness to Big Jacquet was striking . . . terrifying . . .

The man's anger blazed up again; he bent down and was drawing the boy toward him when suddenly an oath strangled in his throat.

There, near the cheek, almost at the corner of the mouth, was a light brown mole, smaller, but a mole exactly like the bigger one Big Jacquet called his "Beauty-Spot."

The last vestige of doubt vanished. No, this was not his child; he was the child of the other man . . . Everything round him seemed to fade away, and the blaze on the hearth seemed to enter his chest and burn his flesh. He seized the boy by the collar.

"Get out . . . Never let me see you again . . . Out with you!"

The child resisted, but he dragged him with one hand to the door, pulled it open and flung him out as one would some unclean beast, and banged it to again.

A ferocious growl . . . a cry of agony rang through the darkness. The man stood stupefied, unable to think. But the mother, who had been listening in the next room, came hurrying out. Not seeing the child and noting the wildness in her husband's eyes, she shouted:

"What have you done?"

Another cry rang out:

"Mother . . Moth . . ."

She rushed outside calling:

"My little one! My little one!"

The child lay panting at the bottom of the steps, his face all torn by the dog's fangs. The beast tried to keep its grip on its prey, but she paid no attention to it, and seizing the boy in her arms dragged him away.

She laid him on the table. His throat was open, his breath came in short gasps. She showered passionate kisses on his poor mud-filled hair, on his poor little blood-covered face, on his open mouth from which the death-rattle was coming . . .

. . . Crouched in a heap on the floor, his eyes shut, his fingers in his ears, the man was sobbing:

"My little one, Holy Virgin, save my little one!"

That Scoundrel Miron

NO ONE ever understood how this woman, who was neither young nor pretty, got complete possession of the heart, the mind, the whole life of Miron. As soon as he met her he broke with his best friends, left off going to his familiar haunts, and instead of devoting himself as formerly to Art for Art's sake, took to painting the rankest potboilers. When a man who had been a great friend in the old days ventured to say:

"You're an idiot, Miron. You are spoiling your style, abusing your talent . . ." he only shrugged his shoulders and said: "Nonsense." When the friend insisted, reminding him of the conscientious work, full of more than promise, he had done in the old days of his dreams of fame, he grew angry.

"My talent? My dreams? You make me laugh. When I had them I slept in a garret, I had one meal a day. I know people will now stop saying: 'You'll see, he'll be rich some day!' but in the meanwhile I can eat as much as I like and am free from sordid worries. I am happy, very happy."

He walked rapidly away. But when he was sure that he was out of sight, he stopped at a café and sat for hours lost in thought with an empty glass in front of him. Miron lied: he was not happy. At first his love had absorbed him to the exclusion of everything else. To get the extra money that was necessary for his new kind of existence he had dashed off little sketches and drawings for the illustrated papers, and when he felt too disgusted with this prostitution of his talent, he had consoled himself by thinking that before long he would return to serious work. But as time flew by he had become morally weak, almost cowardly, and now there was a gnawing bitterness at the bottom of his heart and he was ashamed of himself, ashamed of the soulless love in which he had slowly but surely lost his better self. Debts accumulated, and at last there came a day when, worn out by the threats of those to whom he owed money and by scenes with his mistress, he lost his head and wrote a check he could not meet. He hoped to be able to get the money before the check was presented, but he was not able to do so, and, taking fright, he fled from Paris, from France.

To avoid rousing suspicion he went alone; his mistress was to follow next day. He was so certain she would come he went to bed and fell asleep happily, almost without remorse. He expected a letter from her in the morning telling the time of her arrival; next night there came instead a telegram with just four words: "I am not coming."

At first he was too stunned to take it in; it did not seem possible she could have written that. But on reflection he told himself without bitterness that after all she was right; he was a thief. Thoughts of the lost love merged themselves in the remembrance of the days when his face was set toward fame, and a great weariness, mental and physical, made him feel like a child that has lost itself. You need courage to make an effort to save yourself. He had none left. He resolved to go back to Paris, to be arrested, to be punished. Nothing could be worse than what he had already suffered because of his voluntary artistic downfall. Indeed, it would only seem natural, right, that he should be publicly disgraced. He hesitated a little at the thought of the court, prison, the dishonor from which it was still possible to save himself. But why should he mind? A man might make an effort if he had to consider a wife, parents, friends, anyone he respected; or even if he were well known, his name stood for something good . . . But he?

He took up the newspaper, looked at it without interest, and became very pale. There was a big headline: DISAPPEARANCE OF THE ARTIST·MIRON. It was a long article, and a new thought came to him as he read and re-read it. Every day a dishonest cashier disappears; every day a forger is arrested—did people take any real interest in them? This article made it clear that his flight had aroused unusual interest, that his loss caused regret; if so much space were devoted to him, it showed that the public had begun to recognize his talent and valued it. He was not unknown. He was "Somebody"; he had a name.

His infamy was the revelation of his glory. The idea of prison that had before weighed so lightly now horrified him. He was tortured by shame, fear, and pride. For days he shut himself up in his room, watching suspiciously anyone who stopped under his window, reading with passionate interest all that the papers continued to say about his disappearance and, above all, about his work. Before long he was relegated to the second page of the newspapers, then to the third; two succeeding days there was no mention of him; twice or thrice his name cropped up at intervals; then—silence. People ceased talking of him, the authorities left off looking for him. He felt sure he had escaped, that he could come and go as he liked. He was free.

It was only then that he realized how completely alone in the world he was.

Then came want; he was penniless. He must do something to earn a living. But what could he do? Drawing? Painting? And give them a chance to recognize his style and so lead to his arrest? How could he run the risk of reviving memories of himself only to blacken afresh a name he had now become proud of! Never had he been so aware of his real talent as now when he dare not show a new picture. But he must do something to get the money to support life. He thought of giving lessons, but no one cared to have them; he tried to obtain work in an office, but he had not the necessary certificates. He did all sorts of odd jobs, even the humblest, those that demand nothing but physical strength. His clothes wore out, became covered with stains; he lost his looks, his hair and beard grew gray. Over and over again he determined to kill himself, but resolution failed him at the last moment. His mind would travel back to the old days, to the little studio where he had dreamed such great dreams, and a vague feeling of hope would change the current of his thoughts.

The vision of himself evoked by this remembrance of himself as he used to be only grew more vivid as the years passed, and by slow degrees he became possessed by a longing either to become that old self again or to create another personality on the same lines. This longing sustained him through the long, dreary months of hardship in which he tried to save some money, economizing in food, sometimes even sleeping in the open. Halfpenny by halfpenny the little hoard accumulated, and at last he found himself in possession of a small sum. The enthusiasm of youth had come back to him; he took to making sketches, on a white wall, on the corner of a table, anywhere; everything he saw presented itself as a picture, and when he had a hundred francs he took the train and returned to France. Fifteen years had gone by since he left Paris. Who would remember him? Who would recognize him with his white hair, his long beard, his bent shoulders!

At first he hardly dared go out, but when confidence came his steps were drawn irresistibly toward the windows of the shops of the picture-dealers. There he saw new names, others that were familiar to him, and he found himself—he who had never in bygone days spoken of his talent—comparing himself with these painters and saying: "I can do better than that."

He bought a canvas, some colors and brushes, and began to work in his little attic. He painted feverishly, hesitating as does a convalescent who fears movement after a long illness. When he had finished the picture he spent a whole day looking at it, asking himself:

"Is it good? Is it bad?"

He no longer felt the ability to criticize his own work. At length he pulled himself together, signed the picture with the first name that came into his head—Loriot—put the canvas under his arm and set off for a dealer's shop. When he got there he was almost too agitated to speak, and he stammered as he said:

"I am a painter . . . I have no money . . . I wondered if you would buy a picture . . ."

"By whom?"

"By—by me."

"What's your name?"

"Loriot."

"I'm sorry, but we are not buying anything just at present."

He grew pale and his throat was dry as he held out the canvas:

"You might at least look at it."

The dealer glanced at it, came forward, took it in his hands, and called his partner.

"Look at this. What do you think of it?"

"Not at all bad."

"You mean remarkably good," said the other.

"Do you mean to say it's the work of that old fellow?"

"Yes."

They stood together near the mantelshelf examining it closely, and Miron heard one say:

"Astonishing—amazing! Do you know what it reminds me of? It's like the work of that scoundrel Miron, only ten times better."

Miron, standing motionless in a corner near the door, drew himself up sharply.

"What did you say?" he asked.

The dealer smiled. "We weren't talking of you. I was telling my partner that your work recalls that of a painter called Miron."

Miron repeated reflectively:

"Miron . . . Miron . . ."

"I have a little thing of his here . . . Did you know him?"

"Yes," murmured Miron.

"You have his style, his quality, but your work is better than his—though as a dealer I ought not tell you so."

"Oh, no. It's not better," stammered Miron, his eyes on the picture they had taken from the window to show him.

"Yes, it is. Miron painted instinctively. You are a finished artist. The proof of my opinion is that I am prepared not only to take this picture of yours, but as many more as you can paint. I will sell them all for you. In two months your work will be known, in two years you will be celebrated, and I guarantee Miron will be quickly forgotten."

Miron became paler as he listened. The words of high praise that would have delighted him in the old days now tortured him. He suddenly realized that all he cared for, all he respected in himself was the man he had been before his fall, the Miron he could no longer be, the Miron he had just heard condemned to death. What did the success or the failure of "Loriot" mean to him? He was not Loriot; Loriot was a stranger who was invited to come forward as the successful rival of his real self, an Unknown who would efface his name and what it stood for in the art world. The dealer went on talking, but he did not listen, did not hear. He imagined a buyer coming in and asking for a Miron, and this man replying, with his abominable smile, as he showed Loriot's canvas:

"Miron? . . . Here's something much better. Look at this."

He could not stand the thought. He grieved for his dead self as a man mourns the loss of a last love.

"Let us come to terms," the dealer was saying. "How much do you want?"

Miron raised his sad eyes, but made no reply. He did not seem to grasp the meaning of the question.

"Of course you understand that I can't offer much for the first picture. It will be some time before people understand the difference between Loriot and Miron. Most buyers need guidance. But it will end by Miron's going to the wall."

The painter was still silent. The other believed he was considering the price.

"What do you say to—"

Miron stretched out his hand.

"I'd rather wait. I'll come back some other time . . ."

"All right. But leave the picture. I'll put it in the window instead of the Miron."

"No," said Miron.

"You are making a great mistake. A man doesn't hesitate when a chance like this comes his way. Why, if I had offered that scoundrel Miron what I am offering you, it is more than likely he'd be here now, would never have done what he did."

"That's true," Miron murmured. He was trembling.

"You can't possibly refuse my offer. It would be childish."

"I do refuse it. Give me the picture."

"But I—"

"Give me the picture," repeated Miron. His voice was hoarse, and there was a curious gleam in the depths of his eyes.

"It's a great pity," declared the dealer. "I repeat I would have made a bigger name for you than Miron made."

"That's true," replied Miron for the second time, and he left the shop.

It was growing dark. Some people who were hurrying along stumbled up against him. It was a damp, dreary evening, very like the night of his flight. He stood on the curbstone, his picture in his hand. He held it for a second at arm's length, then threw it in the road in front of a passing carriage.

"You've dropped something," said a man.

"I know . . . it's nothing . . . thank you," replied Miron.

At that moment the hoof of the horse struck the frame . . . then came the wheel. The noise it made as it passed over the picture was hardly audible, but it split the canvas and crushed it in the mud so that little remained of it but a gray mass like crumpled paper.

Miron went back to the shop window. There in a place of honor hung his picture; through the mist that blurred the lights he could see the glimmer of the little plaque on the frame that bore his name: Miron. He looked at it for a long time with eyes that shone with tenderness, thoughts of the past filling his mind. A tear rolled down his cheek as he turned and walked away in the slow rain that was making the pavement shine.

The Taint

THE PRISONER had listened to the charge in complete silence and had replied to the questions of the judge in evasive phrases.

"I was alone when my child was born. I tried to get up, to call for help. I had not the strength. I put it beside me in my bed . . . Afterwards I must have lost consciousness. When I came to myself in the morning, its body was cold . . . Had I overlain and suffocated it! . . . Was it dead when I placed it by my side? . . . How could I possibly know seeing I hardly remember anything that happened before I fainted? . . ."

"Did it cry?"

"I don't know."

"How do you explain your composure in the presence of your maid? Witnesses will tell you presently that you were quite calm when you saw the little corpse. Let us suppose for a moment that it was an accident. You buried its father three months before the child was born. Having lost your husband, his child ought to have been doubly dear to you, for it seems—if I speak of the evidence of one witness, I neither can nor will pass over in silence that of others—it seems your marriage was one of inclination, of love, and that you had been perfectly happy in the union. Yet if we leave these moral considerations and turn to material proofs, the doctors will tell you that the neck showed marks of strangulation, scratches like those made by fingernails, and that not only was the child likely to live, but that it had lived, you understand, had lived for a considerable time . . ."

She lost her assurance and burst into sobs. When she was calmer, the judge went on:

"Come now, think: what have you to say in reply?"

With a gesture of weariness she lifted her long widow's veil, and at the sight of her face, pretty in spite of being swollen with tears, her trembling lips and reddened eyes, a feeling of pity passed through the court, and the silence became intense, almost respectful.

"You must please forgive me for having evaded your questions for so long," she said. "I can't lie anymore. This suffering is too much for me. Perhaps it will comfort me if I tell the truth. I confess: it was I, yes, I, who killed my child."

The judge made a gesture. She stretched out her hands as if to stop a coming accusation.

"But my crime was not premeditated, I swear it was not. I will explain as quickly as I can so as to end it all as quickly as possible, never again to hear any one speak of it . . . never . . . never . . .

"I was pregnant when my husband fell ill. Till then his health had been perfect. At first I believed it was some passing indisposition and attached no importance to it. He himself tried to behave as if he were quite well. But I ended by becoming anxious, more because of his curiously preoccupied manner than because of any actual suffering. He had always been so good-tempered, so light-hearted, but when I begged him to tell me what was wrong with him, he replied nervously, almost angrily:

"'Nothing at all . . . I assure you it's nothing . . . Don't worry me . . . I'm just a little out of sorts . . . Nothing of any importance . . . In a few days I shall be all right again . . .'

"I asked him to see a doctor: he became violently angry.

"Finding him so changed in manner, so changed in his attitude toward me, I began to wonder whether I had been mistaken in my estimate of him. Was it possible his character was so different from what I had believed it to be?

"Then came an evening when, just as we were finishing dinner, he complained of violent pains in his head. Almost at once his eyes became glazed, he jumped up, upsetting his chair, and without any warning fell flat on the ground, dragging the plates and glasses from the table with him. He struggled, making inarticulate cries, foaming at the mouth. The servants were terrified. I knelt down and spoke to him: he did not hear me, did not know me.

"The doctor who came—they had brought the nearest one—made a very slight examination. I know now that there was no need to look long to understand. He asked me if he were subject to attacks of the kind. I replied:

" 'This is the first. What can it be?'

"He looked curiously at me, no doubt very astonished by my question, shook his head, and said gently:

" 'Sooner or later you will have to know. It is epilepsy.'

"Ah! that word, that terrible word. It still rings in my ears. I remembered how I had never heard it without feeling terror and a sort of disgust. Once, passing a crowd in the street with my father, we stopped to see what had happened, but my father drew me away quickly. 'Don't look . . . it's an epileptic . . .'

"And here my husband was one . . . I stood stupefied, not daring to go near the unfortunate being they were holding down on the floor.

" 'I am very sorry,' said the doctor, probably regretting his brutal frankness, 'but you must not let the word make the thing seem more terrible than it really is. It is useless to deny that it is a grave form of illness, but it is much more common than is usually believed, and there is little real danger for those who are able to be properly looked after. Your husband will recover from this attack and will probably not have another for months, for years . . . All I can do is to warn you that for some time to come you must not let there be any chance of your having a child.'

" 'I have been pregnant for two months . . .'

"He bit his lips, prescribed a sleeping draught, and left. My husband recovered consciousness during the night. When he saw me by his bedside he hardly dared to hold out his hand to me, hardly dared I put mine in his . . . I had become convinced that he had known all along about his disease, and that his refusals to allow himself to be looked after, his black moods, his ill-temper, had all been due to the fear that in the end I must inevitably know the truth.

"I did not say anything to my parents. I was divided between the fear of finding myself alone with my husband and that of revealing the nature of his illness to others. But the desire to know for certain had got possession of me. Nor was it difficult to find out. People are always only too happy to tell you about the misfortunes of others. And in a few days I had learned the history of my husband's family.

"His father—died of epilepsy.

"One of his brothers, who was supposed to have gone abroad and had never been heard of since, was shut up in a lunatic asylum.

"Another—an idiot who died at twenty.

"My husband—epileptic since the age of fourteen.

"This was the horrible family line that stretched itself out before me. The same taint had affected them one and all, and I became terrified as I wondered whether the child I was carrying in me might come into the world cursed in the same way.

"Now that I am confessing, I will make a clean breast of it. You may condemn me as a bad wife and unworthy daughter if you like before you pass judgment on me as a criminal mother— what does it matter, I wish you to understand that from that moment my life was a hell; that I lived through weeks of perpetual nightmare; that I grew to hate equally the parents of my husband who had forced this terrible inheritance on him, my husband himself for having cruelly deceived me, and my own parents who had neglected the chief of their duties, that of knowing to whom they gave me.

"Nevertheless, because I respected myself, and also because I felt ashamed, I remained silent.

"Six weeks later my husband had another attack, more violent than the last. After that the fits became more frequent. He soon had one every day, then two. Nothing did him any good, and at last he died in horrible convulsions.

"His death effaced my bitterness. I was overwhelmed with sorrow. I excused the poor dead soul, knowing that it was his great love that had made him hide the truth from me.

"The months that followed had no special interest. I lived through them absorbed in my own thoughts as I waited for the birth of my child.

"I must have made a mistake in my calculations, for it came ten or fifteen days sooner than I expected. That explains the absence of a nurse, midwife, or doctor. I had not the strength to get to the bell. But the thought of the child that would so soon be mine comforted me, and I was almost happy in my agony.

"But just as it was born a frightful clearness of vision came to me. I said just now that I didn't hear it cry. I lied. I heard the sharp little cry, and it was that cry that pierced my brain like an arrow.

"Awful visions flashed before my eyes. I saw its father and his ghastly agonies. I imagined I saw the brother struggling in his straight waistcoat; the other, the repulsive idiot, and the grandfather, the root from which these branches sprang, epileptic also. I saw clearly what my child in his turn would be. I was afraid both of what I seemed to see and of what I probably should see in the future.

"But that was nothing compared with what followed. Suddenly, as I felt the little piece of living flesh move against my side, a mad terror overwhelmed me. I tried to soothe myself by saying it was my child, my own child. But a voice seemed to hiss in my ears:

"'Child of a madman! Child of a madman!'

"I began to shudder as one would at the touch of some loathly reptile . . . It is unbelievable . . . How can anyone understand? . . . A mother afraid of *her own child* . . . of a thing so fragile, hardly alive . . . But it was so, and I could not dominate the feeling. I pulled myself away from it, and it seemed as if I was bound to defend myself against something terrible . . . something monstrous . . . I flung myself on it . . . I seized the little neck that slipped under my fingers, and stretching out my arms so that if there were any instinctive resistance it could not even touch me, I . . . miserable wretch . . . savage . . . criminal . . . I tightened my fingers . . ."

She broke off, and falling on her knees, her face in her hands, sobbed:

"Oh! my baby . . . my little baby . . . afraid of you . . ."

The Kiss

"YES, SISTER, it was for a woman he did it, my poor boy. Soon after he knew her he changed completely. He had always been so quiet and good-tempered, and he suddenly became irritable and short in his answers. He invented all sorts of stories so that he wouldn't have to give me his wages on Saturdays. Sometimes I waited up for him till two in the morning, and when I heard the door shut and knew he was in bed, I used to go quietly to his room, and I could see that his eyes were swollen. Once the tears were still wet on his face.

"At first I thought he had got into trouble at the factory. I went to see the master, and he told me there was nothing wrong there, but that the boy didn't work as well as he used to and that it was to be feared he had fallen into the hands of bad companions. I took care not to let him see that I was watching him, but I made inquiries, and I found that he was often with a woman, a low woman, a prostitute—excuse me, Sister—who walked the streets at night.

"If it had only been a working-girl like himself, in spite of my being old and needing all the help he can give me, I would have married them. But that! One day I went to see her. I asked her to leave him alone; I told her he was all I had in the world. She used awful language and turned me out, and as I went downstairs she called after me:

"'I have taken him away from you, have I? All right. You shall have him back right enough—you'll see . . .'

"Next day they brought the poor child home on a stretcher. He had a shot in his chest. From what I could learn or guess they had quarreled because of me, and because he didn't give her enough money. When he realized that he no longer amused her, that she didn't want to see him again, he lost his head, and without thinking of himself, or me, or anything, he tried to kill himself. Ah! it is hard to bear such things at my age."

Standing near the narrow hospital bed, the nun had listened in silence. The sick youth, who had been in a state of coma, was beginning to give little broken cries like calls. Trembling, the mother asked:

"What does the doctor say? Is there any chance of his getting well?"

"I'm afraid, poor mother, that he is very ill. But we haven't lost hope. He is young . . . Now you must go home. He must not have the excitement of seeing you when he first recovers conscious-ness. You may be quite sure he will be well looked after. You can come again tomorrow for a few minutes . . . every day if you like."

Weeping bitterly, but biting her lips to prevent her sobs being heard by those in the other beds, the old woman walked slowly away, turning every few steps to look back.

A deep silence fell on the ward. The shadows of night were creeping in. The whisperings and turnings caused by an exit or an entrance gradually died away. It was the hour when the sick, tired by a long, weary day, fall gently asleep. The nun sat down by the pillow of the boy.

She was very young. Her eyes were clear as crystal, and there was still in them something of the wonder you see in those of children. Her lips were curved; there had been no time for them to take the lines given by the never-ceasing murmur of prayers. Her face was round and rosy; little curls with golden lights in them sometimes escaped from under the white band that cir-cled her forehead. But notwithstanding her fresh young laugh-ter, she knew all the words and ways that soothe pain. When she spoke to the sick men her voice had tender inflections like those of a mother or elder sister.

Toward the middle of the night the boy recovered conscious-ness. The nun had not left his side. He wanted to ask questions, but she told him he must keep quiet. He obeyed, docile as a child, and fell asleep.

During the first days he saw her constantly, for she rarely left his side. Timid, almost ashamed, he hardly ever spoke, lying

motionless for hours with his eyes shut. It was only when the
door opened or shut that he raised his eyelids, and they would
fall again immediately.

More than once on these occasions he had spoken, saying
shyly:

"Sister . . ."

But when the nun had bent over him with a: "What is it, little
one?" he turned away his head, murmuring:

"Nothing . . . Nothing . . ."

One morning he had more courage:

"Tell me, please, Sister, if anyone has come to ask about me
since I came here?"

"But of course. Your mother—you know that, don't you?"

"Yes . . . But anyone else?"

"No, nobody."

He turned away his head, but she saw there were tears in his
eyes.

"Come, come, little one, this won't do. What's the matter?"

A pressing need to confide in someone after his long silence
drew the confession from him:

"It is so unkind. I can tell you anything . . . you are so good to
me . . . and I shall feel better if you know . . . Mother doesn't
know, she thinks it was an accident . . . But it wasn't. I tried to
kill myself . . ."

The nun stopped him with a gesture:

"She knows all about it."

"Ah!"

For some time he was silent, slowly shaking his head.

"My poor old mother . . . I have given her so much trouble.
She will forgive me, for she knows it wasn't my fault . . . I was so
unhappy. When that woman turned me away, I thought I
couldn't go on living without her. I loved her so much . . . She
could have done anything she liked with me . . . And you see that
even though she knows it is because of her I am here, she has
never even come to ask how I am. Whenever I heard the door
open I thought I should see her walking toward me . . . But now
I know she will never come . . . I don't want her to, either . . . I
shall leave off thinking of her . . . I shall leave off loving her . . .
No, I don't love her at all now . . ."

The tears that were in his eyes gave the lie to his words. Presently he asked:

"It is a great sin, isn't it, Sister, to try to kill yourself?"

"A very great sin. The greatest of all."

"But if you are too unhappy . . . wouldn't God know that, and understand? . . ."

She bowed her head and clasped her hands; her shoulders moved, and the wings of her white head-dress trembled as she replied in a low voice:

"Shh . . . Shh . . . You must not tire yourself, little one . . . You must shut your eyes and go to sleep . . ."

He seemed to do so, but about two in the morning he became very restless. They sent for the nun.

"Well, and what's all this about?" she said as she bent over him. "You are not being good?"

He burst into harsh, incoherent words that came in gasps.

She took one of his hands in hers and with the other gently wiped the perspiration from his forehead, trying to calm him.

Soothed as if by a caress, he grew quiet. He breathed more easily, his voice was even, his words intelligible.

"Yes, I know I am late . . . It was my work that kept me . . . I will come earlier next time. You don't like the flowers? . . . On Sunday we will pick a lot . . . We will go to the river for the day, we will have dinner on the grass . . . We will go home early, and you will see how much I love you . . . If you only knew how much I love you! I love your eyes and your hair . . . all of you. Your skin smells like flowers."

This was said in a tone of supplication, and it sounded like a passionate prayer. But soon he was talking too quickly again, the words running into one another.

The nun, her eyes anxious, let him talk on, and the prayers she murmured mechanically sounded like the accompaniment to a Song of Love.

He began to moan and shudder, and suddenly he sprang up:

"What! Going away? Never see you again! . . ."

He was panting now, the breath coming in short, painful gasps. The nun hurriedly brought a light and looked carefully at him.

He was livid, and his eyes were wild. Deep shadows stretched from the eyes to the corner of the lips; the temples seemed to have fallen in. Drenched with perspiration, his hair was sticking in wisps to his forehead, and his palpitating nostrils seemed to draw all the rest of his face to them.

Ah! she knew them, these agonized faces that looked as if the mind were trying in one minute to live over again the whole of a life . . .

Softly, so as not to disturb those in the other beds, she said to a night-nurse:

"Quick . . . quick . . . bring the doctor and send for the chaplain . . . No. 6 is very ill . . ."

Kneeling by the bed, she began to pray: "Thy will be done, O God, but pardon, oh, pardon this poor child."

The dying boy had taken her folded hands in his and went on talking, but his voice was now quiet, far, far away.

"Don't go . . . I will give you everything you want . . . Anything, if you only will stay with me . . . If you leave me, I shall die . . . Come . . ."

His head brushed against the forehead of the nun. His neck stretched forwards, he bent toward her.

"Come . . . I adore you . . ."

He was touching her eyes and cheeks . . . He reached her lips— She started back and tried to rise.

But he grasped her shoulders, and his dream carrying him right over the threshold of eternity, he implored:

"Oh, stay . . . I love you . . ."

She shut her eyes and bent her head. He pressed his lips on hers in a long, fervent, noiseless kiss, one of those deep kisses in which two beings merge their identity, a kiss like those he had learned in the arms of the prostitute.

Under it the trembling lips of the nun opened—was it in a last prayer? Or had her thoughts flashed back to the fiancé whose death had turned her life to God?

A Maniac

H E WAS neither malicious nor bloodthirsty. It was only that he had conceived a very special idea of the pleasures of existence. Perhaps it was that, having tried them all, he no longer found the thrill of the unexpected in any of them.

He went to the theatre, not to follow the piece, or to look through his opera-glasses at the spectators, but because he hoped that some day a fire might break out. At the fair of Neuilly he visited the various menageries in anticipation of a catastrophe: the tamer attacked by the beasts. He had tried bullfights, but soon tired of them; the slaughter appeared too well-regulated, too natural, and it disgusted him to watch suffering.

What he was always looking for was the quick and keen anguish caused by some unexpected disaster, some new kind of accident; so much so that, having been at the Opéra Comique on the night of the great fire, from which he escaped unhurt; that, having been a couple of steps from the cage the day the celebrated Fred was devoured by his lions, he lost almost all interest in theatres and menageries. To those who were astonished at this apparent change in his tastes, he replied:

"But there's nothing more to see there. They don't give me the slightest sensation. All that I care for is the effect produced on others and on me."

When he was deprived of these two favorite pleasures—it had taken him ten years to get what he wanted from them—he fell into a state of mental and physical depression, and for some months rarely left his house.

Then came a morning when the walls of Paris were covered with multi-colored posters that showed, on an azure background, a curious inclined track that came down, wound round, and fell like a ribbon. Up at the top, little bigger than a dot, a cyclist seemed to be waiting for a signal to rush down the giddy descent. At the same time the newspapers gave accounts of an extraordinary feat that explained the meaning of this weird picture.

It seemed that the cyclist dashed down the narrow path at full speed, went up round the loop, then down to the bottom. For a second during this fantastic performance he was head downwards, his feet up in the air.

The acrobat invited the press to come and examine the track and the machine so that they might see there was no trickery about it, and he explained that his ability to perform the feat was due to calculations of extreme precision, and that so long as he kept his nerve nothing could prevent its accomplishment.

Now it is certain that when the life of a man hangs on keeping his nerve, it hangs on a very insecure peg!

Since the appearance of the advertisement, our maniac had recovered some of his good humor. He went to the private demonstration, and becoming convinced that a new sensation awaited him, was in a seat on the first night to watch closely this looping the loop.

He had taken a box that faced the end of the track, and he sat there alone, not wishing to have near him anyone who might distract his close attention.

The whole thing was over in a few minutes. He had just time to see the black speck appear on the end of the track, a formidable spurt, a plunge, a gigantic bound, and that was all. It gave him a thrill, swift and vivid as lightning.

But as he went out with the crowd, he reflected that though he might feel this sensation twice or thrice, it must eventually fail, as all the others had done. He had not found what he was looking for. Then came the thought that a man's nerve has limitations, that the strength of a bicycle is, after all, only relative, and that there is no track of the kind, however secure it may seem, that may not some time give way. And he arrived at the conclusion that it was inevitable that some day an accident must occur.

From this to deciding to watch for that accident was a very small step.

"I will go to see this looping of the loop every night," he decided. "I will go till I see that man break his head. If it doesn't

happen during this three months in Paris, I will follow him elsewhere till it does."

For two months, every evening at the same time, he went to
the same box and in the same seat. The management had grown
to know him. He had taken the box for the whole period of the
turn, and they wondered vainly what could account for this
costly whim.

One evening when the acrobat had gone through his performance earlier than usual, he saw him in a corridor and went up
to him. There was no need for an introduction.

"I know you already," said the bicyclist. "You are always at the
hall. You come every night."

Surprised, he asked:

"It is true I am deeply interested in your performance. But
who has told you so?"

The man smiled:

"No one. I see you."

"That is very surprising. At such a height at such a moment
. . . your mind is sufficiently free to pick out the spectators down
below?"

"Certainly not. I don't see the spectators down below. It
would be extremely dangerous for me to pay any attention to a
crowd that moves and chatters. In all matters connected with
my profession, in addition to the turn itself, its theory and practice, there is something else, a kind of trick . . ."

He started.

"A trick?"

"Don't misunderstand me. I don't mean trickery. I mean
something of which the public has no suspicion, something that
is perhaps the most delicate part of the whole performance.
Shall I explain? Well, I accept it as a fact that it is not possible
to empty the brain till it contains but one idea, impossible to
keep the mind fixed on any one thought. As complete concen-
tration is necessary, I choose in the hall some one object on
which I fix my eyes. I see nothing but that object. From the
second I have my gaze on it, nothing else exists. I get on the
saddle. My hands gripping the bars, I think of nothing; neither
of my balance, nor my direction. I am sure of my muscles; they
are as firm as steel. There is only one part of me I am afraid of:

my eyes. But once I have fixed them on something, I am sure of them as well. Now, the first night I performed here, it happened that my eyes fell on your box. I saw you. I saw nothing but you. Without knowing it, you caught and held my eyes . . . You became the point, the object of which I have told you. The second day I looked for you at the same place. The following days it was the same. And so it happens that now, as soon as I appear, by instinct my eyes turn to you. You help me; you are the precious aid indispensable to my performance. Now do you understand why I know you?"

Next day the maniac was in his usual seat. In the hall there were the usual movements and murmurs of keen anticipation. Suddenly a dense silence fell; that profound silence when you feel that an audience is holding its breath. The acrobat was on his machine, which was held by two men, waiting for the signal to set off. He was balanced to perfection, his hands grasping the bar, his head up, his gaze fixed straight ahead.

He cried "Hop!" and the men pushed him off.

Just at that moment, in the most natural way possible, the maniac rose, pushed back his seat, and went to one at the other side of the box. Then a terrible thing happened. The cyclist was thrown violently up in the air. His machine rushed forwards, flew up, and lurching out into the midst of the shrieks of terror that filled the hall, fell among the crowd.

With a methodical gesture the maniac put on his overcoat, smoothed his hat on the cuff of his sleeve, and went out.

The 10:50 Express

"THEY SAY you are leaving us today, sir?" the cripple said to me.

"I must. I have to be at Marseilles on Monday morning. I shall go by the 10:50 express tonight from the Gare de Lyon. It's a good train . . . but you ought to know it—you were employed by the P. L. M. before you fell ill, weren't you?"

He shut his eyes, and his face became suddenly very pale as he replied:

"Yes . . . I know it . . . too well . . ."

There were tears under his eyelids as, after a moment's silence, he added:

"No one knows it as well as I do! . . ."

Thinking he was moved by regret for the work he was no longer able to do, I said:

"It must have been an interesting job. Fine work needing plenty of intelligence."

He shuddered; his paralyzed body strained violently, and there was a look of horror in his eyes as he protested:

"Don't say that, sir! Fine work? You mean work of terror and death . . . of horror and nightmare . . . Sir, I am nothing to you, but I am going to ask you a favor—don't go by that train. Take any other train you like, but don't go by the 10:50 . . ."

"Why?" I queried smiling. "Are you superstitious?"

"I'm not superstitious . . . but I was the driver in charge of the express the day of the disaster of 24th July, 1894. I will tell you about it and you will understand . . .

"We left the Gare de Lyon at the usual time, and had been running about two hours. The day had been suffocatingly hot. In spite of the speed we were going at, the breeze that came to me on the platform was stifling, the heavy, sultry air that goes before a storm . . .

"All at once, as if an electric light had been switched off, everything went out in the sky. Not a star left. The moon gone, and great flashes of lightning cutting the night with a light clear enough to make the darkness that followed black as ink.

"I said to my stoker:

"'We're in for it! There'll be a mighty downpour.'

"'Not before time. I couldn't stand this furnace much longer. You'll have to keep your eyes peeled for the signals.'

"'No fear. I can see right enough.'

"The thunder was so loud I couldn't hear the hammering of the wheels, nor the exhaust of the engine. The rain still kept off and the storm came nearer. We were running right into it. It seemed as if we were running after it.

"You needn't be a coward to feel a bit queer when you find yourself being hurled into a great storm on a monster of steel that rushes on like a madman.

"In front of us, quite close, a flash of lightning pierced the ground, and at the same time a terrible thunderclap sounded, then another, so violent that I shut my eyes and sank on my knees.

"I remained like that for some seconds, all of a heap, stunned, feeling as if I'd had a heavy blow on the back of the neck.

"At last I came to myself. I was still on my knees, my back against the partition of the platform. It seemed as if I had come back from hundreds of miles away. I tried to get up. Impossible. My legs were doubled under me, useless. I thought I must have broken something in my fall, but I felt no pain of any kind. I tried to help myself up with my hands . . . my arms were hanging powerless by my sides.

"There I was, stupefied, with the extraordinary feeling that my arms and legs didn't belong to me; that I had no command over them . . . that they refused to obey me . . . that they were things with no more life in them than my clothes which the draught was blowing about . . . Some power I didn't understand prevented my opening my eyes.

"We were running full speed. The storm was still raging, but not so violently, further away. It began to rain. I heard it hissing on the steel, and I felt the warm drops on my face.

"Suddenly something in me relaxed and I felt all right again, quite well, just a little tired. I remembered where I was and my work, and that brought me back to realities with a jerk, and not yet understanding what had happened, why I felt as if I were paralyzed, I called to my stoker to help me to get up.

"No reply.

"The noise is deafening on an engine going at full speed. I shouted louder:

"'François! Hullo there, François! Give me a hand.'

"Still no reply. Then an awful fear gripped me. Fear of what? I didn't know, but the shock of it made me open my eyes and give a yell. It was a yell of terror, and there was every reason for it.

"The platform was empty. My stoker had disappeared.

"In one second I understood exactly what had happened.

"The flash of lightning had struck us; it had killed the stoker and he had fallen out on the line. I—I was paralyzed . . .

"No, sir, not even if I were a great scholar and searched and searched for words, could I give you an idea of the horror I felt. The mate who ought to have been beside me, able to help me, had disappeared as if by magic, and behind me two hundred passengers were sleeping or chatting peacefully in their carriages with no suspicion that they were being whirled onwards in a mad rush to certain death. For the man in charge of the train, their driver, was a helpless mass, unable to stretch out an arm, paralyzed . . . a cripple . . . Me! . . .

"My brain grew as active as my body was inert. First I saw clearly the line stretching before me. I saw the rails shining in the moonlight. We were rushing along . . . how we tore along! . . . I became aware of the sensation of speed that habit had made me lose. The train passed a little station like a flash of lightning, but not too quickly for me to see a signalman dozing in his box near a telegraphic apparatus. A jolt or two on the turntable; a clanging of plates; the line marked by rails that crossed each other, suddenly large, then small . . . the deep cutting, and once more the dash into darkness.

"Then came the tunnel into which we plunged like a raging hurricane . . . Once again the open line. Now I knew where we were, and I told myself we were bound to derail, that in two minutes we should come to a sharp curve, and that at the rate we were going at we were certain to bound off . . .

"But the good God didn't mean it to be that. The engine, the whole train, leaned over . . . the rails ground frantically against the wheels . . . and we passed . . .

"This curve had been my chief fear. I breathed again. The fire would go out for want of fuel . . . The engine would stop . . . The guard would hurry round to the front of the train . . . I would tell him what had happened . . . He would put fog-signals in front of and behind us . . . we would be saved! . . .

"But my relief did not last long. We had just dashed through a station when I saw something that made my hair stand on end: the signal was against us! The block I was entering wasn't free . . .

"I don't know why I didn't go mad. Imagine what can go through a man's mind when, tearing along on an engine going at seventy miles an hour, he is warned that an obstacle bars the road . . .

"I said to myself: 'If you don't stop, you, and with you the whole train, will be smashed to pieces . . . to stop this awful thing, you need only make a slight movement, the simple movement of taking hold of that lever two feet away from you . . . but you won't make the movement . . . you can't make it . . . and you will see the whole thing happen, will have the agony, a hundred times worse than death itself, of sighting the thing on which you will smash . . . of watching it grow larger . . . of rushing on to it . . .

"I tried to shut my eyes . . . I couldn't . . . In spite of myself I kept watching, watching . . . and I saw it all, sir, I saw it all! I guessed what the obstacle was before it appeared, and soon there was no doubt about it . . . It was a train that had broken down that was blocking our way. I could see its shadow, its rear-lights. It came nearer . . . It came nearer! Why did I shriek? 'Help! Stop!' Who could hear? It came nearer. All of me was dead except my head. And that was alive with the terrible life of eyes that could see everything even in the blackness of the night, of ears that could hear everything even through the roaring of the wheels, of a frantic will that kept giving me orders like those an officer gives to routed soldiers he is trying to rally.

"It came nearer . . . Only five hundred yards away . . . only three hundred . . . shadowy forms ran about the line . . . only one hundred . . . one hundred yards . . . just a flash! . . . It was the end . . . the crash . . . the charnel heap . . . Annihilation!

"Sir, those who haven't seen it . . .

". . . I came to myself under a pile of wreckage. Agonized calls for help filled the air. I could see people running through the fields carrying lanterns, and others with the injured in their arms . . . and shrieks . . . and moans . . . and weeping . . .

"I saw, I heard all that, and I didn't care. I was no longer thinking. I didn't call for help . . .

"Between two beams that crossed over my head, so close that my lips touched them, I could see a little bit of sky, very soft, very pure; I just lay looking at a tiny star that trembled there, bright, pretty . . . it amused me . . ."

Blue Eyes

WRAPPED IN a loose hospital wrap that made her seem even thinner than she was, the sick girl was standing lost in thought at the foot of her bed.

Her childish face was wasted, and her blue eyes, sad, fathomless and circled with dark rings, were so unnaturally large they seemed to light up her whole face. Her cheeks burned with a hectic flush, and the deep lines that ran down to her mouth looked as if they had been worn there by the flow of unceasing tears.

She hung her head when the house-surgeon stopped beside her.

"Well, little No. 4, what's this I hear? You want to go out?"

"Yes, sir . . ." The voice was hardly more than a whisper.

"But that's very foolish . . . You've only been up two or three days. In weather like this, too. You'd certainly fall ill again. Wait a day or two. You're not unhappy here? . . . has anyone been unkind to you?"

"No . . . oh, no, sir . . ."

"What is it, then? . . ."

There was more energy in her tone as she said:

"I must go out."

And as if anticipating his question she continued quickly:

"This is All Saints' Day. I promised to take some flowers to my sweetheart's grave . . . I promised . . . He has only me . . . If I don't go, no one will . . . I promised . . ."

A tear shone under her eyelid. She wiped it away with a finger.

The house-surgeon was touched, and either out of curiosity, or so as not to seem awkward and leave her without some word of comfort, he asked:

"Is it long since he died?"

"Nearly a year . . ."

"What was the matter with him?"

She seemed to shrink, to become more frail, her chest more hollow, her hands thinner as, her eyes half closed, her lips trembling, she murmured:

"He was executed . . ."

The house-surgeon bit his lip and said in a low voice:

"Poor child . . . I'm very sorry. If you really must go out, go . . . But take care not to catch cold. You must come back tomorrow."

Once outside the hospital gates, she began to shiver.

It was a dreary autumn morning. Moisture trickled down the walls. Everything was gray: the sky, the houses, the naked trees and the misty distance where people hurried along anxious to get out of the damp streets.

It had been the middle of summer when she had fallen ill, and her dress was a brightly hued one of thin cotton. The crumpled ribbon that encircled her wasted neck made her look even more pitiable. The skirt, blouse and necktie might have smiled back at the sunshine, but they seemed to droop in sadness in the chill gray setting.

She started off with an uncertain walk, stopping every now and then because she was out of breath and her head swimming.

The people she passed turned to look after her. She seemed to hesitate as if wishing to speak to them, then, afraid, walked on, glancing nervously from right to left. In this way she crossed half of Paris. She stopped when she came to the Quais, standing to watch the slow, muddy flow of the river. The piercing cold cut through her, and feeling she could not bear much more, she started off again.

When she got to Place Maubert and the Avenue des Gobelins she felt almost at home, for she was now in the neighborhood in which she had lived. Soon she began to see faces she knew, and she heard someone say as she passed:

"Surely that's Vandat's girl . . . How she has changed!"

"Which Vandat?"

"Vandat the murd . . ."

She quickened her steps, pressing her hands against her face so as not to hear the end of the word . . .

It was getting dark when she at last arrived at the wretched little hotel where she had lodged before she fell ill. She went in. Street girls and the men they kept were playing cards in the little café downstairs. When they saw her they called out:

"Hullo! Here's Blue Eyes"—that used to be her nickname. "Come and have a drink, Blue Eyes. Here's a seat . . . come along . . ."

Their welcome touched her, but the thick, rank smoke made her cough, and she could hardly breathe as she replied:

"No . . . I've no time now . . . Is Madame in?"

"Yes, there she is."

She smiled timidly at the manageress.

"I wanted to ask you, Madame, if I could get at my things. The clothes I have on aren't warm enough . . ."

"Any clothes you left were taken up to the attic; they'll be there somewhere. I'll send someone to look for them . . . Sit down by the stove and warm yourself."

"No . . . I've no time now. I'll come back presently."

She went to the door. One of the men jeered:

"At the old business already? You aren't wasting much time."

She went out, and the short stay in the stifling room made the cold outside seem more piercing than ever. People were hurrying along laden with bead-wreaths and bouquets of flowers; others, dressed in their best clothes, talked and laughed, and one saw at a glance that they were carrying their offerings to the cemetery as a matter of habit, that time had taken the edge from their grief.

All along the side of the pavement barrows of flowers were drawn up. Chrysanthemums with curled petals drooped over clusters of roses; here and there mimosa shed its golden powder over bunches of violets. Nearer to the cemetery, in front of the shops of the marble masons, pots of flowers were arranged on the shelves of stands, insignificant, with neat foliage and restrained colors; further on were immortelles and large bead-wreaths . . .

She looked at all this with eyes that glowed with envy. If only she could get some for him, just a little bunch . . . for him where

he was lying at the far end of the cemetery in his poor, uncon-
secrated grave, a bare mound, without a single word to show
that he was lying there.

"Murderer" . . . that meant nothing to her. He was the being
she adored, her Man, the lover who had possessed not only her
body but her whole soul . . . In a moment of madness he had
killed someone . . . Had he not paid his horrible debt in full?

The day he had been arrested she had sworn never to have
anything to do with any other man, never; to give up the life she
had been leading, to work, to become an honest girl once more
. . . to live in memories of him . . .

She kept on looking at the flowers. A seller held out a bunch
of roses: "A bouquet? Some chrysanthemums then? Violets?"

She passed without replying, for she did not poosess one farthing. Yet there was but one idea in her mind—flowers. She
must have some flowers . . . she must get some flowers for him
somehow . . . she had sworn she would.

She was nearly fainting with hunger and fatigue, but she was
no longer aware of it. She was thinking only of the bare strip of
earth in the cemetery, imagining it with some flowers brighten-
ing it up. But the money . . . how was she to get it? What could
she do?

The way that suggested itself was the obvious one, nor did it
seem to clash with her vow to remain true to his memory.

Just as a good artisan returns to his factory, takes up his tools
and starts on his work, she mechanically patted her hair into
order, arranged her poor dress and began to walk the street as
she used to in the old days when her man, sitting playing cards
in the café, was the only thing in the world she cared about.

On she walked, her eye watchful, swaying her waist as she
whispered between her teeth:

"Stop! . . . I want to speak to you . . ."

But she was too emaciated: one glance at her and the men
hurried away. And indeed her face was no longer a face for pleasure; nor was her body, its sharp angles and deep hollows showing clearly under her thin cotton dress.

In bygone days when she was pretty, when she really was the
"Blue Eyes" everyone admired, it was different. Now she was
only an object of pity.

The daylight was fading. Suppose the cemetery was shut before she was able to buy the flowers . . .

A thin, misty rain was falling, silent, impalpable, and everything was becoming wrapped in gray shadows. You could see nothing of her thin face now except her eyes, two great eyes burning with fever.

A man was passing the corner of a quiet street, his coat-collar up, his hands in his pockets. She brushed up against him and said softly, her whole heart's craving vibrating in her voice:

"Stop! . . . Won't you come with me? . . ."

He looked at her for a moment. She had gone close up to him, her eyes penetrating his with the inspired expression of one conscious of a high mission.

He took her arm, and she guided him to the low hotel she had recently left. Through the half open door she said quickly:

"My key . . . A candle . . ."

The manageress replied in a low voice: "No. 23, second floor, third door."

The men and the girls in the café bent forward to see who was there, and as she went upstairs she heard exclamations and bursts of laughter.

. . . It was almost dark when she came down again. She threw a hasty goodbye at her companion and set off at a run. Stopping before the first flower-seller she came to, she seized the nearest bunch and threw down the two pieces of silver that clinked in her hands.

Quickly, quickly, she ran to the cemetery. People were coming away in little groups. She trembled. Would there still be time?

At the entrance the gate-keeper said: "Too late! We're closing now."

"Oh! please, please. I only want to run in and out again. Just two minutes . . ."

"Very well. But—quick."

Down the path she rushed, stumbling over the stones in the dark. It was a long way. She could hardly breathe, something was burning so painfully in her chest. She stopped by the wall where those who are executed are buried, and fell on her knees, scattering her flowers on the earth. Her tears streamed from her eyes, dripping between the hands she pressed against her face.

She tried to pray, but she could not remember any of the proper words, and she just sobbed, her lips on the ground:

"Oh! my man . . . my man . . ."

Then, so worn out she had lost all sensation in her limbs, but with a feeling of ease, almost of joy in her heart, she rose and hurried away. She even smiled at the gatekeeper as she said:

"You see I haven't been long."

But now that it was over, now she had kept her promise, had been near her man, she became aware again of the cold and her exhaustion. She could hardly drag herself along, her cough was so bad: every now and then she had to stop and lean against the wall . . .

At last she got back to the hotel and stumbled into the door. The girls and men were still playing cards in the overheated, smoke-filled room. A dead silence fell on them all when they saw her. She tried to laugh.

A woman at the far end of the room threw herself back on her chair and cried:

"You've made a fine start, Blue Eyes. Needed a bit of nerve, didn't it?"

She shrugged her shoulders. The other went on:

"Did you know who it was?"

"No . . ."

"Well, I'll tell you. It was Le Bingue."

Blue Eyes stammered:

"What do you say? Le . . ."

Emptying her glass and taking up her cards again, the girl called back:

"Yes, Le Bingue . . . You know, the Executioner!"

The Empty House

WHEN HE had picked the lock, the man went in, shut the door carefully and stood listening intently. Although he knew the house was empty, the complete silence and inky darkness made an extraordinary impression on him. Never before had he experienced at one and the same time such a longing for and fear of solitude. He stretched out his hand, felt about the wall and fastened the bolt of the door. A little reassured, he took from his pocket a small electric lamp and looked round. The white patches of light that broke the darkness moved up and down with the beating of his heart. To give himself courage he murmured:

"It's like being in my own house."

Forcing a smile, he stepped cautiously into the dining-room.

Everything was in the most scrupulous order. Four chairs were pushed in round the table; the reflections of the legs of another were mirrored in the shining parquet floor. Vague odors of tobacco and fruit floated in the air.

He opened the drawers of a sideboard where table-silver stood in orderly piles: "That's better than nothing," he thought as he put it in his pocket. But at every movement the spoons and forks jingled, and though he knew that the house was empty and he could not disturb anyone, the noise agitated him and he turned away on tiptoe, leaving untouched a case of silver and enamel fruit knives and forks.

"That is not what I have come to get," was what he said to himself to excuse his hesitation.

But the same want of resolution kept him standing by the table fingering the silver that weighed heavily in his pocket as he looked at the door of the little salon where the closely drawn, heavy curtains made the darkness still more dense. He made a supreme effort to dominate this unusual cowardice; and finally he walked calmly into the room with the easy step of a man who is returning to his own home after an evening with friends. He had suddenly lost the sensation of fear, and seeing a candelabra on an old chest he struck a match, lit the candles, and carried the light round to examine the pictures on the walls, the gold photograph frames, the ornaments, the piano, the mantelpiece from beneath which there came the smell of cinders and soot. He glanced at some papers that he raised with a finger, weighed a silver statuette in his hand and put it down again, then with a last look round the room, placed the candelabra on the table, blew out the candles and opened the door of the bedroom.

There was no longer any shadow of hesitation. Under pretext of looking over the house, which was to let, he had some days before been able to find out where every piece of furniture stood, and its nature. At one glance his practiced eye had noted the bureau where the old man was sure to keep his valuable documents, the chest where his money ought to be, the bed in the alcove, and the big wardrobe with glass doors and many drawers, the contents of which he would probably find it well worth while to examine. He put out his lamp, stretched out his arm, and without knocking against even a chair, walked toward the bureau. He felt the top, drew his hand along the front, placed one finger of the left hand on the lock and felt in his pocket for his keys.

He had lost a little of his calm. It was not that he had any return of the curious fear of the darkness and silence of the house he had broken into; he now felt the feverish haste of the gambler who fingers his card before turning it up. What would he find? . . . Title-deeds? . . . Banknotes? . . . And how much? What fortune lay waiting for him here behind this plank of wood? . . .

But he could not get at his keys. He had forgotten to take them out of his pocket before putting in the silver, and they had become entangled in it. As he fumbled, the spoons got into the rings of the keys, the prongs of the forks bent and pierced the lining of his coat, scratching his flesh. His impatience increased his clumsiness; he stamped his foot, swore, clenched his teeth and pulled so violently that the stuff gave way, and the keys and silver flew out and scattered over the floor with a sound like that of old iron . . . He was losing his nerve again . . . he had so nearly attained his object, and time was flying! . . . He did not know the exact hour, and it seemed as if he had been there a very long time. For the first time he became aware of the tick-tock of a clock, and the minutes seemed to be galloping along . . .

He knelt down, took a key, and tried it, his ear close to the lock; no use. He took another, then a third, still another, trying them with careful movements . . . No good. No use at all! . . . His anger blazed up again, and he laughed harshly:

"Enough of that . . . Why should I spare the furniture?"

And seizing his jimmy, with one skillful movement he had the lock off. Then he opened the drawer and turned on his lamp.

A sigh of joy burst from him as his eyes fell on a collection of notes pinned together in packets. Slowly, methodically, he took them up, counted them, held them up to the light, then smoothed them with the back of his hand. He drew up a chair, sat down, and continued to search at ease. Under a bag of gold there was a thick packet of share-certificates made out in the name of the holder, shares that amounted to twenty thousand francs—a fortune! . . .

"What a pity to leave them," he thought. "But they're no use to me . . ."

He replaced them. Sure now of his booty, he took his time; weighing the gold coins in his hand, comparing the surfaces and inscriptions on the forty- and fifty-franc pieces before putting them in his breast pocket. There was no longer any haste or agitation; success had ousted every feeling but those of relief and exultation. A heavy cart passed along the street, rattling the windows, shaking the furniture, making the silver on the floor vibrate. The familiar sound brought him back to a sense of where he was, and he took out his watch. Four o'clock—it was growing late! Gathering up the money without counting it, he looked quickly through the other drawers. There was nothing of any value to him. Some loose money had strayed among the papers and letters, and this he put in his vest pocket, murmuring:

"For out-of-pocket expenses."

A beautiful bronze paperweight lay on the table. He had been wise enough to leave the share-certificates and some jewelry, but this—might he not take this as a charming little souvenir? . . . He was stretching out his hand when a noise startled him; the clock was striking, four sharp little strokes. He stood still, his hand out, his fingers open . . . the silence, broken for a moment by the decisive sounds, seemed suddenly to become oppressive, solemn. There was not a vibration within the four walls, not even the imperceptible murmur of hangings when the folds stir, not a crack from the dry boards that seem to sleep by day and wake into a sort of attempt at life during the night . . . Nothing but the beating of his own pulses, the sound of the quickened tide of the blood that throbbed in his temples . . . Fear gripped him again, a stupid, unusual fear—surely there was something abnormal about the nature of this silence? Why did he feel that he dare not disturb it by even a gesture? . . . He had ceased pressing the button of his lamp and stood there in the darkness, his shoulders bent, his neck stretched forwards, his nostrils dilated, his ears straining as he bent toward the mantelshelf where the little clock had ticked so quickly . . . The ticking had ceased! Well, the clock had stopped, that was all. Was there anything terrifying about that? . . . Nevertheless, a shiver ran down his back; some immediate and terrible danger seemed to be threatening him, and he seized his knife, turned on the lamp, and wheeled quickly round.

In the alcove, half hidden in the shadow, he saw the face of an old man. The mouth was half open, and two terrible eyes were looking fixedly at him. There was no expression of fear; the eyes looked unflinchingly into his own, the hand that was stretched out over the sheet did not tremble, the leg that hung down below the covering was steady. Someone was going to take him by the throat; in a moment he would feel on his face the breath of this pale and silent adversary.

Without daring to move his head, he turned his eyes to look for the door. The banknotes had fallen to the floor, forgotten; he had but one idea—to flee! But from the menace in the eyes he saw that he would never manage to reach the door, that the old man was opening his mouth to cry for help, and that once the cry had sounded, it would be too late to escape; and without a second's hesitation, like a beast defending itself, he rushed to the bed, raised the knife, and with a gasp of rage thrust it twice in the body up to the hilt. There was no moan, not a sound; a pillow fell softly to the ground and the head slipped sideways on the bolster, the lips half open, the chin on the chest.

Still trembling with fear and passion, he drew back and looked at his victim. The light of the lamp was too small to allow him to distinguish either the rent made by the knife in the disordered shirt or any trace of blood. Apparently the stroke had gone straight to the heart, for the expression of the face had not changed. The first thrust, well-aimed and lightning-swift, had stopped life as if it had been a shot from a revolver. Proud of his skill, he muttered menacingly:

"So you were at home watching me! Well, you have seen, haven't you?"

But as he bent over the quiet face and noted that the expression was the same, it flashed into his mind that the knife might only have pierced the coverings, that perhaps the old man was still alive, still watching him with the same supreme irony.

He raised the knife again and drove it in, drew it out and brought it down with savage frenzy, and intoxicated by the dull sound it made as it entered the chest, he continued to strike, exciting himself by oaths and exclamations that he forgot to stifle. The shirt was now in rags, the flesh one large wound. But untouched by the knife, the face still kept its impassive calm, its terrifying stare. He lost his head, and flinging his lamp away, seized the old man by the throat to give a last certain stroke.

But his right hand remained up in the air and the cry of rage did not pass his lips, for under the other hand he felt, not the damp and throbbing flesh from which life was escaping in a flow of blood, but flesh that had no last quiver of life in it, which was cold with the awful iciness that is like nothing else in the world—dead flesh, dead for long hours! . . . His arm fell.

He had never been afraid of crime. His knife had often been red: his face had been wet with the warm stream that leaped from severed arteries: he knew the smell of blood, the death-rattle that comes when life is flowing from the body . . . Death caused by his own hands was nothing . . . But this! . . . And instinctive respect for the Dead suddenly rose from some obscure depth in his murderer's soul, and a superstitious fear of the Great Mystery froze him . . . He had believed the house was empty, and he had shut himself in with a corpse! . . . A corpse . . . this, then, accounted for the unearthly silence and the pall-like mystery of the darkness! . . .

Somewhere in the far distance a clock struck five, and without daring to turn his head toward the abandoned spoils, with his hat in his hand and vague memories of prayers rising in his ter-rified mind, he stumbled over the furniture and fled from the house . . .

The Last Kiss

"FORGIVE ME . . . Forgive me."

His voice was less assured as he replied:

"Get up, dry your eyes. I, too, have a good deal to reproach myself with."

"No, no," she sobbed.

He shook his head.

"I ought never to have left you; you loved me. Just at first after it all happened . . . when I could still feel the fire of the vitriol burning my face, when I began to realize that I should never see again, that all my life I should be a thing of horror, of Death, certainly I wasn't able to think of it like that. It isn't possible to resign oneself all at once to such a fate . . . But living in this eternal darkness, a man's thoughts pierce far below the surface and grow quiet like those of a person falling asleep, and gradually calm comes. Today, no longer able to use my eyes, I see with my imagination. I see again our little house, our peaceful days, and your smile. I see your poor little face the night I said that last goodbye. The judge couldn't imagine any of that, could he? And it was only fair to try to explain, for they thought only of your action, the action that made me into . . . what I am. They were going to send you to prison where you would slowly have faded . . . No years of such punishment for you could have given me back my eyes . . . When you saw me go into the witness-box you were afraid, weren't you? You believed that I would charge you, have you condemned? No, I could never have done that, never . . ."

She was still crying, her face buried in her hands.

"How good you are! . . ."

"I am just . . ."

In a voice that came in jerks she repeated:

"I repent, I repent; I have done the most awful thing to you that a woman could do, and you—you begged for my acquittal! And now you can even find words of pity for me! What can I do to prove my sorrow? Oh, you are wonderful . . . wonderful . . ."

He let her go on talking and weeping; his head thrown back, his hands on the arms of his chair, he listened apparently without emotion. When she was calm again, he asked:

"What are you going to do now?"

"I don't know . . . I shall rest for a few days . . . I am so tired . . . Then I shall go back to work. I shall try to find a place in a shop or as a mannequin."

His voice was a little stifled as he asked: "You are still as pretty as ever?"

She did not reply.

"I want to know if you are as pretty as you used to be?"

She remained silent. With a slight shiver, he murmured: "It is dark now, isn't it? Turn on the light. Though I can no longer see, I like to feel that there is light around me . . . Where are you? . . . Near the mantelpiece? . . . Stretch out your hand. You will find the switch there."

No sense even of light could penetrate his eyelids, but from the sudden sound of horror she stifled, he knew that the lamp was on. For the first time she was able to see the result of her work, the terrifying face streaked with white swellings, seamed with red furrows, a narrow black band round the eyes. While he had pleaded for her in court, she had crouched on her seat weeping, not daring to look at him; now, before this abominable thing, she grew sick with a kind of disgust. But it was without any anger that he murmured:

"I am very different from the man you knew in the old days—I horrify you now, don't I? You shrink from me? . . ."

She tried to keep her voice steady. "Certainly not. I am here, in the same place . . ."

"Yes, now . . . and I want you to come still nearer. If you knew how the thought of your hands tempt me in my darkness. How I should love to feel their softness once again. But I dare not . . . And yet that is what I wanted to ask you: to let me feel your

hand for a minute in mine. We, the blind, can get such marvel-
ous memories from just a touch."

Turning her head away, she held out her arm. Caressing her
fingers, he murmured:

"Ah, how good. Don't tremble. Let me try to imagine we are
lovers again just as we used to be . . . but you are not wearing
my ring. Why? I have not taken yours off. Do you remember?
You said, 'It is our wedding-ring.' Why have you taken it off?"

"I dare not wear it . . ."

"You must put it on again. You will wear it? Promise me."

She stammered:

"I promise you."

He was silent for a little while; then in a calmer voice:

"It must be quite dark now. How cold I am! If you only
knew how cold it feels when one is blind. Your hands are
warm; mine are frozen. I have not yet developed the fuller
sense of touch. It takes time, they say . . . At present I am like
a little child learning."

She let her fingers remain in his, sighing:

"Oh, my God . . . my God . . ."

Speaking like a man in a dream, he went on:

"How glad I am that you came. I wondered whether you
would, and I felt I wanted to keep you with me for a long, long
time: always . . . But that wouldn't be possible. Life with me
would be too sad. You see, little one, when people have memories like ours, they must be careful not to spoil them, and it must
be horrible to look at me now, isn't it?"

She tried to protest; what might have been a smile passed
over his face.

"Why lie? I remember I once saw a man whose mistress had
thrown vitriol over him. His face was not human. Women
turned their heads away as they passed, while he, not being able
to see and so not knowing, went on talking to the people who
were shrinking away from him. I must be, I am like that poor
wretch, am I not? Even you who knew me as I used to be, you
tremble with disgust; I can feel it. For a long time you will be
haunted by the remembrance of my face . . . it will come in
between you and everything else . . . How the thought hurts . . .
but don't let us go on talking about me . . . You said just now that

you were going back to work. Tell me your plans; come nearer, I don't hear as well as I used to . . . Well?"

Their two armchairs were almost touching. She was silent. He sighed:

"Ah, I can smell your scent! How I have longed for it. I bought a bottle of the perfume you always used, but on me it didn't smell the same. From you it comes mixed with the scent of your skin and hair. Come nearer, let me drink it in . . . You are going away, you will never come back again; let me draw in for the last time as much of you as I can . . . You shiver . . . am I then so horrible?"

She stammered:

"No . . . it is cold . . ."

"Why are you so lightly dressed? I don't believe you brought a cloak. In November, too. It must be damp and dreary in the streets. How you tremble! How warm and comfortable it was in our little home . . . do you remember? You used to lay your face on my shoulder, and I used to hold you close to me. Who would want to sleep in my arms now? Come nearer. Give me your hand . . . There . . . What did you think when your lawyer told you I had asked to see you?"

"I thought I ought to come."

"Do you still love me? . . ."

Her voice was only a breath:

"Yes . . ."

Very slowly, his voice full of supplication, he said:

"I want to kiss you for the last time. I know it will be almost torture for you . . . Afterwards I won't ask anything more. You can go . . . May I? . . . Will you let me? . . ."

Involuntarily she shrank back; then, moved by shame and pity, not daring to refuse a joy to the poor wretch, she laid her head on his shoulder, held up her mouth and shut her eyes. He pressed her gently to him, silent, prolonging the happy moment. She opened her eyes, and seeing the terrible face so near, almost touching her own, for the second time she shivered with disgust and would have drawn sharply away. But he pressed her closer to him, passionately.

"You would go away so soon? . . . Stay a little longer . . . You haven't seen enough of me . . . Look at me . . . and give me your mouth again . . . more of it than that . . . It is horrible, isn't it?"

She moaned:

"You hurt me . . ."

"Oh, no," he sneered, "I frighten you."

She struggled.

"You hurt me! You hurt me!"

In a low voice he said:

"Sh-h. No noise; be quiet. I've got you now and I'll keep you. For how many days have I waited for this moment . . . Keep still, I say, keep still! No nonsense! You know I am much stronger than you."

He seized both her hands in one of his, took a little bottle from the pocket of his coat, drew out the stopper with his teeth, and went on in the same quiet voice:

"Yes, it is vitriol; bend your head . . . there . . . You will see; we are going to be incomparable lovers, made for each other . . . Ah, you tremble? Do you understand now why I had you acquitted, and why I made you come here today? Your pretty face will be exactly like mine. You will be a monstrous thing, and like me, blind! . . . Ah, yes, it hurts, hurts terribly."

She opened her mouth to implore. He ordered:

"No! Not that! Shut your mouth! I don't want to kill you, that would make it too easy for you."

Gripping her in the bend of his arm, he pressed his hand on her mouth and poured the acid slowly over her forehead, her eyes, her cheeks. She struggled desperately, but he held her too firmly and kept on pouring as he talked:

"There . . . a little more . . . you bite, but that's nothing . . . It hurts, doesn't it! It is hell . . ."

Suddenly he flung her away, crying: "I am burning myself."

She fell writhing on the floor. Already her face was nothing but a red rag.

Then he straightened himself, stumbled over her, felt about the wall to find the switch, and put out the light. And round them, as in them, was a great Darkness . . .

Under Ether

IN THE evenings, when the wounded were asleep, when there were left burning in the halls only the Argand lamps, shaded by hoods of cardboard, the old doctor used to take a little turn up and down the road.

His pipe stuck between his teeth, he used to climb the little hill, from which through the trees he could see the denuded plain, the villages, whose mutilated profiles made strange, sharp-drawn figures against the sky, and, further off, St. Quentin, which for eight days past had been illuminated by the glare of incendiary fires.

Then, his back bent forward, his hands in his pockets, he watched going up in smoke the city in which for twenty years he had visited the poor and the rich—the peaceful little city where formerly the old people whom he had cared for and the children whom he had brought into the world greeted him as he passed by; the sorrowful little city, now in captivity, where his mother awaited him. Now and then, as the wind blew aside the smoke and the flames licked the black horizon, he would say:

"It is the factory which is afire. Or maybe it is the city hall—or the church."

Clenching his fists, his lips trembling, he made his way back to the hospital—older, more weary, heavier at heart.

On the mornings of the days of the attacks, when the cannon passed at a gallop, when the tread of regiments on the march echoed through the silence, he stole softly from his bed to watch, buoyed with the hope that this time at last they were going to retake his city; that he would re-enter it and see there once more his old mother, his old home and his old friends.

But when he saw the soldiers coming back, when the thunder of the cannonade slackened and died away, he would sigh, "Not this time, either," and resume his tasks.

One day when there had been sharp fighting, they brought into the hospital a batch of wounded prisoners. One of them, a Feldwebel (sergeant-major), whose shoulder was shattered by a shell, astonished him by the dignity of his bearing and the refinement of his talk. Examining the wound, he asked the prisoner in German:

"Where do you come from?"

"From Magdeburg, in Saxony, Monsieur le Médecin-Majeur," replied the sub-officer, in good French.

"Ah," said the doctor, with an intonation of regret, for he had hoped that the wounded man was an Alsatian, conscripted by force. The latter seemed to understand, and murmured:

"What can you expect, Doctor? War is war. But that doesn't prevent me from loving France, where I grew up."

Of a sudden the blood mounted to the face of the old surgeon. Pushing up his glasses and looking sternly at the prisoner, he hurled at him this question:

"And are you not ashamed to ravage this country, to ruin these poor people, who before the war, received you with kindness?"

"Yes," the other answered softly. "I am often ashamed. For my part I have always striven to be humane, to be just, to avoid mistreating anybody and to alleviate mistreatment by others as far as lay in my power. The combat over, one becomes a human being again; and the inhabitants of the occupied regions are not responsible. Their persons and their property ought to be sacred. I have to apologize for those of my companions who have not understood this. For instance, my regiment has been for the last six months at St. Quentin—"

The doctor gave a start.

"You have been at St. Quentin for six months? I come from St. Quentin. Perhaps you can give me some news. Often in the evenings I see fires—now in one quarter of the city, now in another. You haven't destroyed the place systematically, have you, as you did Noyon, Péronne and Bapaume?"

"Alas, Doctor, that is a foul blot on our arms."

"But," pursued the surgeon, his voice almost choked, "you have been burning only public buildings, haven't you? Not private houses?"

"No; the private houses are practically untouched up to now."

"Ah! Do you know a street called Beffroi Street?"

"I know it very well. It is there—"

"It is there that my old mother lives," said the doctor slowly. "My name is Journau. Do you know my mother?"

"I was quartered in her house."

"Ah! *Mon Dieu*! How is she?"

"She is well—very well. She is a very worthy person and I suffered from the annoyance which our presence caused her. I, too, have an old mother in Magdeburg, and I thought of her when I saw your mother weeping. But such is war!"

The doctor breathed freely. Big tears ran down his cheeks. But he collected himself, and, bending again over the wound, he announced:

"We are going to put you to sleep right away. It is nothing serious. You will soon be well."

While they washed the wound with tincture of iodine and an assistant got ready to administer ether, the wounded man gave some more details:

"Yes, your mother is well and suffers no inconveniences. The house is always in order, as if for a *fête*. Her rooms are so neat and the floors so scrupulously polished that it is a pleasure to look at them in passing. She waters her flowers; she trims her rose bushes. An attractive house! A fine woman!"

Then his voice wavered a little; he grew stiff; soon he relaxed and softly passed into slumber.

In the midst of the operation he gave a start, turned his head to one side and babbled some meaningless words. The assistant was about to administer more gas, but the surgeon stopped him.

"Not too much. We are nearly through."

The prisoner began to talk again. This time his words were precise, his phrases clean-cut. His voice, which a little while before had been so calm, became harsh and imperious, and he smiled between his phrases with a huge smile which shook his abdomen and his arms.

"Go ahead! Go ahead! Take that old wardrobe out and burn it! Break it open for me first! Linen? That's good to wipe our shoes with. What does she say? A spigot for the wine casks? Ho, there, the rest of you! Get an ax and draw the wine out in buckets."

The doctor's hand trembled.

"Hurrah!" the wounded man went on. "Seize the old woman! Tie her to a chair if she is obstinate! She has a son who is an officer? Ha! Ha! Slap her on the head till she gives us the key to her strong box!"

The old doctor stood erect, very pale. For an instant his terrible eyes ran from his fingers to the neck of the Boche. Then, in a very low voice he said to his assistant, as he bent down again:

"Give him a little more gas. Unless you do so I am afraid I can't go ahead."

The Spirit of Alsace

THE HOUSE of M. Hermann was the third to the left on the Place au Cuir, facing the market. A shop occupied the ground floor—a gloomy ground floor, where it was often necessary to light the lamps before sunset.

In the springtime the linden trees on the sidewalk filled it with a perfume of honey, which mingled with the crude odor of linens and cottons. When winter came, one saw the storks, abandoning Alsace, fly by just over the roofs in a long, noisy train.

Hidden in the back of his shop, ignoring Sundays and feast days, M. Hermann came and went, pushing his ladder, rolling and unrolling his pieces, stopping only to verify his change, to measure his cloth twice, to sell to his patrons bodices and blue blouses, or trousers, which kept for weeks, in spite of the rain and wind, the deep creases worn in them on the shelves. Once a year he closed his shutters and disappeared. Then the neighbors said:

"M. Hermann has gone to Haguenau to gather his hops."

Because M. Hermann had still down there his old parents, a little farm and a house—a fine house, which the Prussians had turned into a casino for the officers, since it stood near the new barracks.

He was there on July 30, 1914, and returned on the day when they posted on the walls the notice of mobilization. The whole village was celebrating. The old people smiled and rubbed their hands. The young people went away singing, their bags over their shoulders. Standing on his front doorstep, he watched what was going on, but said nothing. Presently the Mayor, M. Schmoll, a veteran of the War of 1870–71, came up to him and slapped him on the shoulder, exclaiming:

"This time, Monsieur Hermann, they are going to get back our old country for us. And the thing will not be dragged out.

Before the storks sing their farewell I wish to see, in Strasburg, if my chop is still waiting for me in the Café à la Mésange, at my old table near the wine tun."

M. Hermann nodded his head gravely and answered:

"I hope you may find it there, Monsieur Schmoll."

That same evening a squadron of dragoons passed through the village on a trot. The next morning a battalion of *chasseurs* made a brief halt. The people pressed about them on the main road, throwing them flowers, and crying *"au revoir"* to the soldiers.

Then for two days one heard nothing and saw nothing but a French airplane, which wheeled for a moment in the sky and then disappeared. But on the third day, early in the morning, they heard a distant cannonade, and about 2 o'clock the chasseurs passed through again without singing, gray with dust, followed soon by *gendarmes*, weary and begrimed. The *gendarmes* stopped in the village square. The inhabitants came running to hear the news. M. Schmoll, the mayor, very pale, came up and asked:

"Have things gone wrong, brigadier?"

"They didn't go very well, Mayor. We are retreating, and the *Boches* are following us closely. The women and children and all the young men between sixteen and nineteen will have to leave the village. They must start within two hours. It is the provost's order."

M. Schmoll read the paper, folded it, and put it into his pocket. Then, turning to the group around him, he said:

"My friends, you have heard what the brigadier said. You must leave. Only those whom duty or advanced age detains may stay behind. You others, put your most valuable possessions in wagons, lock your doors and go!"

He stopped there, because his emotion choked him. Gathering himself together again he added:

"But it will not be for long, if it please God."

About 5 o'clock the Germans entered, playing their fifes and beating on their flat drums. Before the mayor's office, wearing his scarf, his military medal, and his medal of 1870 pinned on his coat, M. Schmoll awaited them.

First they seized the post office and the railroad station. Then they requisitioned forage and wine. Finally, the sentinels having been placed, the officer who commanded the troop said:

"You will guarantee with your person the security of my soldiers. If one of them is insulted I shall arrest you. If one of them is injured you shall be hanged."

M. Schmoll straightened out his angular figure.

"So long as your men respect the lives and honor of the inhabitants, no one will do them any harm. That is all that I can guarantee you."

The officer slapped his boot and grinned.

"Agreed. And now take me to Hermann, the draper."

M. Schmoll was speechless for a minute.

"Hermann, the draper? Do you know him?"

"Probably. Let's go."

M. Schmoll bit his lips and obeyed.

When he saw the officer and the mayor enter, M. Hermann came to the door of his shop, putting on his spectacles. The officer took a seat at the counter, looked around, and said:

"Your house at Haguenau is more comfortable than this one, M. Hermann. But, no matter. Take a chair. You are an intelligent man. I want to talk with you. How many head of cattle are there in the village?"

M. Schmoll interrupted.

"Monsieur Hermann is not authorized to answer that. I alone—"

"You will speak when I address you," said the officer. "Answer me, Monsieur Hermann."

"But, Monsieur le Commandant," the merchant protested, "it is very difficult for me to give you anything like an exact answer. I do not know very precisely."

"Good, good. You will inform yourself and tell me tomorrow. Besides, I need wine, beer, and groceries. I count on you to make your mayor understand what I want. He appears not to have a correct notion of his obligations to His Majesty's troops, or to realize that what he is not ready to deliver to us voluntarily we will certainly take from him by force."

M. Schmoll clenched his fists.

"I have no obligation to fulfill to the enemies of my country. As for the duties with which I am charged, I do not need anybody to inform me about them."

The officer did not deign to understand. He lifted his eyes to the shelves.

"On my word, Monsieur Hermann, you have a fine stock here."

"It is at your service, Monsieur le Commandant," answered the draper with a bow.

The officer now inquired about a watering place for the horses and about the vehicles available in the village. He also asked what had become of the three canvases by distinguished painters that were known to hang in the château of M. de Pignerol.

"The watering place is a hundred meters beyond the slaughterhouse. You will find some carriages at the shop of Mathias, the blacksmith. As for the paintings, I think that the servants of M. le Marquis have carried them away."

"Too bad! Too bad!" said the officer, half to himself. "They were to be sent to the museum in Berlin. But we shall be quits if we find them a little further on."

Having said this he reflected a second, and recapitulated, under his breath:

"The wine, the beer, the groceries, the vehicles, the watering place."

Then he arose.

Night had come. M. Hermann placed a lamp on the counter. The officer lighted a cigarette and went on:

"One thing more. By what road did the French leave?"

"By the main road, I suppose."

"I doubt it. But I don't mean the civilians. I mean the soldiers."

M. Hermann hesitated.

"My God! Monsieur le Commandant, I don't know."

The officer shrugged his shoulders.

"Come, come! No foolishness!"

He said this in so brutal a tone that the merchant was visibly troubled.

"Well—"

He stopped, shamed by the look on M. Schmoll's face. But he was afraid of the Prussian, and answered slowly:

"Well, they had to take—"

"You mustn't tell that! You have no right to!" cried M. Schmoll.

"Be quiet!" shouted the officer. "Continue, Monsieur Hermann."

But M. Schmoll burst in:

"Monsieur Hermann, be silent! I order you to say nothing. While I am alive no one shall betray our soldiers. Monsieur Hermann, I forbid you to do it. Besides, you don't know. You know nothing. He knows nothing whatever, Monsieur."

The officer took a step toward him.

"But you? You know, don't you?"

"I do. But if you put twenty bayonets at my breast I will not tell."

M. Hermann bent his head and turned his skull cap between his fingers.

The officer yawned and stretched himself and then said, without paying any attention to the protests of M. Schmoll:

"You hesitate? So be it! I am going to let you reflect for a while—the time it takes me to smoke a cigarette outside. I shall be back in five minutes. Try to decide by then. I give you that advice."

When he was gone M. Schmoll took the merchant's hands.

"You won't say anything, will you, Monsieur Hermann? It was only for the sake of gaining time that you seemed to yield?"

M. Hermann disengaged himself and passed behind the counter. He had raised his head and spoke with precision.

"I am going to tell him. If I could I should remain silent. All that I possess is in the hands of the Germans, both on this side of the frontier and on the other. He has told you. What we do not do voluntarily they will make us do by force. The law of the victor is a terrible law. Believe me, Monsieur Schmoll, at our age we must know how to incline ourselves to it."

M. Schmoll lifted his arms.

"Is it you who talk like that? You!"

The officer, who was walking before the door, stopped to relight his cigarette. M. Hermann answered:

"What would you have me do? I am only an old dry-goods merchant. We have not wished the war, you or I. We were living in peace. Then why—"

"Be silent!" cried M. Schmoll. "Be silent! I am ashamed of you."

The officer re-entered.

"Have you decided?"

"I am at your orders," murmured M. Hermann.

"The sooner the better! Get your hat and let's go. You know the road?"

"Very well."

"You will serve us then as a guide. Let us get under way—and quickly."

M. Schmoll stammered:

"Wretch! Wretch!"

The officer pushed him into the street.

"You, Mayor, come with us!"

M. Hermann exchanged his slippers for heavy shoes, drew on his cloak, locked his cash drawer, put up the shop shutters, extinguished the lamp, and followed the others out.

In the Place four companies were assembled. They put M. Schmoll between two men and the troop set out, M. Hermann leading. M. Schmoll tried to escape. They pushed him back into the ranks with the butts of their rifles. He cried aloud, pointing to M. Hermann:

"Look at the traitor! *Vive la France!*"

Leaving the village, they followed the national road. Then they took a road leading across the fields. Some distance away, to the left, a bridge crossed the river. But M. Hermann showed them a ford, over which the whole troop passed, scarcely wetting themselves.

"My faith!" exclaimed the officer. "We have gained almost four good kilometers. At this rate we ought to fall on their rear guard before daylight."

The night was so black that one could hardly see three feet ahead of him. Each time in the course of the march that they came near together M. Schmoll hissed at the dark figure of the guide:

"*Boche!* Prussian!"

At first M. Hermann simply shrugged his shoulders. Finally, becoming annoyed, he asked the soldiers to put a handkerchief over the mayor's mouth.

After having marched a good hour they entered a wood. At a junction where three roads crossed M. Hermann said:

"One second, so that I am sure I don't make a mistake. In the daylight I should have no trouble, but in pitchy blackness like this!"

They advanced very carefully. The company to the rear, which had not preserved its distance, pushed against the company preceding it. The company in the lead had almost come to a halt. The column was thrown into confusion. M. Schmoll found himself against M. Hermann. The trees were so tangled that the troops could neither advance nor retire.

In the semi-panic M. Hermann gave a command in an under-tone to M. Schmoll:

"Lie down! For God's sake, lie down!"

Then, turning about and waving his hat, he shouted at the top of his voice:

"*Chasseurs* of the 10th! I have brought them to you! Fire into their ranks!"

At the Movies

IN SIMPLE little phrases, such as one uses who has repeated the same thing over and over again, the woman in mourning was telling her story to a neighbor during the intermission at the moving picture show. In these war times one makes acquaintances very easily. Any one individual's sufferings are but a part and parcel of the sufferings of the community at large.

"Yes, madam, I lost my husband two years ago—my husband that was to be, the father of my little boy. We were to be married in the autumn. He was killed at once—at the very beginning of the war."

"If he had to go, it was better that he shouldn't have suffered the hardships of the trenches for a couple of years."

"Perhaps, yes; perhaps, no. For, at least, we should have seen him again, and he would have written. While this way— My little son here, who is nearly seven years old—he hardly remembers his father. Think of it! My husband was mobilized among the very first. He was not yet twenty-six. Already for eight days he had told me: 'It will be war. You will see.' But, like so many others, I wouldn't believe it.

"One evening, returning from his office, he said to me: 'It has come. I am off tonight.' I wanted to make him up a bundle of clothing, with some linen. But he wouldn't wait. He scarcely listened to me. At such a time one could almost believe that nothing counts any longer with a man! I had just put the little one to bed. He kissed the boy, he kissed me and then he made for the street on the run. In the street he turned to wave me a goodbye and then jumped into a cab. It was the 31st of July. Since then I have heard no news of him. Without doubt he was killed in one of the first battles. I know neither where, nor how, nor even whether they were able to find and bury him. Not one thing."

"Perhaps he is a prisoner! How can anybody tell? I have known persons who have gotten news after many months."

"Oh! I no longer have any hope. It is more than two years, remember. Well, that was to be my fate. At any rate, I have my little boy; he helps me to live. Poor little fellow! A childhood like his is not very cheerful. To see always about the house a sad figure, with reddened eyes! Until recently I didn't care to go out. Then I decided to take him to the picture shows in order to amuse him. The picture show is not like the theatre. One can go to it, even if one is in mourning."

The electric bell sounded. The people took their places again. A soldier passed by. He wore a military medal, the Croix de Guerre. The child, leaning over to his mother, asked:

"Is he like that, my papa?"

She stroked his hair softly.

"Yes, my dear."

"With medals like that, too?"

For a child a brave soldier ought always to have medals. The mother answered:

"Yes, dear."

With his head turned, his hand in his mother's hand, the child gazed eagerly at the soldier.

The lights went out and a picture title appeared on the screen.

"The War in 1914."

"Are we going to see the war?" asked the child.

"Yes, my dear. Look."

At first streets were shown—a chaos of half-demolished houses, beams smashed, walls shattered, a mass of black ruins almost without form.

"What is that?" asked the child.

"A village."

"That a village? There is nothing there."

But a dog ran about among the ruins, and a little boy also, who stumbled over the stones. Then came a wide plain. The shells had dug enormous holes in it and along the road as far as the eye could reach—even to the horizon, where heavy clouds of smoke gathered and then dissolved—one could see only the big trees, razed almost to the ground, tumbled right and left among the fields. On the trunks, already dead, some leaves still fluttered in the wind.

"And that? What is that?" asked the child.

"The country, my dear."

"Is that the country? There is nothing there."

"It was beautiful once," said the mother, trembling. "The Germans have destroyed everything."

The boy gave a sidelong glance at the soldier.

But already, in another film, troops defiled. In a heavy rain cavalrymen trotted along the roads bordered by ruins, field artillery guns were dragged at a gallop, jolting, rolling, plunging into and rising out of the ruts. In passing one saw the artillerymen laugh and the officers lift their arms, turning in their saddles.

"What is that?" asked the boy.

"The pursuit, my dear," murmured the mother, pressing him close against her.

"Are they running after the *Boches* to capture them?"

"Yes, my dear."

And behind the cavalrymen appeared the infantrymen, spattered with mud, their shoulders sagging under their heavy packs.

"Are they going to fight?" the child asked.

"Yes, dear."

To her all the soldiers were like her poor, missing husband. In their ranks, under each helmet, in each movement, it was he whom she saw. And the little fellow, more collected, more grave, asked in an almost inaudible voice:

"Was papa like that?"

Then when all—artillerymen, cavalrymen and infantrymen— had passed, a long file of prisoners appeared. One saw them first fleeing under the fire of their own cannon to our lines, then in the camps, then in huddled groups about the coffee kettles. Some were very young and others were old; some with stupefied faces and a melancholy bearing, others with an air of insolence. Still others lay on the ground, a miry horde, conquered, disarmed. The mother sighed.

"See them. Look at them well, my son. They are *Boches*."

And the film unrolled their story. They were neither present-able nor brilliant. They were no longer swaggerers. Famished, gesticulating, jostling one another, they crowded about a French soldier, who was distributing rations, and as they got their allow-ance they scattered to eat it, shamefacedly and apart.

"Are they soldiers?" asked the child.

But the mother was weeping too much to answer.

Suddenly among those downcast figures a bestial and joyous figure appeared. He was a clean-shaven trooper, his cap over his ear, who, in the face of the public, alone on the screen, cynically, his eyes batted, his cheeks protruding, consumed with huge bites his piece of bread.

"Oh, mama," said the child. "Mama, see how ugly that one is."

And the mother, having looked up through her tears, gave a cry—a terrible, heartrending cry.

For that German glutton, that man who laughed at the hate of a whole hallful of people, was her husband—her husband, who, she believed, had died in our ranks.

The Little Soldier

S HE LISTENED, her elbow on the table, her chin in her hands. While he spoke he gazed at her with eager eyes—the eyes of amorous youth. He was telling her the story of his life—of his brief memories of boyhood, of college, the ending of his studies; the war, his ardent desire to fight, his mother's fears and, finally, his dream of fighting realized.

She interrupted him:

"How old are you?"

"Eighteen years."

She smiled and laid her finger on the narrow ribbon which he wore on his coat.

"What is this?"

"That is the emblem of those wounded in battle."

"Have you been wounded?"

"Yes," he answered, without attaching any importance to it.

Moved by the thought of this mere boy stricken down, lying in a ditch, she murmured, with an air of almost maternal interest and concern:

"Poor little fellow! And when were you wounded?"

"At the Marne."

"Was it a serious wound?"

He answered negligently, pointing to his breast:

"A piece of shell went through there."

And as she insisted, anxious to have all the details, he told her what he knew about the war: The hard retreat; the triple daily marches to the rear; then the advance, the roads encumbered with wreckage and bodies, the trees uprooted; the men struggling against fatigue and sleep and able to see nothing ahead of them but a dead plain and a gray horizon; the sudden thunder of the artillery; the blow which one never sees or knows of, but

which strikes one to the ground; then the awakening to consciousness at a relief station, removal to a distant hospital, long
months of rest under a gracious sky, convalescence and, finally,
the furlough home.

She took one of his hands in hers and repeated:

"Poor little fellow! And will you return to the front?"

"I hope to."

They got up. The wood, this springtime night, was filled with
shadows and perfumes. She walked along, leaning on his arm,
stroking with her ungloved hand the rude cloth of his cloak. At
moments, when the moon shone on them from between the
trees, she glanced admiringly at his delicate little figure, his shining eyes and his beardless cheeks. He scarcely spoke now, forgetting the war, surrendering himself to the tenderness of the
moment, seeking words and promises, but finding only soft pres-
sures and sighs with which to express the feelings of his heart.

Then suddenly the sky became black, the trees tossed, the
wind bent the small ones double and whistled among the great
oaks with a noise like bullets. She said:

"A storm is coming. We must hurry home."

"Why? It is so pleasant here."

In fact, they were happy there, in spite of the storm—happy
to be alone in the wood, so alone that the wood seemed to
belong to them. She smiled as they made a little detour from the
main path.

"If I were not with a soldier I should be afraid."

These words filled him with pride and he pressed her arm
softly. Then the rain began to fall, and they sought shelter under
some trees. With her thin dress and her light taffeta mantle she
could not help trembling. They thought that they were sheltered, but the drops reached them gradually and then the
shower turned into a steady downpour. He expressed concern
about her being so lightly clothed. She answered:

"That is nothing. But how about you?"

"Me? I have been in worse storms than this."

She excused herself for having asked him such a question.

"It was foolish, of course. You are a soldier."

Time passed. The rain beat through their leafy covering. The far-off street lamps seemed enveloped in a watery haze. No conveyances were in sight.

"We must go home, all the same," she said.

"You are right," he replied. "But you cannot walk through the rain this way. You are already drenched. You are cold. It is dark. Nobody will see you. I am going to put my cloak over your shoulders."

She refused.

"And how about yourself?"

"Nonsense. Let me do it, please."

He unbuttoned his cloak and softly laid it over her. This time it was he who was maternal in manner. They hurried along, smiling, through the rain, but each one worried about the other.

"Are you all right?"

"All right. And you? Aren't you cold?"

"Not at all."

"I should never forgive myself if you were taken ill again."

At a roadhouse they found a carriage. As he shivered a little she put her hand on his jacket.

"You are wet through."

"It is nothing at all."

"When you get home you must change your clothes at once."

"I promise you that I will."

She heard his teeth chatter.

"I am heartbroken. If you should fall ill—"

"But you didn't catch cold; that was the only important thing."

He thought of nothing else than of gazing at her, of cuddling up against her, stroking affectionately the big cloak which for a few minutes had sheltered her. On parting with him she said:

"Above all, let me hear from you soon."

Then he kissed her hand and let her enter her house.

A week went by without her hearing anything from him. She did not dare to go herself and inquire about him. One day she passed by the house in which he lived. They had put straw in the street. That evening she decided to telephone.

They told her that the little soldier was ill—in fact, very ill. And one morning she received a letter, the envelope bordered in black. He was dead. Stupefied, she read and re-read that frightful line:

"Jean Louis Verrier, corporal of the 7th Infantry."

Her little soldier! Her poor little soldier! She followed the funeral procession, her eyes fixed on the hearse, which went jolting along draped with a tri-color bunting and with the blue cloak with which he had covered her.

Afterward a desire to know something more about this poor youth, of whom she really knew so little, led her to pass again by the house in which he had lived. Some men had just removed the furnishings. She approached the janitress and said to her:

"My God, but he went quickly."

"Alas!" sighed the good woman. "They had little hope that he would pull through."

"It was his wound, I suppose?"

"Oh! his wound—that would never have carried him off. That would have healed. But he had weak lungs. In spite of that, they could never prevent him from taking risks. All those fatigues, all those hardships—they were too much for him. He got pneumonia. He was passed along for six months from one hospital to another, refusing always to be mustered out. They thought that he was better. He must have committed some imprudence. He got pneumonia again, and that finished him."

She answered:

"Thank you, madame."

And thinking of the spirit of that adolescent, who had marched toward death for a beautiful ideal, and then, for the simple joy of being gallant toward a woman, had carried with him to the tomb no other trophies than a piece of ribbon and a woman's smile, she sighed:

"He was a man."

The Great Scene

A VOICE mounted from the depths of the obscurity in which the main floor of the theatre was left, despite the glare of the six dusty stage lamps.

"That's not the way, Monsieur Fanjard. Won't you do it over again?"

Fanjard, who had been perched on a chair, which represented the staircase of a château, jumped down and made his way to the front of the stage. Respectfully, yet not without a certain hauteur—his foot on the prompter's cubbyhole, his elbow on his knee and his hand held to his ear like an ear trumpet—he asked:

"What is it, monsieur?"

The author called back at the top of his voice, as if making head against a tumult:

"I should like to have in that passage more ardor, more passion, more grief. Do you understand?"

"I understand," answered Fanjard, with a bow.

The author would have been glad to elaborate his meaning. But Fanjard, having already returned to his chair staircase and said to his comrades, "Let us do it over, my friends," played the climax of the scene again just as he had played it before.

"That's not right yet! That's not right yet!" cried the author. "You are on the first step. Mlle. Ravignan lifts her arms toward you. You stop her with a gesture. 'What is it?' A silence, you understand, mademoiselle? A silence, a simple silence! You, Monsieur Fanjard, you ask her, almost in a whisper: 'Your brother? My son?' You bow your head, mademoiselle. That is enough. He has understood you. Then you, Monsieur Fanjard, you utter a cry, a harrowing cry; all the rest of the scene is only a sob. You see what I want. Let's try it again!"

With a glacial patience Fanjard played the scene over. But this time his articulation was hardly any more impassioned, and his gestures, barely sketched out, seemed to die away, as if succumbing to some invisible obstacle.

Five o'clock sounded and the players left the stage. The author rejoined Fanjard in the wings. After having gesticulated, shouted, and fumed for three hours, he had a moist skin, a dry tongue, and a hoarse voice. Fanjard, as he made his way toward his dressing room, listened to the other composedly. He was an old actor, reckoned as one of the glories of the stage, and all its noblest traditions survived in him. The author had thrown an arm across his shoulders and talked to him as they walked along.

"It is the capital scene, my dear sir. If it doesn't go the whole piece will fail. What it needs is emotion, grandeur, despair. Don't hesitate to let yourself go. You can make, and you ought to make, something sensational out of it. It is just the scene for you."

"I see—I see very well what you wish. But at rehearsal I can't let myself go. I need costume, light, atmosphere. But don't worry."

Still the author insisted, timid and firm at the same time:

"Certainly I won't worry. Certainly. But I should like to have you, once before the first night, only once, show me your real quality. Only once; just once. Think of it. We are only three days from the première."

"Don't worry," repeated Fanjard.

Then he went away.

At this moment the director passed by. He asked with a pleasant smile:

"Well, how does it go? Are you satisfied?"

"Satisfied? My dear man, my piece is ruined—you understand, ruined. Mlle. Ravignan is passable. The light effects are a fizzle; Fanjard is bad, bad, bad!"

The director tried to calm him. He had heard many others talk that way, and he knew that in the theatre, better than anywhere else, everything somehow works out. Fanjard was an artist, sure, conscientious, incapable of slighting his roles, let him play them two hundred times. Obstinate? Yes. Unequal at rehearsals? Possibly. But exceeding all expectations when the curtain went up.

The author, still skeptical, shook his head.

"Let's wait and see, my dear master," the director protested. (And when a director thus addresses an author who has only a vague claim to such a title, he is using his ultimate argument.) Let's wait and see. Have more confidence. I am as much interested in the success of your piece as you are. Don't get worried yourself—and don't worry him. He is so-so now, perhaps; only so-so. But he will be superb. That I guarantee you."

❊ ❊ ❊

The first night arrived.

In the back of a box, alongside the director, the author listened to his play. The first part of it was a torture. With each spectator who entered late, with each seat slammed down, he had the feeling that humanity in general was in a conspiracy to ruin him. Yet the director kept whispering to him:

"It's a go. It's a go."

After the first curtain he wanted to go up to the dressing rooms and give some last suggestions to the actors. But the director dissuaded him.

"Let them alone. Don't bother them. Believe me, it will be a success."

The second act had a *succès d'estime,* and the curtain rose for the third act. Fanjard finally appeared, descending the staircase with an air of nobility. Mlle. Ravignan stretched out her arms toward him. He stopped her with a gesture and said, "What is it?" And then, in a low tone, "Your brother? My son?" She bowed her head, and he, just as at the rehearsals, without a cry, without a sob, began his set speech.

Clinging to the arms of his velvet-covered seat, arching his shoulders, the author growled out, as if he thought he could communicate his own fire to the actor:

"Let go! Let go! Let go!"

But Fanjard continued to the end in a colorless voice. While the curtain descended amid merely courteous applause, the author ran to the wings. The fury which he had held back for eight days nearly strangled him. Fanjard was returning to his dressing room.

"Well, are you satisfied?" the author shouted at him. "You have wrecked my play. Yes, you were going to reserve yourself for the first performance! You should have talent, my dear sir, before you have genius. Effects are not improvised. They are produced by hard work. And, besides, what a role you had! What a scene! A scene to raise the house. A father, a father, who has only one love, one joy in the world—his son. They tell him of his son's death, and you stand there tranquil, half stupefied! I declaimed the scene, even in writing it. I shouted it."

Then the old actor answered softly, without anger, without indignation, without any show of wounded pride:

"You are wrong, monsieur; and that is because, fortunately for you, you don't know. I learned only four hours ago of the death of my son, killed at Craonne; and I did not cry aloud then any more than I do now."

After the War

ALTHOUGH HE was a colonel, a Prussian baron, a veteran officer of the Guard and the possessor of a castle on the banks
of the Rhine, at which His Majesty the Kaiser had once stopped
for a few hours, in other respects this *Boche* had a spirit rather
generous for a Boche.

Having served two years at Paris as an embassy attaché, he
recalled that sojourn with infinite graciousness, and never
advertised more than was necessary the fact that he had spent
two other years in the same city as an employee in a little restaurant near the Champ-de-Mars, frequented by orderlies of
the officers of the École de Guerre. In this capacity he had
acquired a real respect for the French soldier—for his discre-
tion and the affectionate attachment which he bears his chiefs.

Certainly, war seemed to him a legitimate thing. But he practiced it, to use his own expression, "in a chivalrous manner."

In the house that he occupied he would have felt himself at
fault if he had not left his card once a month on his involuntary
hostesses, if he had not sent them invitations, with a program,
for the military musicals, and, on Sedan Day, a card for the
review. At that, he was astonished that these ladies were not
more appreciative of such delicate attentions.

In the line of service he showed himself strict (as was proper),
but not brutal. He went so far as to speak to the under-officers
as if they were almost human beings, and, in the evening, on the
Mall, to converse with lieutenants who were neither noble nor
long connected with the army (the war had so decimated the
ranks of the others!). He even struck up a friendship, so to
speak, with one of these, an attractive fellow, obsequious, correct, well educated, too, for an ordinary plebeian. With him the
colonel talked freely and confidentially.

162

"When we shall have won the war I should like to live in Paris again. It is a very agreeable city. The Bois de Boulogne is exquisite at all seasons of the year; the theatres show excellent taste, and the women are charming."

"I was highly delighted with the visit I made there in July, 1914," answered the lieutenant. "One can do business easily, the people are hospitable, and, if one wishes to live the sort of life there that he lives at home, our compatriots are so numerous that, in the evenings, we can gather together just like a family. I speak of conditions before the war, of course."

"Before the war! Before the war!" repeated the colonel a little abstractedly. "I feel that after the war all that will be considerably changed. Sometimes I read the Paris newspapers, and I am pained to see what a hostile feeling there is against us. The devil! War is war. We did not wish to make war, did we? We were forced to make it.

"Our superiority in all branches of human activity is such that no people can resist us. That is a fact. Why don't the French admit it? Since we are the most cultured nation on earth—the chosen people, you might say—why don't they let themselves be guided by us? We should realize great things together. But there the old Latin obstinacy comes in. How regrettable it is on their part! For—I tell you this between ourselves—I am very fond of the French."

"So am I, Colonel."

Thus exchanging ideas they regained the town, where in the twilight the demolished houses stood out jagged against the sky, since the horizon was lighted everywhere with conflagrations. The colonel sighed:

"Look at that. Don't you believe that it cuts a sensitive German to the heart to see such a spectacle? There is the farm with the big mill on it—a fine farm, a perfect milling establishment, a magnificent investment. But it will all be in ashes tomorrow. Whose fault will that be?"

"It is war," the lieutenant suggested, urbanely.

"Indispensable destructions, which the superior interest of our armies amply justifies. That is another thing which the French fail to understand."

"Yet it is all very simple."

The colonel threw away his cigar, which had gone out, stopped and lifted his finger.

"Under all circumstances, Lieutenant, remember this," he said. "It may be that for strategic reasons we shall abandon this country. Let us root up the roads, destroy the bridges, turn the streams out of their courses, fell the trees and throw them across the highways—let us do everything, in a word, which the security of our armies requires. But let us commit no depredations on the inhabitants. For myself, I intend to set an example. In the house in which I live I shall see to it that nobody touches anything. In proportion as you have found me paternal and considerate, you will find me, if my orders are not scrupulously obeyed, a man of iron."

The event which the colonel foresaw arrived. His regiment retreated. In conformity with instructions, not a tree was left standing, nor a bridge on its arches, nor a stream in its bed. The work was accomplished methodically; explosions succeeded one another at regular intervals. The house which the colonel lived in alone remained intact, with its old balconies of wrought iron, its garden of flowers, its windows hung with curtains.

The colonel departed with regret, carrying with him a few souvenirs—two silver candlesticks, a clock, a silver gilded water glass—mere trifles. But he left the furniture shining, the table linen carefully folded, the floors waxed like glass.

He had already reached the open country when he recalled that he had forgotten to leave a P. P. C. card. Desirous of being impeccable to the last extreme, he retraced his steps. But on entering his apartments he stopped, stupefied at first, then bursting with fury.

With blows from a pick four soldiers were demolishing the bathroom and the water pipes. Seeing him, the men redoubled their ardor. He shouted to them:

"Swine! I shall have you shot!"

A fifth man appeared, his sleeves rolled up, a hammer in his hand. It was the lieutenant who had been so amiable and correct.

"You? Is it you I find here?" bellowed the colonel. "You, who know my ideas? I shall send you before a court-martial!"

"At your orders," answered the officer, clicking his heels. "But excuse me, Colonel. All this installation comes from the firm of Schwein, Boelleri & Co., of Mannheim, of which I am the representative for Northern France. Our house alone possesses these replacement parts. And after the war, I thought, how simple it would be for these people to apply to us for the plumbing fittings. It would be a very natural way of resuming business relations. As trifling as the thing seems, it concerns our industry in the highest degree."

"Well, that is different," said the colonel gravely. "*Deutschland über alles!* Consider that I have said nothing at all."

Reassured by these words, the lieutenant finished demolishing, with a well-directed blow of his hammer, a syphon which had hitherto resisted his attack.

The Appalling Gift

M. AND MME. Jutelier recoiled in horror as they unpacked Aunt Sophie's gift. M. Jutelier was the first to recover his powers of speech, but it was only to enunciate in accents of despair, "And to think that now we have to put that thing somewhere where she can see it!" Whereupon Mme. Jutelier, whose temperament led her to dare extreme measures, cried out, "Never! I'd rather have her cut us out of her will and be done with it." But her husband shrugged his shoulders. "Don't talk nonsense."

Once again they stood in despairing silence while on the table in front of them the vase spread out its enormous lacquered paunch, decorated with flowers, with fruit, and with seashells. In the middle of these decorations, a coiled serpent darted out a long red tongue, and here and there the leaves of waterplants hung in festoons that were intended to be decorative. The base was blue and the inside was salmon pink. "There is no doubt about it," murmured M. Jutelier, "that thing has no equal for ugliness."

"It simply means," said Mme. Jutelier, "that our apartment is ruined."

"Oh, la, la la!" groaned M. Jutelier, "and it was all so nice and cosy."

Giving free rein to his despair he cast his eyes about the room for some place to put the terrifying gift with results that would not be too disastrous. The mantelpiece—impossible. The table—less possible still. The buffet—the thought brought tears to his eyes. He suggested the salon, but Mme. Jutelier announced firmly, "If that thing goes through the door of the salon, I go through the street door."

"In the bedroom," he ventured.

Mme. Jutelier turned pale with anger.

"Not in my room! Why not in your office?"

166

M. Jutelier explained that was the very last place one could think of. As an architect he was called upon to receive clients, who would flee from the mere presence of such an object. They passed all their rooms in review, and at the mention of each one Mme. Jutelier set up stubborn opposition. She had not been collecting the loveliest bibelots and weeding out everything that was not in perfect taste, for all these years, in order to have this monstrosity thrust in among her treasures. And then suddenly M. Jutelier smote his forehead.

"How many times a year does Aunt Sophie come to visit us? Twice, or say three times. In the winter she does not go out because of her rheumatism, and from July to October she is in the country. Being a personage above the common station, and expecting to be received with the ceremonies due her, she always announces her visits in advance. All we have to do is to put this horror in the attic and bring it down when we hear she is coming. That way we can arrange everything, and later on, at the very last, when the poor old lady is dead, why then, if we have a country house, it will do to put it in the guest chamber."

"To give our guests the nightmare? No, sir, when that time comes we'll smash it."

"All right then; smash it if you want to"—and having made mutual concessions they embraced each other.

Next Sunday Aunt Sophie arrived. They had carefully put chairs on each landing so that the dear lady could rest on her way up, and they had set the vase on the table so that her eye would fall on it the very first thing. But being a discreet old soul, she pretended not to see it at once, and her niece had to remark, with an ecstatic smile, "Do you think your vase is in the right place?"

"Yes," murmured Aunt Sophie, "but I think I should have preferred the mantelpiece. Then you can see it a second time in the mirror."

"Your aunt is right," said Mme. Jutelier to her husband, "and if we put a green plant in it—"

"Well, do as you want to," said Aunt Sophie, "but for my part I'd rather see a little moss with artificial roses stuck in it. They look so pretty if you use all the colors. I'll send you some. I have a lot."

The household burst into a chorus of thanks, and Aunt Sophie departed, charmed.

"Well," said M. Jutelier when they were alone again, "everything went off very well, and we are all right for the moment. You will see; everything will arrange itself."

They put the vase out of sight, and life went on as usual. About Easter time Aunt Sophie came back. This time she brought the promised flowers, and this was the occasion of an affectionate and delightful discussion. Ought the artificial roses to be arranged according to color or according to size? Aunt Sophie's opinion prevailed, and with her own hands she erected a hanging garden of the most ravishing description.

Summer came and brought vacation. Autumn came and brought rheumatism. As New Year's Day approached the household trembled before a new fear. Suppose Aunt Sophie took it into her head to make them another New Year's gift! She did not have this idea, however, but another one, a hundred times more dreadful. One day she called without sending word ahead; but fortunately Mme. Jutelier had seen her getting out of the taxi, and had just time to climb to the sixth story and bring down the object of art.

This alarm served its purpose. Since such an incident might occur again, they practiced the maneuver until it was all carefully worked out. As soon as a new maid was engaged, before they showed her in which closet Monsieur kept his coats, or where Madame kept her hats, they showed her, the very first thing, where the vase belonged, and told her how if by any chance a fat lady—dressed in black, wearing a capote, and carrying an umbrella no matter what the weather—should arrive when they were away, she must first of all lock the door of the dining-room and not open it on any pretext whatever until she had put the vase on the mantelpiece.

And yet this did not keep Madame Jutelier from saying to Aunt Sophie every time she called, "Come and see us oftener, my dear aunt; you are neglecting us."

On the third Monday in February, after her usual custom, Aunt Sophie wrote a letter to announce her coming. As soon as they received it, everybody got ready to greet her. Madame

Jutelier said to her maid after lunch, "Josephine, go to the sixth story, get the vase, dust it, and bring it down here."

She was just getting its place ready on the mantelpiece when a terrible crash made her leap up and rush out to the landing, with her heart in her mouth and a terrible foreboding in her soul.

The misfortune exceeded the worst that she could imagine. Hanging over the banister, with round eyes, Josephine was staring down upon the shattered fragments of the vase. It had been smashed so small that the whole stairway was powdered with it. At his wife's shriek of dismay, M. Jutelier came running. For a moment he was too stupefied to speak, and then he had the most absurd ideas.

"Why don't you send a telegram to say you're very sick?"

"But Aunt Sophie is already on the way!"

"Suppose I try to find another vase like it?"

"In an hour?"

They waited, overwhelmed. At three o'clock Aunt Sophie came. Immediately the pallor of her young relatives struck her.

"What is wrong, my children? You look out of sorts."

"Henri will explain," sobbed Mme. Jutelier. And Henri explained. "A misfortune, a great misfortune. The beautiful vase that you gave us, the vase we loved so much—all broken! That miserable maid of ours. We told her never to dust it with a feather duster, and she knocked it off on the floor this very morning."

He burst into tears, which were almost genuine. Aunt Sophie drew herself up and murmured, "That is certainly too bad. That is certainly too bad."

"Oh," groaned her niece, "I shall never feel the same again."

"You must never utter such words except over human beings," said her aunt with a certain dryness.

"And yet—oh aunt, aunt, you do not know—you can't know how much we liked it. It was so pretty, and then, besides, it came from you."

Aunt Sophie had not yet accepted the armchair that her nephew was delicately pushing up behind her. Madame Jutelier waited for a gesture, for a word, but Aunt Sophie crossed her cloak over her breast and started toward the door. M. and Mme. Jutelier held out suppliant arms toward her. She paused and lifted her finger: "Never mind. I know where to find one just like it, and I will go there right away. Only this time you must do what I do with my own valuable things. You must have it cemented fast to the mantelpiece. All you have to do is to hunt up my workman. In fact, it will be simpler if I send him to you myself."

Night and Silence

THEY WERE old, crippled, horrible. The woman hobbled about on two crutches; one of the men, blind, walked with his eyes shut, his hands outstretched, his fingers spread open; the other, a deaf-mute, followed with his head lowered, rarely raising the sad, restless eyes that were the only sign of life in his impassive face.

It was said that they were two brothers and a sister, and that they were united by a savage affection. One was never seen without the other; at the church doors they shrank back into the shadows, keeping away from those professional beggars who stand boldly in the full light so that passersby may be ashamed to ignore their importunacy. They did not ask for anything. Their appearance alone was a prayer for help. As they moved silently through the narrow, gloomy streets, a mysterious trio, they seemed to personify Age, Night and Silence.

One evening, in their hovel near the gates of the city, the woman died peacefully in their arms, without a cry, with just one long look of distress which the deaf-mute saw, and one violent shudder which the blind man felt because her hand clasped his wrist. Without a sound she passed into eternal silence.

Next day, for the first time, the two men were seen without her. They dragged about all day without even stopping at the baker's shop where they usually received doles of bread. Toward dusk, when lights began to twinkle at the dark crossroads, when the reflection of lamps gave the houses the appearance of a smile, they bought with the few halfpence they had received two poor little candles, and they returned to the desolate hovel where the old sister lay on her pallet with no one to watch or pray for her.

They kissed the dead woman. The man came to put her in her coffin. The deal boards were fastened down and the coffin was placed on two wooden trestles; then, once more alone, the two brothers laid a sprig of boxwood on a plate, lighted their candles, and sat down for the last all-too-short vigil.

Outside, the cold wind played round the joints of the ill-fitting door. Inside, the small trembling flames barely broke the darkness with their yellow light. . . . Not a sound. . . .

For a long time they remained like this, praying, remembering, meditating. . . .

Tired out with weeping, at last they fell asleep.

When they woke it was still night. The lights of the candles still glimmered, but they were lower. The cold that is the precursor of dawn made them shiver. But there was something else—what was it? They leaned forward, the one trying to see, the other to hear. For some time they remained motionless; then, there being no repetition of what had roused them, they lay down again and began to pray.

Suddenly, for the second time, they sat up. Had either of them been alone, he would have thought himself the plaything of some fugitive hallucination. When one sees without hearing, or hears without seeing, illusion is easily created. But something abnormal was taking place; there could be no doubt about it, since both were affected, since it appealed both to eyes and ears at the same time; they were fully conscious of this, but were unable to understand.

Between them they had the power of complete comprehension. Singly, each had but a partial, agonizing conception.

The deaf-mute got up and walked about. Forgetting his brother's infirmity, the blind man asked in a voice choked with fear:

"What is it? What's the matter? Why have you got up?"

He heard him moving, coming and going, stopping, starting off again, and again stopping; and having nothing but these sounds to guide his reason, his terror increased till his teeth began to chatter. He was on the point of speaking again, but remembered, and relapsed into a muttering:

"What can he see? What is it?"

The deaf-mute took a few more steps, rubbed his eyes, and, presumably reassured, went back to his mattress and fell asleep.

The blind man heaved a sigh of relief, and silence fell once more, broken only by the prayers he mumbled in a monotonous undertone, his soul benumbed by grief as he waited till sleep should come and pour light into his darkness.

He was almost sleeping when the murmurs that had before made him tremble wrenched him from an uneasy doze.

It sounded like a soft scratching mingled with light blows on a plank, curious rubbings, and stifled moans.

He leaped up. The deaf-mute had not moved. Feeling that the fear that culminates in panic was threatening him, he strove to reason with himself:

"Why should this noise terrify me? . . . The night is always full of sounds. . . . My brother is moving uneasily in his sleep . . . yes, that's it. . . . Just now I heard him walking up and down, and there was the same noise. . . . It must have been the wind. . . . But I know the sound of the wind, and it has never been like that . . . it was a noise I had never heard. . . . What could it have been? No . . . it could not be . . ."

He bit his fists. An awful suspicion had come to him.

"Suppose . . . no, it's not possible. . . . Suppose it was . . . there it is again! . . . Again . . . louder and louder . . . someone is scratching, scratching, knocking. . . . My God! A voice . . . her voice! She is calling! She is crying! Help, help!"

He threw himself out of bed and roared:

"François! . . . quick! Help! . . . Look! . . ."

He was half mad with fear. He tore wildly at his hair, shouting:

"Look! . . . You've got eyes, you, you can see! . . ."

The moans became louder, the raps firmer. Feeling his way, stumbling against the walls, knocking against the packing-cases that served as furniture, tripping in the holes in the floor, he staggered about trying to find his sleeping brother.

He fell and got up again, bruised, covered with blood, sobbing: "I have no eyes! I have no eyes!"

He had upset the plate on which lay the sprig of box, and the sound of the earthenware breaking on the floor gave the finishing touch to his panic.

"Help! What have I done? Help!"

The noises grew louder and more terrifying, and as an agonized cry sounded, his last doubts left him. Behind his empty eyes, he imagined he saw the horrible thing. . . .

He saw the old sister beating against the tightly closed lid of her coffin. He saw her superhuman terror, her agony, a thousand times worse than that of any other death. . . . She was there, alive, yes, alive, a few steps away from him . . . but where? She heard his steps, his voice, and he, blind, could do nothing to help her.

Where was his brother? Flinging his arms from right to left, he knocked over the candles: the wax flowed over his fingers, hot, like blood. The noise grew louder, more despairing; the voice was speaking, saying words that died away in smothered groans. . . .

"Courage!" he shrieked. "I'm here! I'm coming!"

He was now crawling along on his knees, and a sudden turn flung him against a bed; he thrust out his arms, felt a body, seized it by the shoulders and shook it with all the strength that remained in him.

Violently awakened, the deaf-mute sprang up uttering horrible cries and trying to see, but now that the candles were out, he too was plunged into night, the impenetrable darkness that held more terror for him than for the blind man. Stupefied with sleep, he groped about wildly with his hands, which closed in a viselike grip on his brother's throat, stifling cries of:

"Look! Look!"

They rolled together on the floor, upsetting all that came in their way, knotted together, ferociously tearing each other with tooth and nail. In a very short time their hoarse breathing had died away. The voice, so distant and yet so near, was cut short by a spasm . . . there was a cracking noise . . . the imprisoned body was raising itself in one last supreme effort for freedom . . . a grinding noise . . . sobs . . . again the grinding noise . . . silence. . . .

Outside, the trees shuddered as they bowed in the gale; the rain beat against the walls. The late winter's dawn was still crouching on the edge of the horizon. Inside the walls of the hovel, not a sound, not a breath.

Night and Silence.

The Cripple

Because he had good manners, and although there was no one present but Farmer Galot, Trache said on entering:

"Good day, gentlemen!"

"You again!" growled Galot, without turning around.

"To be sure," replied Trache.

He raised his two maimed hands, as if explaining, by their very appearance, his instructions.

Two years ago, in harvest-time, a threshing-machine had caught him up and, by a miracle, dashed him to the ground again instead of crushing him to death. They had borne him off, covered with blood, shrieking, with arms mangled, a rib smashed in, and spitting out his teeth. There remained from the accident a certain dullness of intellect, short breath, a whistling sound that seemed to grope for words at the bottom of his chest, scrape them out of his throat, and jumble them up as they passed his bare gums, and a pair of crooked hands that he held out before him in an awkward and apprehensive manner.

"Well, what do you want?" snapped Galot.

"My compensation money," answered Trache with a weak smile.

"Compensation money! I haven't owed you anything for a long time. There's nothing the matter with you now but laziness and a bad disposition. To begin with, you were drunk when the thing happened. I needn't have given you anything."

"I was *not* drunk," said Trache quietly.

The farmer lost all patience.

"At this moment you can use your hands as well as anybody. You keep up the sham before people, but when you are alone you do what you like with them."

"I don't move them then; I can't," mumbled Trache.

"I tell you, you are an impostor, a trickster, a rascal; I say that you are fleecing me because I have not been firmer with you, that you are making a little fortune out of my money, but that you shall not have another cent. There, that's final. Do you understand?"

"Yes, from your point of view," assented Trache without moving.

Galot flung his cap on the table and began to pace the room with long strides.

Trache shook his head and hunched up his shoulders. At last Galot squared up before him.

"How much do you want to settle for good and all? Suppose we say five hundred francs and make an end of it?"

"I want what is due to me according to the judgment of the court."

Galot became transported with rage:

"Ne'er-do-well, lazy-bones, good-for-nothing; I know what you told the court through the mouth of your doctor, and why you would not let mine examine you."

"It was upon the sworn evidence of the doctors that the case was decided," observed the cripple.

"Ah, it isn't they who have to pay!" sneered Galot. "Let me see your hands. . . . Let me look, I say: I know something about injuries."

Trache stretched out his arms and presented the wrists. Galot took them between his heavy hands, turned them over, turned them back, feeling the bones and the fleshy parts, as he would have done with cattle at a fair. Now and then Trache made a wry face and drew back his shoulder. At last Galot pushed him away with brutal force.

"You are artful, cunning. But look out for yourself: I am keeping my eye on you, and when I have found you out, look out for yourself! You will end by laughing on the other side of your face, and to get your living you will have to work—you hear what I say?—to work."

"I should like nothing better," sighed the cripple.

Pale with wrath, Galot emptied a purse of silver money on the table, counted it and pushed it toward him.

"There's your money; now be off."

"If you would be so good as to put it in my blouse," suggested Trache, "seeing that I can't do it myself. . . ."

Then he said, as on entering: "Good day, gentlemen," and with stuffed pocket, shaking head and unsteady step, he took his departure.

To return to his lodging he had to pass along the riverside. In the fields the patient oxen trudged on their way. Laborers were binding the sheaves amid the shocks of corn; and across the flickering haze of the sultry air the barking of dogs came with softened intonation.

Near a bend of the river, where it deepened into a little pool, a woman was washing linen. The water ran at her feet, flecked with foam and in places clouded with a pearly tint.

"Well, are things going as you wish, Françoise?" asked Trache.

"Oh, well enough," said she. "And you?"

"The same as usual . . . with my miserable hands."

He sighed, and the coins jingled under his blouse. Françoise winked at him.

"All the same it isn't so bad—what the threshing-machine has done for you, eh? . . . And then, to be sure, it's only right; Galot can well afford to pay."

"If I weren't crippled for life, I wouldn't ask for anything."

Thereupon she began to laugh, with shoulders raised and mallet held aloft. She was a handsome girl, and even a good girl, and more than once he had talked to her in the meadow, but now he reddened with anger.

"What is the matter with you all—dropping hints and poking your fun at me?"

She shrugged her shoulders.

"If I gossip it's only for the fun of gossiping."

He sat down near her, mollified, and listened as she beat her linen. Then, wanting to smoke, and unable to use his helpless hands, he asked her:

"Would you mind getting my pouch out of my pocket and filling my pipe for me?"

She wiped her hands on her apron, searched in his blouse, filled his pipe, struck a match and, shielding it with her hand, said jokingly:

"You're lucky in meeting me."

He bent forward to light his pipe. At the same moment she slipped on the bank, lost a sabot, threw up her arms and fell backward into the water.

Seeing her fall, Trache sprang up. She had sunk immediately, dragging her washtub after her, in a place where the water was deep and encumbered with weeds. Then her head reappeared, stretched out into the air, and she cried, already half choking:

"Your hand! Your hand!"

Trache stopped short, his pipe shaking in the corner of his mouth. Shriller, more despairingly came the cry:

"Your hand! I'm drowning. Help! . . ."

Some men in a neighboring field were running. But they were at a great distance and could only be seen as shadows moving over the corn.

Françoise sank again, rose, sank, rose once more. No sound came from her lips now: her face was terrible in its agony of supplication. Then she sank finally; the weeds, scattered in all directions, closed up again; their tangled network lay placid as before under the current. And that was all.

It was only after an hour's search that the body was found, enmeshed in the river growth, the clothes floating over the head. Trache stamped on the ground.

"I, a man, and powerless to do anything! . . . Curses, curses on my miserable hands!"

They tried to calm him as they condoled with him on his wretched lot, accompanying him to his cottage in their desire to soothe. Seeing him approach in this way, his wife uttered a piercing cry. What new disaster had befallen her husband? . . . They told her of the catastrophe, and of his anguish at not being able to save Françoise, whereupon she joined her lamentations to his.

But when they were alone behind closed doors, taking off his hat with a brisk movement, Trache rubbed his benumbed hands, stretched out his fingers, worked his joints, drew forth his pouch full of coins, flung it on the table and said:

"No, damn it. A fine business if I had given her my hand and she had gone and chattered to Galot! . . . No! damn it . . ."

The Look

THE LOG fire was dying in the grate. About the whole room, lighted by a too heavily shaded lamp, there was something vaguely menacing that chilled my blood the moment I entered it.

My friend came forward. "I am glad to see you, very glad," he said, holding out his hand.

He had aged and altered so that I hardly recognized him. Extending his hand in the direction of the fireplace, he said in a low voice, "My friend Janville . . . my wife."

I discerned a very pale face and a slender form that bowed slightly, while a subdued voice, a melancholy, weary voice, murmured, "We are pleased to see you here, Monsieur."

My friend offered me a chair. The white form relapsed into immobility; and silence, a deadened silence through which flitted indefinable thoughts, fell upon us.

I could think of nothing to say. These two had been man and wife for some months. They had been in love for years before they were free to marry. And this was how I found them now!

My friend broke the silence with a hesitating inquiry as to my health, and his thought seemed far from the words that fell from his lips.

"Fine," I replied, and speaking lower, I added, "You are happy?"

"Yes," he muttered.

His wife coughed slightly and rose.

"Forgive me, Monsieur, but I am a little tired. You will excuse me, I am sure. . . . Please do not go."

She crossed the dining-room, presented her forehead to her husband, and left us.

My friend got up and paced the floor with long strides, gnawing his mustache, then, stopping abruptly before me, put his hand on my shoulder.

"I said I was happy. That's a lie!"

I looked at him in mute astonishment.

"No doubt you think I am out of my mind," he continued. "Not yet, but I'm likely to be before long. . . . Don't you feel some sinister influence brooding over this house?"

"Your wife and you appear to be under some cloud, certainly. Some worry, no doubt, the importance of which you exaggerate."

"No! No! No! There's a horror hanging to these walls . . . there's a terror creeping about these floors. Between my wife and me there's the shadow of Crime . . . of Crime!

"As you know, she who today is my wife was for long months my mistress. You know how desperately I loved her . . . or rather you do *not* know . . . no one can know. . . . I worshipped her, that creature, worshipped her to the point of devotion . . . of frenzy. From the day she came into my life, there was no other life for me. She became a need in my nature, a flaw in my sanity, a vice in my blood.

"I thought of running away with her, of challenging the voice of scandal. But neither of us had any means. I had only my profession to support me. And our being together openly in Paris was not to be thought of . . . so I put aside honor, every moral scruple. To see her more frequently, I obtained an introduction to the husband. I cultivated his acquaintance, I came to be his constant guest, his intimate friend.

"I made that despicable third in a household who, under the shelter of its welcome, steals in cold blood from its master his peace and happiness.

"I spent my holidays with them. He was a great sportsman; while he was out in the woods and fields I passed my time with her.

"One day we two were startled by loud cries. I ran downstairs, and found the terrified servants gathered around the husband.

"Stretched upon a couch, he was fighting for breath with quick, short gasps, as he clutched at a wound in his abdomen.

"'Ah, Monsieur,' faltered the man who carried his game-bag, 'how suddenly it happened! Monsieur had just shot a woodcock

. . . it fell in the rushes, he ran toward the spot, and all in a moment, I don't know how it happened, but I heard a report—a cry—and I saw Monsieur fall forward. . . . I brought him here.'

"I cut away the clothes and examined his injuries. The charge had plowed through his side. Blood flowed in jets from a terrible wound extending from above the hip to the thigh.

"Years of training made me regard him solely as a patient. I examined him as if it had been a hospital case. I even gave a sigh of satisfaction as I learned that his injuries were really superficial. The intestines did not appear to be involved, but on the wound's internal surface a small artery was spurting freely.

"Hearing footsteps, I looked up, and saw Her standing in the doorway. A strange and unaccountable agony gripped my heart. It was with a great effort that I said, 'Don't come here. . . . Go away.'

"'No,' she said, and drew nearer.

"I could not take my eyes from hers—she had fascinated them. My finger still pressing upon the artery, the sufferer full in her view, I watched that look of hers as a man watches a dagger pointed at his throat, a wavering dagger, the gleam of which hypnotizes him.

"She drew still nearer, and a cloudy impotence fell upon my will. That look spoke things of terrible import. It seized upon my soul, that look; it spoke—no need of words to make me understand what it asked of me. It said:

"'You can have me for your own. . . . You can take me and keep me. . . . I shall thrill to no other joy, faint under no other fondness . . . if only you will—'

"Once more I faltered: 'You must not stay here. . . . Go away.'

"But the look spoke again:

"'Soul without resolution . . . heart that dares not . . . what have you always longed for? . . . Look! . . . Chance changes your dream to reality.'

"The artery pulsed under my finger and, little by little, strive as I would to maintain it, the pressure diminished.

"She was close to me. She bent above me. Her breath played in my hair; the emanation from her body stole into every fiber of my being, impregnated my hands, my lips—that exhalation was madness to me.

"All conception of time, of danger, of duty, fled from my mind.

"Suddenly the door opened, and a servant appeared with my surgical case. The stupor was dispelled.

"'Quick! Give it to me!' I shouted rather than called.

"But then . . . I saw that my finger had deserted its post . . . that there was now no pulsation under it . . . that the stricken man's lip was drawn upward into the mocking semblance of a smile . . . and . . . that it was all over.

"Our eyes met. And in that moment a shadow fell between us, a shadow with a mocking smile—the shadow of the dead man. . . .

"I thought at first that this nightmare would fade away. I strove to assure myself that the fatal issue was an accident, unavoidable. But since she became my wife, that shadow is between us, always, everywhere. Neither speaks of it, but it comes between our meeting eyes.

"I—I see once more her eyes, the look, saying, 'Take me. Let us be free.' She—she sees once more my hand, as, by slow degrees, it lets the life of her husband ebb away. And hatred has come, a silent hatred, the hatred of two murderers who are in the bonds of a mutual fear.

"We remain for hours as you have seen us tonight. Words rush up within us, smite asunder the clenched teeth, half open the lips—and we keep silence."

He took a dagger from the table, tried the edge with his finger.

"Cowards . . . both of us!"

He flung the weapon, clanging, to the table, and burying his face in his hands, burst into tears.

The Horror on the Night Express

THE TRAIN hurtled through the black night toward the Swiss frontier. My three companions in the compartment, an elderly gentleman and a young couple, were not asleep. From time to time, the young woman, almost a girl, spoke a few words to the young man, who answered with a nod or a gesture. Then all would be silent again.

I suppose it is impossible for a man to get away from his profession. I was going to Switzerland on a much-needed vacation. Aside from my private practice as a physician, my services had been called for several times during the preceding months as medical expert for the Paris Police. Upon concluding my work on the last case, some hours before, I had thrown a few belongings into a bag and started off. Yet I found myself speculating as to the identities, background, and professions of those forced into almost intimate contact with me for the duration of the voyage, due to the division of a railroad car into compartments prevailing on European lines.

I dismissed the elderly gentleman very soon as an ordinary type; the sort of well-to-do old chap, retired from active business, that one might expect to find traveling for his pleasure in a first-class compartment. The girl was pretty, sweet, but obviously without individuality, for the present at least, for she was engrossed in her husband. I assumed that they were on a wedding trip.

The young man held my attention longer. He was a handsome fellow, perhaps thirty years old, solid yet dapper, with a fine, energetic face, soft eyes and an expression of gentleness that increased when he glanced at his beautiful companion. Thus far, beyond the banal words of politeness when adjusting baggage or shifting positions on the seats, there had been no conversation.

183

It was about two o'clock; the train passed by a small station without slowing. The lights flickered swiftly, darted through the windows, as our car jostled over turning plates. This jarring, this noise, aroused the girl, who had been drowsing. At her slight movement, the young man smiled, wiped the plate glass with the fingers of his gloved hand, leaned to peer out. But the station clock, the lamps, the name of the depot had flashed out of sight.

"Where are we, Jacques?" the young woman asked in a weary voice.

"I don't know exactly," he said, glancing at his watch. "Pontarlier is the next stop."

"We're not there yet," the old gentleman said. He had been waiting for a chance to talk, to while away the minutes, and took the slight opportunity:

"We have not passed through the tunnel yet."

"This trip is endless," the girl sighed. "I can't sleep. If only you had thought of buying papers or magazines—"

"Allow me?" the old gentleman said eagerly, holding out several newspapers.

She accepted with a grateful smile. Her husband drew a blanket over her knees, adjusted the lamp so that the light would be easier on her eyes. She opened one of the papers and soon was absorbed in what she was reading. The young man drew a cigarette case, which he snapped open and held out to his neighbor: "A cigarette, Monsieur?"

"With pleasure—"

"Really, I'm much obliged to you, sir. This trip is long and hard, especially for my wife who is not used to traveling at night."

"Especially as day breaks so late at this season," the old gentleman replied courteously. "So late it will be dark when we reach Vallorbe, where we must go through the customs. I take it you're going to Italy?"

"My wife is not well, and the doctors have advised mountain air, so we're going to Switzerland. However, if it is too cold up there, we shall go down to the lakes. She needs care, rest, and as for myself I've been so occupied in the past few weeks that I need a vacation."

I refrained from smiling. There is something about travel in a compartment that renders men loquacious. Enough to give to an absolute stranger, whom one is not likely to meet again, information withheld from all but the most intimate friends at home. I knew it was inevitable that I should be drawn into the conversation, and wondered just how that would be effected.

Within a few minutes, the young woman dropped the paper.

"Nothing in all that," she said with visible disappointment, adding in rapid apology to the kind old man, "I mean nothing on what I'm interested in. You see, I'm following that crime as one follows a fiction story—a mystery serial—"

"The murder in Pergolese Street?" the old gentleman asked, unwilling to drop the conversation.

"Yes, Monsieur. Isn't it fascinating?"

"Extremely fascinating, yes—"

"I don't see what's so intriguing about it," the husband said with a shrug.

"What's intriguing?" she exclaimed. "Why, everything about it! The skull of the murderer, the mystery—the—well, everything—"

"I dare say." The young man picked up a newspaper. He opened it and spoke without lifting his eyes: "But I don't know anything about it, darling."

"You don't know? You read about it as I did. Remember, between the acts at the theatre, the other night? This morning, before we left—"

"Come!" He dropped the paper and looked at her in amazement. "Are you losing your mind? As long as I tell you I didn't read it, it means I didn't read it!"

I noted that this man, who appeared so soft and tender, was not patient and could not bear contradiction, for he uttered the words in a hard voice, almost harshly. His eyes, so caressing a moment before, suddenly turned to a sharp, blue glitter which embarrassed me. I thought I guessed his motive; his wife was nervous and he did not like to have her discuss such a gruesome subject with strangers. I could have told him that the best course would have been to humor her. He must have noticed my surprise, my instinct to give advice, for he resumed in a lighter tone:

"Of course I saw something of it in the papers. Who didn't? Some lady of easy virtue stabbed in the middle of the night—"

"In broad daylight," his wife corrected him.

"In broad daylight, as you wish. Money, jewels stolen—such crimes occur every day—"

"It's very mysterious," she insisted.

"Ah!" he sighed, "how you do love mystery!"

And he resumed reading *Le Temps*. His wife addressed the other traveler, eager to prove her point:

"To think that someone rang the poor woman's door while she was being killed!"

"Eh? What makes you think that?" the old gentleman asked.

"That's probable," she declared. "Not a jewel missing, yet they were right there, within reach. Two magnificent rings were found on her dressing-table, with a gold purse and a diamond pin. Not a single one of the precious trinkets on the shelves was touched or taken. Only the money. There was no disorder. The murderer must have been frightened away by some noise, for he fled without taking time to collect all the loot. The crime did not earn him much!"

"Oh, yes, Madame, it did!" The old man nodded in self-approval. "It was one of the most profitable crimes committed in recent years. And the assassin took his time, believe me."

"Then why did he leave the jewels?"

"Simply because he was an intelligent man who reasoned that the coin and banknotes he stole could not be identified, while jewels, whether you keep them or sell them, lead to eventual discovery and arrest. The telegraph, telephone, radio, have complicated the task of the criminal. Just remember that he can be reported at once to ships at sea, arrested, and held before having a chance to land in a country refusing extradition."

"And this murderer," the wife resumed, "figured out this job in advance so thoroughly that he will not be found for a long time?"

"He—" the old gentleman paused, smiled quietly—"will never be caught."

I had been amused by my companions' eagerness to talk. I had expected to be drawn in by a question, a glance. To my own astonishment, I spoke without thought, unguardedly. Perhaps I can stand isolation no better than the next man, perhaps lingering vanity, the pride of having something new, authentic to bring into the discussion, prompted me.

"That's not so certain as it was yesterday," I declared.

They had not expected me to speak. The young woman started, the old man turned toward me suddenly, and the young man's eyes met mine above the newspaper.

"Yet," insisted the old man, "I've read everything concerning this case, followed it with great attention in a dozen newspapers and failed to see anything to make me believe that—"

"Because the clue of which I speak is most recent," I replied. "It will not be in the papers until tomorrow."

"Are you a reporter, Monsieur?" the young woman asked me with quick curiosity.

"No, Madame. But I'm well informed, nevertheless. I was called in as medical expert. During the first inspection of the premises, only one fact was evident, for the room in which the woman was killed happened to be quite dark, and that was that the victim had been slain with a single stabbing blow in the chest.

"But when the corpse was brought to me for autopsy at the morgue, I discovered a rather large stain under the left breast, a reddish spot that appeared to be shaped like a hand. I took a photograph of this stain, treated the negative to make it sharper, clearer, and when I obtained a print, I saw that it was indeed the design of a human hand, of a long, slim hand, so precise that not a detail, not a crease, not a line, not a single fingerprint was lacking."

"Perhaps one of the policemen who lifted the body touched it," the old gentleman said slowly. "Such people wear no gloves. I grant that it may be the trace of a dirty hand, but admit it may be that of an innocent hand."

At this, the young man who was reading laughed. I did not take offense, aware that it was customary to laugh at the theories of physicians in general and of medical experts in particular. Moreover, I was sure of my facts, so I continued my demonstration.

"Where the human eye might be mistaken, chemistry makes no error. That stain was made by blood. It is very faint, I admit, but it is a bloodstain nevertheless. Naturally, I immediately ascertained that it did not match the hand of any of the persons who had entered the room since the discovery of the crime.

"Also, a moist towel was found on the washstand, very soiled, and it did not take much imagination to reconstruct that part of the crime. The murderer killed with a single, clean stab, that is true, but he found his right hand covered with blood. He wiped it on the towel. When about to leave, he wished to make sure that his victim was quite dead, ready to dispatch her with another blow.

"He laid his hand over her heart. When he did not feel the slightest beat, he left as he had come, noiselessly. Unfortunately for him, he had forgotten that blood sticks to skin tenaciously, and that, without knowing it, he had placed on his work the least questionable of signatures."

"Extraordinary," the young woman breathed.

"Very curious, as a matter of fact," her husband added.

As for the old gentleman, he murmured: "Bah! Unless the killer's fingerprints are on record in the police files, that's a worthless clue. If I were the assassin, I would sleep in peace!"

"Tonight, perhaps!" I resumed. "But not tomorrow. For all the newspapers will reproduce the picture I took in the morning. Throughout France tomorrow, throughout Europe within two days, that hand will be known and sought for. And the murderer will be betrayed by his right hand, unless he decides to wear gloves all his life, or, showing heroism in his own fashion, he strikes it off himself at the wrist.

"For that hand, aside from the characteristics that would be sufficient for any expert to know it from all other right hands, has a marking that calls attention when you see it. A scar, running from the end of the ring-finger to the base of that line which palmistry terms 'life-line.' A scar which must be so plain that it cannot be unnoticed. So, God forbid, if one of us were the murderer and chanced to draw off his gloves, there would be every chance in the world for you, gentlemen, for me, to identify that hand immediately and ask for the man's arrest at the next station."

"Oh!" the young woman gasped.

The two men stared at their gloved hands instinctively.

"And," the younger man spoke, "that photograph is to appear in the morning papers?"

"We'll see it when we arrive?" the old gentleman wondered.

"No," I explained, "the print was given to the press only tonight, and the Paris papers won't reach us until tomorrow."

My information appeared to have disturbed the young woman. She spoke after a moment of hesitation, yielding to curiosity:

"I'd like to see it."

"Nothing easier than that," I assured her. "I have a print in my briefcase. Here it is."

She took it.

Her husband looked over her shoulder. The old gentleman, after murmuring: "Will you permit me?" crossed the compartment and sat at her side for a closer glance. All three stared at the print intently. Such attention tensed their faces that I might have believed they were staring at the real hand. But as the light was not too strong, I leaned over to indicate the details.

"See that white streak? Isn't it clear? That's the scar, see? And over here—"

"Growing stuffy in here," the young man said. "Mind if I open the window?"

He slid the pane of glass into its groove in the door panel, and cool air rushed in. The old man wiped his forehead and said: "Oh, how good that feels!"

I was about to go on with my explanation, but at this moment the locomotive shrilled piercingly and a formidable uproar started. I spoke loudly, for the tumult increased and covered my voice: "We are entering the tunnel. I shall resume when we're out of it—can't hear anything now—"

The old gentleman sank back on the seat. The young woman kept her eyes on the photograph. The husband leaned against the side of the car, and I saw his lips move, guessed the words: "It's stuffy."

And he leaned out of the window, as if to place his face in the rush of air. It seemed to me then that I heard an odd sound, something like a muffled cry or a moan, with another, slighter, indescribable noise, a crunching, squishing sound. My companions must have heard it also, through that thunderous din, for all three lifted their heads questioningly. Then, as it was not repeated, we looked at the print again. For a minute, the train crashed on in the tunnel, then the sounds lessened, the air felt lighter, and the steam which had whirled into our compartment through the open window drifted and dissolved. We were rolling under the open sky again.

But as I was about to resume my explanation, I suddenly noticed that the young man, braced in his corner near the window, one arm hanging outside, had grown dreadfully pale. He swept us, his wife, with an insane stare.

"You feel faint, Monsieur?" I risked.

He lurched, and I scarcely had time to catch him as he fell face forward. It was then that I noticed at the end of his right arm something bloody, broken, shapeless, a mass of flesh and smashed bones dripping blood.

"Oh! The poor fellow!" the old gentleman cried out. "He slipped and struck the wall of the tunnel. His hand's gone!"

The young wife rose.

Already, ripping the sleeve of the wounded man, I was applying a tourniquet improvised with my handkerchief to stop the spurting blood. He opened his eyes, his bewildered eyes, and his glance swept down his arm to his horrible wound. Then he looked wildly at the motionless girl. She dropped back on the seat, and with chattering teeth she clutched him against her breast without speaking a word.

Suddenly, the old man's sentence echoed in my ears: *His hand is gone.* And I looked down at the photograph fallen to the floor of the car. The wounded man followed my eyes with his own. And I remembered that I had said: *he will be discovered unless he strikes off his hand at the wrist.*

The suspicion, then the certainty, entered my consciousness almost together. But before those pleading eyes in the tortured face, I had neither the will, nor perhaps the wish, to speak. And we waited for daylight without exchanging another word.

As it was still dark when the train reached Vallorbe, the wounded man was not taken off the train until we arrived at Lausanne. I never heard of him again.

But I know that the murderer of Pergolese Street was never found.

Thirty Hours with a Corpse

D AY HAD come at last. The two men looked at each other and although they did not move or speak, each read in the eyes of his companion relief—followed quickly by fear. With the growing light a murmur of voices came up from the newly awakened street. They waited tensely almost as if they expected some unknown accuser to burst open the door, rush in, and seize them.

An interruption such as that, or death, even, at the hands of an infuriated mob would have been welcome, anything that would somehow, some way, break the continuity of horror that had held them for hours speechless and motionless beside the dead body of a woman lying face downward on the floor.

But life was resuming its activities casually enough in the streets, sounds of opening shutters, the shrill cry of a vegetable vendor. It was this last sound that seemed to arouse the younger of the two men, Armand Barthe. Barthe's eyes held a staring fixity of expression, but his lips trembled now. He hesitated for a moment, looked toward the window, then with a quick, convulsive movement picked up his overcoat and put on his hat.

"Where are you going?" Guiret asked sharply, before he had reached the door.

"Out—out—come with me—"

"You must be crazy. It won't be long before the concierge will be up to do our rooms. He would find it and the police would be on our tracks before we could get out of Paris—"

"But—but we are lost, we are lost—"

"No!" Guiret denied vigorously, even though he could not, at the moment, see any way to escape the consequences of the crime.

Barthe usually deferred to his roommate on important questions. He appeared to gain a momentary composure, to feel almost reassured. He did not speak because he felt that Guiret

191

had not yet made definite plans. Guiret was thinking, he knew that, and while he waited to hear the results of that thinking, he put his palms over his eyes, pressing them on the eyeballs, but even then he seemed to see the body.

"Armand—" Guiret said, so abruptly that Barthe started violently, as if awakened from sleep.

"What is it?"

"Get your big trunk—it's empty, isn't it?"

"Yes—" Barthe replied, but made no move to go.

Guiret got up impatiently, went into Barthe's bedroom, and came out dragging the high, round-topped trunk after him. The sweat was running from his temples, for the trunk was heavy even though it was empty. He took out his handkerchief and wiped his forehead, then unfastened the straps and lifted the cover.

"Yes, it will do," he said. "Help me—"

"Help you?" Barthe questioned stupidly.

"Yes, yes!" Guiret cried out, suddenly tense, unnerved for a moment through the contagion of his friend's terror.

"I—I can't—"

"But we must!" Guiret insisted. "We must cram it inside some way. It's our only chance. There is a train for Switzerland in two hours, another one later if we miss that. We'll buy three tickets, two for us to Lausanne, the third to check the trunk somewhere else. We'll be far away when the customs inspector tries to open it. We'll cross Germany, go as far as Hamburg. There we will get a boat for somewhere."

"But if we are suspected?"

"Why should we—two tourists—who would bother us? Come on, now—you take the head."

For a few moments there was no sound in the room save their labored breathing.

"Wait—wait!" Barthe cried out nervously.

"What's the matter now?"

"The head has fallen back—"

"Hold it up, then. Now—now press down. There, you see, it was quite simple—"

Barthe drew his hands back from the head that he had supported almost tenderly, a strange gentleness that grew out of his horrified remorse. He stepped back and, when he heard the snapping of the lock into place, he grasped the table for support. Guiret buckled the straps, then straightened up briskly.

"Call the concierge," he said. Then he noticed that Barthe held his hat in his hand, his overcoat over his arm. "Never mind," he said hastily, "I'll tell him." He opened the door, stepped into the hall, and called down the stairs: "Monsieur Legros—Monsieur Legros!"

The loud voice of the concierge responded: "What is it?"

"Will you give us a hand to take down a trunk?"

"I'll be right up."

Guiret came back into the room, closed the door, and hurriedly took his wallet from his coat pocket. "Take some money," he said: "One never can tell. We might get separated."

Barthe accepted the notes without counting them and put them in his pocket mechanically.

The heavy step of the concierge was heard on the stairs and Guiret swung the door wide.

"Good morning, Messieurs," Legros said, under his habitual cordiality a note of surprise and disapproval: "Are you leaving?"

"For a little vacation only, to the south of France."

Legros smiled cautiously: "You're lucky. I wish I were in your shoes. I'd like to take a vacation."

"That will come, my man, that will come," Guiret said absentmindedly.

"Not at my age. I'm lucky to have a job when times are so hard—" He sighed regretfully and meaningly, thinking of the tip. "So this is the trunk—" He grasped one of the handles, lifted the trunk from the floor, and then allowed it to fall back again with a thud: "It weighs something, all right!"

Barthe became if possible more pallid, and Guiret felt called upon to explain: "Our study books are in there, and books are heavy."

"That's right," Legros agreed amiably.

"It's not too heavy for you, is it?" Guiret asked anxiously.

"No, oh, no—" the concierge protested. "I am over sixty, but there are few men who can lift more than I. Give me a hand. As soon as I have it on my back I can go it alone. Take hold, will you, Monsieur Barthe?"

Barthe came forward weakly, but Guiret pushed him aside. "I'll do it. Come on, let's go, Monsieur Legros."

But Legros straightened up, no longer offering his broad back.

"You know I would like to help you, Monsieur Guiret, but I have remembered—I cannot take the trunk down."

"Why not?" both Guiret and Barthe asked as if with the same breath.

"You owe three months rent, that's why. Oh, I understand how it is with students. One has money from home to pay and it goes for amusements. That's not a crime with young men like you. But the proprietor is very strict on these matters. Last month when you sold that mahogany chest of drawers he pulled me up about it, said that nothing was to go out of here until you had paid your back bill."

"But we are leaving the rest of our things here, the rug, the curtains, the pictures."

"I know all that, but—just the same I cannot take the trunk down."

"But we're going to pay the rent before we leave."

"Oh, that's different! Why didn't you say so?" He stooped over as if to take the trunk, then straightened up again, his hands on his back.

"It can't be much more than two thousand francs—" Guiret said lightly, taking out his wallet.

"That I do not know," Legros replied, somewhat indifferently. "I'll give you three thousand and you can keep the change for yourself."

"Oh, no, I could not do that, Monsieur."

"Why not?"

"You know as well as I that the bill must be made out by the proprietor."

"Very well, very well!" Guiret said impatiently. "Ask him to make it out, then."

"But he is not in Paris."

"Not in Paris?"

"He will not be back until day after tomorrow. You should have let me know before. This is not like a hotel by the day where the proprietor always sits in the office. The rents are by the month, you know that, and you are three months—"

"But we want to leave right away—"

The concierge shrugged then smiled again genially as a solution offered itself: "Why don't you go, then, take your small baggage and leave the trunk behind? I will send you the bill, you can send the money, and then I will forward the trunk."

"Yes, and how many days will that take?" Guiret muttered after a moment, without glancing at Barthe. "We will be a week without our books. No, you must telegraph the proprietor at once to send the bill. How long will it take for it to get around?"

"Twenty-four hours, or a day and a half at most."

"I don't know what else we can do," Guiret agreed, in a tone that he tried to make nonchalant.

The concierge cocked his ear and listened. "I am wanted below," he said, and went out.

As soon as the door closed Barthe gave way to a spasm of trembling. "We are lost," he whispered.

"Don't be stupid. We are delayed, that is all. We cannot help it. Tell me how we can help it?"

"We cannot," Barthe agreed, without abandoning his hopeless manner.

"Then what is there to do but wait calmly?" Guiret asked with irritation. "We both run the same risk. If I can be calm, why can't you?"

"If I could get out for a little fresh air—I'll go down, take a few turns, it doesn't matter where—"

"No?" Guiret questioned sarcastically. "I suppose it doesn't matter where you go to behave like a fool and attract attention to yourself?"

"Then come down with me. It would do you good, too, to get some air."

"I'm all right. What's wrong with me? Someone must stay here."

"But it's locked."

"There's blood here."

"Where!" Barthe exclaimed, as if startled all over again.

"Don't talk so loud. Here—on the rug. I've covered it with the big chair. But if Legros started to clean—"

"Yes. You're right. But I—"

He watched Guiret as he crossed to the door, turned the key in the lock, and then put it in his pocket.

❖ ❖ ❖

The interminable hours must be passing. It could not be that Time stood still. By an unhappy coincidence the clock on the mantel had stopped, and neither Guiret nor Barthe had had their own watches for months. They heard the hour of midday strike. Fatigue immobilized them, but fear and hunger kept them awake. They did not realize that they were hungry, and their physical exhaustion was so great that there was no place for remorse.

Guiret would get up now and then, go into his bedroom, and wash his hands. He did this when Barthe stared at the trunk, Barthe who thought at one time that he saw the cover move. Guiret would stay in the bedroom until he believed that Barthe was not looking at the trunk, and then to justify his brisk return he would say:

"Did you speak, Armand?"

The first time, Barthe leaped to his feet and cried out nervously: "I didn't speak, no, I didn't say anything—no!"

After that he did not respond to the question. Somehow it seemed to mark an indefinite passage of time.

Suddenly Guiret burst out unexpectedly in a thin voice: "Will the day never end?"

Immediately he regretted his words, for Barthe passed into a sort of muffled hysteria. He threw himself downward on the divan, rolling his head among the pillows.

"Legros must have heard by now," Guiret said cheerfully, trying to calm him. "Surely he will show up any moment now. Don't let him find you like this."

Barthe did not seem to hear. He remained face downward among the silken pillows, his shoulders lifting and falling with spasmodic shivers.

A little later Guiret spoke again: "It will be dark soon." And again he regretted his words and resolved to remain silent. Barthe repeated the words with new terror: "Yes, you are right, it will be dark soon."

The day seemed eternal. At last the shadows descended the length of the windows and gathered in the corners of the room. One by one the chairs became blurred, the trunk, however, in the middle of the room remaining visible, illuminated by a beam of light that seemed to come from nowhere. Guiret got up and went to the window and located the light from an apartment house window. He sighed and sat down again.

For a while the darkness brought peace to both of them, for it blotted out the trunk. Barthe tried to forget that it was there and succeeded until the obscurity suddenly became peopled with ghosts. He got up jerkily and fumbled about for the cord that lighted the reading lamp.

They faced each other again. The day was over, yes, but the night as many hours long was before them. Barthe stretched himself on the divan, turning toward the wall. His breathing became regular in sleep, then he lurched up with a choking gasp, awakened by the beginning of a nightmare that started with the events of the day before unrolling in memory toward that time when he had bent over her where she lay on the rug, and saw that she was dead.

At daylight Barthe got up, raised the shades, turned out the light, took his place again on the divan, face to the wall, and seemed to be soundly asleep.

"Now that he's quiet, I can sleep," thought Guiret, and lifted his feet on a stool, his head in the comfortable curved back of the armchair. In the beginning of that torpor where the will held but fragile control, he recalled vividly the events of the night before, events that he dare not think of in his waking moments for fear that once started on the path of memory he would find himself unable to stop when he reached the first premises of that terrible climax, the result of which was now securely locked and strapped in Barthe's large trunk.

It had been a gay evening at the start. Guiret and Barthe had gone by special invitation to the apartment of Roland Marousse, a wealthy merchant, who found, in common with the two students, pleasure in card-playing and gambling. It was the first of the month and both Guiret and his roommate had received their allowances. It was planned that the three of them would go together to another apartment where they would meet other acquaintances. They had expected to find Marousse alone. . . .

Guiret, half-conscious, knew that he was breathing heavily, as he had heard Barthe breathe when he first tried to sleep, and he knew that if he could not throw off the torpor of weariness, pull himself out of the swoon that he was in, he would like Barthe go on and on until he, too, awakened with a hoarse, strangled cry.

"No—no—no—" he muttered, and that was what he was saying when suddenly he sat bolt upright in his chair, rubbing his eyes with his palms.

How much time had elapsed, he could not tell. Possibly he had slept for a while before the recollections started to turn into the nightmare. He listened, hoping to hear a clock strike. From the sounds below in the street it must be ten o'clock or later.

"Armand—Armand—" he said tensely. "Wake up—someone is coming up the stairs!"

Barthe awakened with a start of fright and Guiret tried to calm him:

"What is there to worry about? It must be Legros. If he's coming here who else could it be?" he asked confusedly.

He went to the door and unlocked it, opened it wide. Then he fell back into the room.

"Who is it?" Barthe asked, from the bedroom where he had gone as if to hide himself.

"Marousse!" Guiret exclaimed. "What on earth has brought you here so early?"

Marousse came into the room wearily. He seemed very tired and somewhat embarrassed.

"I was passing. I hope I do not disturb you."

"No, no!"

Marousse looked at the trunk: "You are leaving—"

"For a short stay at Cannes. We are waiting for the concierge to bring the bill. Sit down—sit down—"

Marousse sat down uneasily and looked around the room. "Where is Barthe?"

"In his bedroom. He—he has a headache. Ill luck, too, when we have planned to take the train this afternoon. Armand—"

"Don't bother him. I know how one feels with a headache. I'm none too well myself," Marousse said wearily.

Guiret noticed that his usual jovial expression was lacking. He showed his age this morning. His body looked as if it had suddenly become emaciated.

A constrained silence seemed to weigh upon them. Guiret was the first to break it.

"Oh, Marousse," he said, fumbling in his pocket. "Don't let me forget that little sum of money I owe you."

"Never mind. Let it go," Marousse protested. "You'll be back, won't you?"

"Of course—but I want you to know that I wouldn't leave— even for a trip without mentioning—"

"Never mind. I cannot think or care about money. I am too much disturbed." He broke off, waiting for Guiret to question him. Guiret did not offer to do so and he went on: "I am terribly worried. Chouchou has not come back."

"I have not seen her, not since she left us night before last."

"But—I don't understand—"

"Neither do I. You recall what happened. I should think you might well remember. Both you and Barthe lost so much at cards. You noticed, no doubt, that—" he hesitated, embarrassed, then forced himself to continue—"that Chouchou and I quarreled."

"Yes, I mean I—I thought no more about it."

"I was jealous, I admit. I should not have been, but I was. She was trying always to—to be alone with—well—" he lowered his voice—"with Barthe—you noticed, did you not?"

"Yes, I did—"

"She had won so much at cards from all of us I thought she should go on playing and I told her so—well, you know how she got angry at me in the taxi on the way home and got out and called a taxi to go to her apartment—I haven't seen her since—"

"But that was night before last—"

"Yes! That's why I am so worried. When I got to my apartment I telephoned her, you know, to find out if she was still angry. No answer. I called later, in an hour. Still no answer. You remember it was very late when we parted. I slept a little, then took a bath and changed my clothes, and telephoned again. Still no Chouchou—"

"Perhaps she was there but did not answer the phone."

"That's what I thought. I called a taxi and went to her place. The maid had not seen her. She had not been back that night. I knew she could not be shopping. She had not been back to change her clothes, and she would not go about in evening clothes in the morning. I waited a while. Ten o'clock, half past ten, then I decided to telephone her friends. No one had seen her. I went down in the street and waited for an hour before the door, watching the taxis go by, expecting, hoping every moment to see her step out."

"And she did not?"

"Would I be here worrying about her if she had? You can understand that I was terribly uneasy—" Marousse seemed to be playing with words, repeating himself in an attempt to reach what he had come to say: "When night came again and the street lamps were on I lost my head completely, or I did the right thing, I don't know. I went to the police."

"You did!" Guiret exclaimed.

"What else could I do? What would anyone have done in my place? A well-dressed woman, with valuable jewels—Chouchou always carries a large sum of money on her. I have known her to go out with four thousand francs to buy a postage stamp. I am sure something terrible has happened to her—or—" He broke off and perspiration beaded his pasty forehead.

Guiret tried to think of something to say to calm him, for his own forehead was damp at the thought of Marousse going again to the police.

"What I am about to say may seem brutal, Marousse, but is it not possible that Chouchou— Are you quite sure that—I mean, if she were deceiving you with someone else that would explain—"

Marousse tapped his shoe with the end of his cane. He showed no resentment or surprise at what Guiret had said. On the contrary, after one or two attempts to speak, he seemed to agree by nodding his head.

"Yes, I have asked myself that," he said, after a while. "And since you are frank with me, I will be frank with you. I had the firm conviction that you know where she is."

"Me!" Guiret exclaimed.

"You need not pretend with me. I am no longer a boy, I am past forty-five, neither handsome nor clever. I have nothing except money to offer a pretty young woman like Chouchou. I understand that and would excuse many things."

"I don't see what you're trying to get at," Guiret said.

"I am neither a fool nor blind. I tell you that I could not help noticing that Chouchou and Barthe—before he lost so heavily at cards that he was depressed—did you not notice? What I mean to say is, I would be the happiest man on earth to learn that she is alive and well. That's how much I have suffered with worry. Even though she had come here to wait for Barthe after she left us—"

"What a mad idea!"

"But you would say just that even if she had. I tell you, I will not make a scene. All I want to know is that nothing terrible has happened to her, that she is here—"

"Here—" Guiret repeated, turning pale. "No, no—I swear it."

"You give me your word?"

"Yes, my word—"

But Marousse continued to stare at the door leading to the bedrooms.

"If it is necessary for you to convince yourself, Marousse—" Guiret said presently.

"Oh, no," Marousse protested, flushing. "I must believe you."

"But I don't want you leaving here unless you really believe me, and there is only one way to prove—" He opened the door and indicated that Marousse might search.

Deeply embarrassed but holding to his firm purpose to purchase peace of mind at all costs, Marousse stepped into the bedroom. Barthe, lying on the bed, his hand over his eyes as if to shut out the light, did not stir, and Marousse tiptoed by him to inspect Guiret's room, which was beyond.

"I must ask your pardon," Marousse said to Guiret when they were again in the sitting-room. He sat down weakly on the trunk. The conviction which had whipped his courage deserted him. Guiret held himself very erect, icy in his manner.

"I can only think the worst now," Marousse said.

"Wait until late tonight," Guiret suggested. "Why make a fool of yourself if she— Anyway, if harm has already come to her what good will it do?"

Marousse did not seem to hear him. He picked up his hat and stick and went out slowly, almost regretfully, as if he sensed that in this room there was something that should have held him back.

"My God—" whispered Guiret, when the door had closed after him. "That time I thought we were surely gone!"

"Yes," Barthe said, for he had come to the doorway and was standing there weakly, as if the strength had left his limbs.

He seemed more composed, however, and Guiret calmed himself, spurred on by what he believed to be a necessity—to tell Barthe of his plans before he could sink again into the hopeless terror that seemed always ready to engulf him.

"If Legros is downstairs when we leave I shall direct the driver of the taxi to the East Station. I can change the order later. Whatever happens do not show surprise by a gesture or word at anything I do. There must be one head to this. Is that understood?"

"It is understood," Barthe agreed, and he added, thinking for the first time of his physical misery, "God, but I'm tired! If I could only snatch a little sleep."

"But you've been sleeping since daylight! We must hold ourselves in readiness. Later, perhaps, but first of all, be ready."

It was not long after that he heard a clock strike ten. He wound and set the clock. The minutes seemed longer with the exact knowledge of their passing.

"I wonder why Legros does not show up?" he said after a while, and restlessly opened the door and went to the landing to look down and listen for voices. When he came back into the room he recoiled and paled, for it seemed to him that the air was already impregnated with a vague and terrible odor.

"What's the matter?" Barthe asked, noticing his sudden pallor. "Is anything wrong?"

"I hope we can get away soon."

He cried out with joy when a few minutes later he heard Legros' steps on the stairs. Legros knocked at the door and showed a smiling face.

"Monsieur Guiret, here is the bill."

"That's fine!"

He went through the formality of verifying the addition, but the figures danced madly before his eyes.

"Two thousand, one hundred and sixty-two francs is correct, is it not?" Legros asked.

Guiret had opened his wallet. There were two one-thousand-franc bills but no change.

"What have you got, Barthe?"

Barthe had no change either.

"We'll have to get this five hundred franc bill changed," Guiret said, and handed it to the concierge.

"That may not be so easy around here. I may have to go to the Post Office."

"Well, go then—"

"But I cannot go just now, Monsieur Guiret. You see I am alone downstairs. My wife has gone to market and I cannot leave the premises. The proprietor is very strict about that. Someone might come to look at the apartments."

"But we can't wait around here until your wife gets back!"

"You could go yourself, or Monsieur Barthe—"

"Monsieur Barthe has a headache and I am waiting here for someone."

"My wife will not be gone long. Surely in half an hour—"

"But we'll miss our train."

"We could gain time this way," the concierge suggested. "I could take your baggage down now and leave it in the corridor. And coming back from getting the change—that is, after my wife returns so that I can go—I could call a taxi."

"Leave the trunk downstairs in the corridor?"

The thought of that seemed to lay an icy hand upon both of the men. Only when they watched it did they feel relatively secure. It seemed to them that peril commenced the moment they ceased to watch it. When that time arrived they must be speeding away in the opposite direction.

"Why not?" Legros asked, and it was then that Guiret realized that he had spoken aloud.

"Because even then there might not be time."

Legros shrugged. Barthe started to pace the floor. Guiret tried to think of something to say to reassure him, although he himself felt that he was perilously near the breaking point. What if the nervous tension that held him together should suddenly desert him at the decisive moment! Already he could see that one could not definitely plan on anything. There were always unexpected delays.

Legros left and went downstairs and Guiret turned to Barthe:

"You see how well I'm planning things? I told him that we were leaving soon. That's to give us plenty of time and also so that he won't know where we are going. Our train does not leave for two hours. We have plenty of time."

"Too much time. Let's get some air. He is downstairs waiting for his wife. He did not clean yesterday because we are giving up the rooms, so why should he want to clean today until we are out?" In the chaos of his thought a single idea persisted, to get out of the room away from the trunk, which he did not wish to see but upon which, in spite of himself, his gaze was constantly fixed.

"You should not make me waste my breath to repeat to you that we should not budge a foot from here until things are settled and we can leave for good. A single false word or gesture—"

"What have I said now?" stammered Barthe. "Did I speak a-again?"

"Do you not know whether you speak or not?" Guiret questioned loudly, then lowered his voice: "Someone is coming."

"More than one, too."

"Well, we aren't the only persons living in the house."

Nevertheless he found himself counting the steps, heard them cross the landing, then started counting again. Strangely enough he had never thought of it before, but now he remembered that there were twenty-three steps. When the last footstep resounded under the heels, Guiret reached for a bottle that was near, half-filled with brandy. His hand closed convulsively over the neck. He stood against the wall by the door. Someone rapped. He did not speak. A second rap, then a voice:

"Open up. I happen to know you're there."

"Who is it?" Guiret asked through the door.

"Marbois, sheriff's officer."

"Sheriff's officer!"

"A judgment was given against you on the sixth of December. I am here at the request of Messieurs Bardier and Gordane, Tailors. Will you be kind enough to let me in?"

With a sigh of relief Guiret put the bottle down and opened the door.

Marbois entered followed by his man.

"It is three thousand, six hundred and sixteen francs and that includes costs," he said. "Can you pay it?"

"No, Monsieur," Guiret said firmly, with a warning glance at Barthe.

"Then I must make an attachment."

"All right. Do so."

Marbois sat down at the table, took out a sheet of stamped paper and a fountain pen.

"The furniture here, it is yours?"

"Not all of it. The bed, the table, the chairs, you cannot touch. You know that. They are our tools of work. The rugs, the draperies, the pictures and the bookcases are ours."

The assistant commenced his inventory in a high-pitched voice:

"A bookcase with glass doors, bronze lamp, Chinese rug—"

"But—" Barthe began nervously.

Guiret scowled at him and he did not speak again until the sheriff's officer and his man had gone into the bedroom.

"But we have money to pay."

"Don't be stupid! What would be left for us, then? We must buy the three tickets, and then there's our living expenses where we're going."

"That's right."

Marbois came back into the living-room briskly. "Will you sign this, please?"

Guiret took the pen in a steady hand. He was about to write his name when the officer interrupted him.

"Wait a moment, we've forgotten something."

"What?"

"This trunk."

"But that is our trunk."

"I know that. But will you be kind enough to open it?"

"Will I—what?"

"Open it."

"Why?" Guiret asked.

"How do I know that it does not contain property that should he inventoried?"

"There's nothing there except our books, our papers. They constitute our tools of work and cannot be attached."

"That is true, but I must assure myself."

"I give you my word, Monsieur."

"Don't waste time. Let's get at it."

"But I say—did you not hear what I told you? It contains our personal belongings—" Guiret's tone was that of a man who would not tolerate that his word should be questioned.

The officer took a pompous voice now: "If my presence here and my insistence on doing my duty annoys you, you can get rid of both by paying."

Guiret drew himself erect proudly: "I have no lessons to take from you, Monsieur."

"I ask you for the last time, will you open it?"

"And if I refuse?"

"I am here to take legal judgment. I will go to the Commissioner of Police who will doubtless authorize me to return with a locksmith."

"All right, do that!" Guiret said angrily, playing for time. "Before the police I will do what is necessary. But I forbid you to so much as put your hand upon it."

The officer drew back slightly before the pallid, distorted, angry face that was lifted defiantly toward him, then with a commanding gesture of warning to Guiret to stay at a distance he spoke to his man:

"Ask the Commissioner to send a gendarme."

But Guiret had been thinking rapidly. A moment before he had intended to get rid of these men some way, any way, and flee with Barthe. That was neither wise nor necessary.

"All right, I'll pay you."

"Why didn't you say that before?"

"And if I do you will not insist on opening the trunk?"

He asked this question in a heavy constricted voice and the officer glanced at him suspiciously and took his time before replying.

"If you pay that annuls the attachment."

"Very well, I will pay."

He opened his wallet, having forgotten for the moment that he had given the concierge a five-hundred franc bill to change. The sweat broke out on his forehead, but he recovered quickly and turned to Barthe.

"What about it, Armand?"

"But you said yourself—that we—" Barthe stammered.

"Will you give me the money and bring this to an end?"

Barthe took out his wallet slowly. "I think you're wrong, but—"

Guiret snatched the bills from him: "How much was it, did you say?"

"Three thousand, six hundred and sixteen francs, including costs."

Guiret found the strength to be ironical: "Justice is not for nothing, I see!"

When he counted the money he saw that he had only three thousand francs.

"Take this and I'll send you the rest," he said.

"You know I cannot do that."

"But I give you my word to send you the rest tomorrow, this afternoon if you wish."

"My orders are formal. And anyway if you intend to pay, it is not important. In a few hours when you get the money as you say you will have it, you can pass by the office and pay. You have twenty-four hours to do that after the attachment.

"So, if you'll let me throw an eye in that trunk—"

"No—no—no!" Guiret stammered. Then as he felt the other's curious gaze resting upon him: "There you go again, doubting my word!"

He felt a sort of madness gaining upon him. It entered his head to throw himself upon the sheriff's officer and strangle him, stop forever that insistence of his on opening the trunk. But the other man was there and at the first gesture he would enter into the struggle and Barthe was trembling so much that he would be of no help, doubtless would run at the first sign of conflict. Reason came at last.

"How stupid I am! Legros, the concierge, has five hundred francs that I gave him to get changed. He is waiting for his wife to get back. Perhaps he's downstairs. Or if he's not then he'll be back soon with the change. Armand, go down and see—" But as Barthe moved eagerly toward the door, Guiret caught a glittering, mad, desperate light in his eyes: "No, no, you stay here, Armand. I'll attend to all this. You realize that I am doing my utmost to get the money, do you not, Monsieur?"

His face was so pale, his eyes so distracted that after he went out, the sheriff's officer spoke to his man: "Follow him," he said.

Barthe, who had seated himself in the armchair, weak with relief when the affair seemed to have been arranged, looked up tensely, when he heard the officer give the order.

"I know who you are," he said.

"Well, I know that myself," Marbois said, shortly. "What's the matter with you fellows, anyway?"

"You'd like to know what's in that trunk?" Barthe asked.

"What's all this about the trunk?"

"You'd like to know, wouldn't you? That's what you say to us. You know all right. Books in the trunk, eh? You know better." He unfastened the straps, took out his key-ring which Guiret had given back to him after he had taken it from him to lock the trunk. "You're a brave man, I hope." With a swift turn of the wrist he turned the key: "Quietly, please. She's asleep, that's all. Yes, she's there, and you'll agree with me she's very pretty."

He lifted the cover with careful deliberation. An odor rose like a cloud into the face of the sheriff's officer. The flesh on the body was mottled, there was a large hole in the breast, the lips of which had already turned purple. Marbois fell back and uttered a startled cry. Barthe laughed:

"It's worse than you thought, eh?"

Just then Guiret pushed the door open, the change in his hand, a smile on his face. He saw the open trunk, he stared for a moment at the two men in the room, then turned to flee. The man who had followed him was coming in the door. They grappled.

"Armand—Armand—help—help me out—why do you stand there—help—"

But Barthe was seated again now: "He's not the sheriff's man. He's from the police. He didn't fool me. Marousse sent him here—Marousse sent him here—"

Guiret passed quickly from frenzy to complete submission. The money was scattered all about him on the floor and he stooped to pick it up.

"I didn't do it, I didn't do it," Barthe was saying. "She came here to see me. She had money, all the money that she had won and we had lost. We asked her to give us some of it—she wouldn't—"

"Yes, yes—" Guiret shouted, eager to shriek in a high voice the story of the events of that horrible night, words that he had repeated in a whisper for over thirty hours: "I killed her, yes. It was for the money and her jewels. Here—here is everything—" He threw on the table the jewels, tied in his handkerchief, a small distorted bundle bulging with bracelets and necklaces. He opened it and spread the jewels out: "See! She flaunted these before us. She wanted to talk to Barthe. Yes, she intended to run away with him. She flaunted her money and these when we had lost everything. I did not intend to kill her. I struck her in anger, then she threatened me—and I struck her again—and then—"

"He shot her—" Barthe said simply. "That was the way it all started."

She Thought of Everything

IT WAS an evening much like any other evening, after a day when nothing had happened that did not happen any day, that Madame Chertier decided to kill her husband. He was reading with one elbow propped on the table, the light on his book, his face in the shadow. Nevertheless, he must have sensed something, for he looked up and spoke.

"Why do you look at me?"

And she replied: "I wasn't looking at you, dear."

"Thought you were," he murmured. His wife sat back in her chair, tilted her head so that the lamplight did not reach her face, with her hands out of sight, so that he did not notice the sudden contraction of her fingers. Mr. Chertier turned a few pages rapidly, doubtless to skip some boring description. His wife shrugged, and he spoke again.

"What makes you laugh?"

"I wasn't laughing," she answered.

"Thought you were," he murmured again. Then he was reading once more, vest loosened to ease his protruding abdomen, legs crossed, one foot swinging a slipper.

When she saw him thus, placid and self-satisfied, Madame Chertier thought ardently of her lover, of the many joys that freedom would bring her, and closing her eyes pictured without emotion that coarse body deprived of life, that smug, fat face motionless, the funeral, the black crepe dress which she would wear, her widow's bonnet trimmed with white.

The idea of the murder had entered her head so gently that she accepted it calmly. It seemed to her that she had always had that idea, that it had been in her forever, fatal and almost natural. Why should she seek explanations, reasons, excuses? Everything was driving her to that end, and having dared to think and consider the idea, she felt a sort of relief, and her brain was strangely lucid.

At eleven o'clock, Mr. Chertier closed his book.

"Bed time?"

They exchanged a few words as they undressed. He kissed her forehead as usual, went to sleep immediately. She turned to the wall and thought things over. All night, she mused, calculated, figured out schemes. Now that she had reached a decision, it was important that she should be careful, patient, meticulous, and wise.

In the morning, she was sweeter than ordinarily. Her husband spoke of this change of humor, congratulated her. And she replied in an absolutely candid voice: "I'm the same as usual. But you seldom notice me."

She had an appointment at a dressmaker that day, which she kept. She selected a brilliantly colored dress. And so that her existence should be unchanged, if there was an investigation later, she went to see her lover, and did not return home before the usual hour. At dinner, while the maid was busy near them, she spoke in a casual way of a visit she planned to their summer home in the country.

Mr. Chertier was surprised.

"If it bothers you at all," she said quietly, "I'll stay—"

He waited until the maid had gone to the kitchen to explain.

"I wouldn't wish to deprive you of a pleasure trip, dear. But you might have picked a better time. My business is not going so well just now—"

"Ah?" she breathed. And pretending that she had not noticed that the maid had reentered the dining-room, she added: "Business is bad, you say? You mustn't worry so—is it very serious?"

He reminded her with a glance that they were not alone, and she showed confusion. But she had planned the remarks, had been careful that she was overheard. The last sentence— recalled at the proper time by the maid—might explain matters, direct suspicions elsewhere. From now on, every word, every act must count. She had planted in a witness's mind the facts that she was going away on a trip and that her husband was worried.

Days and weeks elapsed. And Madame Chertier's preoccupation grew. At times, she wished that chance would interfere, that her husband should die a natural death. But chance never works when it is needed.

As she could not wait forever, she set herself a date, and started methodical preparations. At the end of spring, vacation time drawing near, she retained a berth in a sleeping-car for the following week. The maid would testify that she had planned the trip months ago.

Mr. Chertier did not object, and he even suggested that it would be wise to hire a large taxi to carry all the baggage in one trip. She agreed that this was a good thought, and had the maid order the car, mentioning before her husband that it was his desire. Then she said that it might be a good time to grant the maid and the cook a few days of vacation. Mr. Chertier could live at a hotel, she added.

Her husband was delighted, for as a rule she did not concern herself much with others, and he complimented her on her orderliness and system. She felt some remorse to find him so easy to trick, so attentive to her every wish. But she scorned him for his foolishness, for his stupid lack of instinct; for everything he said or did seemed a new precaution to give her trouble later.

Everything seemed, to outsiders, to originate with him, he appeared to plan for her! With the servants on vacation, with him presumably living in a hotel, he would not be missed for days. His superiors, his employees would think that he had decided to go with her at the last minute. She heard him speak to the office on the telephone, hinting that he was tempted to escort her for a while.

On the morning set for her departure, the apartment was in order; tissue papers shrouded the lamps, the various trinkets, the picture frames. The trunks lined in the hall were full, and the house linen had not been packed! But Madame Chertier had ordered a new trunk, quite large, especially for it. When it was delivered, her husband admired it greatly—said it was handsome, solid, an excellent buy. For the first time, Madame Chertier felt some embarrassment. The servants were ready to go, and she took the occasion to break off his extravagant praise of the trunk she had bought for his coffin. She paid maid and cook, thanked them for their good wishes. Mr. Chertier followed them downstairs, saying that he had to purchase tobacco.

Left alone in the silent, empty apartment, Madame Chertier felt numb and frightened. She did not for a moment think of giving up her plans, but the deed she had to perform perturbed her. In her small handbag, a traveling-clock was ticking impatiently, time was passing, he would return—and she would have to act!

She tested the locks of the massive trunk. They held well, and the lid closed tight. She went through her pocketbook, saw that she had her railroad ticket, her money, a checkbook, smelling-salts. She was about to look once more at the revolver she had concealed in a drawer. She had loaded it very carefully, placed it in readiness, in her boudoir.

She turned as she heard her husband enter. And she answered his question: "Where are you?" in a steady voice. This was the room she had intended for the final episode. There was a thick tarpaulin on the floor—which had been placed there, the servants knew, to keep the metal corners of the trunks from scratching the floor. In the dresser drawer below that in which she had put the gun, she had ropes. And she had asked for waterproof tarpaulin, waterproof, hence bloodproof.

When her husband entered, she faced him, her back to the dresser. He came toward her, stood in the center of the tarpaulin. The time had come, she must reach for the gun and shoot him. Involuntarily, her eyes swept the boudoir.

"I'm not forgetting anything?" she asked to cover her nervousness. She did not expect an answer, her trembling hand was in the open drawer, groping for the revolver.

He smiled.

"What about this?" he said, holding out the gun she sought.

"That's right, I was forgetting that," she stammered.

Mr. Chertier laughed loudly.

"The most important thing!"

She started. She was terrified by the change in his expression. His eyes were hard as steel, and suddenly, he appeared far from stupid, a cool, resolute man. He drew her on the tarpaulin, pressed the gun's muzzle on her forehead, between her eyes.

He fired.

Madame Chertier slumped to the tarpaulin, which was stained with blood. The husband had stepped back calmly, to allow her to drop.

Then he gathered the corpse in the tarpaulin, took the ropes from the drawer, fastened the whole into a bundle, with unshaken, expert fingers. This done, he carried her to the trunk, dropped her inside, packed the loose linen tightly to prevent shaking. Then he opened the pocketbook, took out ticket, money, checkbook and smelling-salts, tossed the empty bag with the body. After which he slammed the lid down, locked the trunk.

The bell rang, he opend the door to the janitor and the taxi chauffeur, who carried the baggage down to the waiting cab. As he saw the big trunk swaying on the porter's shoulders, Mr. Chertier sighed and thought:

"She had thought of everything!"